Everybody loves Dorothy Cannell
and her mysteries!!

Praise for *The Importance of Being Ernestine*

"It is the absurd predicaments of her central characters that readers find themselves recalling, and Cannell is cunning at devising outlandish situations for them."   —*Chicago Sun-Times*

"Cannell orchestrates plenty of laughs along with a clever plot, merrily winking at readers as she pokes fun at numerous genre conventions."   —*Publishers Weekly*

༄

"With its ancient setting, complicated story, mysterious old houses, hidden diaries, simmering passions, spooky emanations and love matches gone awry, [*Bridesmaids Revisited*] sometimes reads like *Wuthering Heights* on steroids. . . . Cannell's smooth narration and her appealing, smart-mouthed characters charm you into suspending disbelief. The result is a thoroughly delightful puzzle."   —*Publishers Weekly*

"Full of gothic touches and the ineffable sweetness of memory."   —*Booklist* (starred)

"Wacky and wonderful."   —*Carolyn Hart*

"Spunky and delightful."   —*Minneapolis Star Tribune*

"Sparkling wit and outlandish characters."   —*Chicago Sun-Times*

"Thoroughly entertaining."   —*Cosmopolitan*

"Wickedly witty good bubbly fun."   —*The Cleveland Plain Dealer*

"Hilariously funny."   —*Boston Globe*

The Importance of Being Ernestine

AN ELLIE HASKELL MYSTERY

Dorothy Cannell

PENGUIN BOOKS

PENGUIN BOOKS

Published by the Penguin Group

Penguin Putnam Inc., 375 Hudson Street,
New York, New York 10014, U.S.A.
Penguin Books Ltd, 80 Strand, London WC2R 0RL, England
Penguin Books Australia Ltd, 250 Camberwell Road,
Camberwell, Victoria 3124, Australia
Penguin Books Canada Ltd, 10 Alcorn Avenue,
Toronto, Ontario, Canada M4V 3B2
Penguin Books India (P) Ltd, 11 Community Centre,
Panchsheel Park, New Delhi – 110 017, India
Penguin Books (N.Z.) Ltd, Cnr Rosedale and Airborne Roads,
Albany, Auckland, New Zealand
Penguin Books (South Africa) (Pty) Ltd, 24 Sturdee Avenue,
Rosebank, Johannesburg 2196, South Africa

Penguin Books Ltd, Registered Offices: Harmondsworth, Middlesex, England

First published in the United States of America by Viking Penguin,
a member of Penguin Putnam Inc. 2002
Published in Penguin Books 2003

10 9 8 7 6 5 4 3 2 1

PUBLISHER'S NOTE
This is a work of fiction. Names, characters, places, and incidents
either are the product of the author's imagination or are used fictitiously,
and any resemblance to actual persons, living or dead, business establishments,
events, or locales is entirely coincidental.

ISBN 0-670-03060-0 (hc.)
ISBN 0 14 20.0284 4 (pbk.)
CIP data available

Printed in the United States of America
Designed by Nancy Resnick

To Julian Ashley Moore and Trevor McNeil Cannell.
Time to take your bows. Here is your book.
With love from Granna

The Importance of Being Ernestine

One

Mata Hari and the other devious divas of history had nothing on me! The plotting with all its secret assignations and whispered telephone conversations was enormously satisfying. Yesterday's heist had been somewhat nerve-racking given that Kathleen Ambleforth, the vicar's wife, had failed to send the van at the appointed time to remove the loot. But now the stage was set.

All day I was exuberantly busy. In the morning I instructed the furniture men where to place the leather sofa that would have done Lord Peter Wimsey proud, made sure the tapestry armchair was angled just right and that the Georgian-style cabinet intended to hide the new computer was positioned squarely under the window. Seeing three burly men close to tears always brings out the best in me. In the space of fifteen minutes I produced three pots of tea, watched an entire fruit-cake be demolished and did not snap when one of them took a chunk out of the wall. Immediately following their departure I hung the Scottish landscape paintings and the gilt-framed mirror, positioned the lamps and potted plants and tied back the topaz velvet curtains with tasseled cords.

My cousin Freddy who lives in the cottage at the bottom of the drive kindly watched two-year-old Rose for me during the afternoon, enabling me to revel in arranging the brass candlesticks and antique finials on the mantelpiece and the Royal

Worcester figurines in the display cabinet that had arrived the previous day. I had just finished positioning the area rug when it was time to collect the twins—son Tam and daughter Abbey—from school.

They would be five in a few weeks, at the beginning of December, and were always bounding with energy when they got home. Having them underfoot made lining up the books in the newly installed walnut bookcases a lengthy process, but I got through it with my sunny mood intact. The only one out of sorts was Tobias the cat who accidentally got shut in the cupboard under the stairs. But fortunately he worked off most of his irritation having a showdown with the Hoover and a couple of mops. All three children ate their supper of toad-in-a-hole and rice pudding without fuss.

I got them bathed and down for the night with a minimum of pillow fighting and jumping on the beds. Hurrying them through their prayers and only reading them one chapter of *Charlotte's Web* left me feeling a little guilty, but the minutes were ticking away. It was time to step into the shower. I resisted the temptation to skip washing my hair because it is long and always takes an age to blow-dry. But I wanted to look my best when the curtain rose on the entrance of the man who played the leading role in my life.

The corduroy dress I put on was forest green, one of my favorite shades. A glance in the mirror showed my eyes sparkling with anticipation and my chignon pinned neatly in place except for the tendrils I had allowed to escape. Usually I didn't fuss unduly about my appearance. I would never be a beauty like my cousin Vanessa, the well-known model. My coloring was too subdued, my features unremarkable. Fresh-faced and wholesome was one way I'd heard myself described. Still, I thought this time I had risen to the occasion.

It had been storming on and off during the day, and rain now beat against the windowpanes as I hurried back down to the study to turn on the gas logs, another new addition. The grandfather clock struck the half-hour: 7:30. He should be here any moment now. I was setting two glasses on the silver tray containing the brandy decanter when I heard the front door open and his footsteps in the hall. My hero! My husband had returned from a week's trip promoting his latest cookery book.

Ben was peeling off his damp coat. Never had he looked more handsome with rain glistening in his dark hair and his blue green eyes alight with the pleasure of being back where he belonged. I stumbled over his suitcase in getting to him and for several moments I was lost to the thrill of being again in his arms and returning his passionate kiss. It's amazing how even a short absence can revitalize a marriage of six years. I was swept back to those first heady days when he had stormed into my life and I had thought him the most insufferably arrogant, infuriating . . . marvelous man alive. But this wasn't just a reunion. It was the moment for which I had been rehearsing all day. Over and over again I had recited my lines and his too, knowing exactly what he would say when I walked him on stage.

"Come with me," I tugged on his arm. "Have I got something to show you, darling! We're going into the study. Promise to close your eyes when we get to the door and not open them until I've walked you into the middle of the room."

"Not a surprise party?" He recoiled, looking aghast. "There isn't a bunch of people in there. I want it to be just you and me and the children."

Hadn't I known that's what he would say?

"The children are in bed. And there's nobody else here except Tobias, and he's too much of a gentleman to intrude." I laughed in cheerful delight. I just couldn't wait to see my beloved's expression when I had shuffled him into position. Across the flagstones we went, past the twin suits of armor against the staircase wall and through the study door. No doubt about it, my labors had paid off. The room was a vision to behold. Those gas logs gave an apricot glow to the newly hung wallpaper and gleamed upon the polished surfaces. The brandy in the decanter seemed to have caught on fire. How could Ben fail to be as delighted as I was? "You can open your eyes now." I moved back to the doorway, eager not to impede an inch of the view.

"My God, Ellie!" It was the exclamation I had anticipated.

"Surprised?"

"You've changed everything!"

"Out with the old. In with the new," I carroled back at him.

"You shouldn't have!"

The very words I had rehearsed for him! But he was supposed to have included an endearment, such as sweetheart or darling. And I hadn't pictured his eyebrows coming down in an iron bar across his nose. Or that his mouth would have firmed into an equally hard line. For several moments he did not move except to fold his arms. Then he began to pace with thundering steps.

"Where's my typewriter?"

"The old manual?" A quiver entered my voice.

"And my filing cabinet?"

"That beaten up, rusty piece of tin?"

"Ellie," menace throbbed through every syllable, "what have you done with my stuff? I can't work in this fussed-up environment. I want my own things. My lumpy armchair, the old jet gas fire. Why the wallpaper? Why the china cabinet and the silver and crystal?" He was now clutching his head and looking as anguished as if I'd given away his mother to the Salvation Army. "How do you expect me to write? With a quill pen?"

"There's a computer in that cabinet?" I pointed a shaking finger. "And all your files are in the drawers."

"I don't want a damn computer!"

"I thought you would be pleased!"

"Then you thought wrong? What really went on here," he

flung out an arm toppling over a vase, "is that you've been itching to get your hands on this room, the one place in this house that I've called my own, because you thought it wasn't up to your standards as a professional interior designer."

"Ben, I went to a lot of effort"—I did not add that I had also spent an unconscionable amount of money—"to do this for you."

"No, Ellie," he had never before spoken to me so coldly, "you did it for you." Before I could summon up an answer the telephone rang. Feeling relieved at having a reason to leave the room and its suddenly icy atmosphere, I went out into the hall to answer it. When I returned Ben was back to standing with his arms folded.

"That was Mrs. Malloy," I said bleakly, "phoning from the detective agency." He continued standing, staring, silent. "She's been cleaning there in the evenings for the past few weeks. She asked if I could bring her a lipstick she left behind when she was here last. And as it seems to me you're not too keen on my company at the moment, perhaps taking it to her now would be a good idea."

"Should I hire her employer to locate my missing items, or am I likely to find them if I rummage in the attic?" He raised what would have been described in a romance novel as a dark, sardonic eyebrow.

"There's no need to be hateful." I blinked away tears and escaped from the room and out of the house with my raincoat half on and my head in a desperate whirl. Would there ever be a good time to tell him the extent of what he deemed my wicked betrayal? Could my once faithful daily helper Mrs. Malloy offer words of wisdom? After all she had been married herself—more times than she could remember, as she was fond of reminding me. Or would she stick to telling me that I'd made a complete hash of things? It didn't matter. Nothing much mattered. There was no point in telling myself that there were real tragedies going on in the world at that very moment: life savings being lost, nice old people being ill-treated by their relatives, murders being plotted. All I could think about was Ben's wretched ingratitude.

As I drove out onto Cliff Road the curtain came down in a heavy gauze of rain, behind which my unhappy thoughts were left wandering on stage like lost souls in search of a script.

Two

It was no fit night for man nor beast, let alone a female in distress, to be out and about in Mucklesby. Rain lashed against the windows as I parked the car. The wind howled at the top of its lungs when I stepped out onto the curb. The moon peeked furtively out from behind a muffler of clouds. Tucking my already drenched hair under my raincoat collar, I stood under a streetlight to study the address on the scrap of paper I had pulled from my pocket. Thirteen Falcon Way. According to the instructions given to me by Mrs. Malloy this should be the street. And a nasty, seedy place it was with its boarded-up shop windows, graffiti-covered walls and a rusted chain-link fence surrounding a vacant parking lot. A couple of straggly haired youths sidled past me followed by a woman who smelled the worse for drink.

On spotting the lighted doorway of a café, I nipped inside. It was crowded with half-a-dozen tables covered with dark green oil cloths upon which sat bottles of tomato sauce and pink plastic salt and pepper shakers. Only one chair at one table was occupied, by a man having a bad hair day. He should have kept on the hat that was set down at his elbow. On glancing my way he buried his face in the dog-eared menu. It didn't surprise me. I had already decided that Mugglesby wasn't the sort of place to welcome strangers—an unfair assessment, as was proved when a door behind the counter opened.

Out came a woman with at least three chins and a beehive hairdo. Her pink overall matched the salt and pepper shakers. When I said I had come in seeking directions she smiled as though I were a long lost friend.

"I'll take this over to the gent and be right back with you, love," she said. And on returning a few seconds later, having received not so much as a grunt from the man behind the menu, she went on brightly: "It's a good thing he's still here, or I'd have closed up a couple of hours ago. In wintertime I don't stay open as a rule past 6:30. Might as well roll up the pavements after dark in this part of town. And just as well. Cuts down on the muggings. But I'm not one to hurry my customers.

"That's kind."

She gave me a concerned look. My puffy eyelids had to give the game away that I had been crying. "Always the silver lining isn't there? Nasty raw evening to be wandering around lost. Now, tell me, where is it you're looking for, love?" She stood nodding as I gave her the address. "You're as near as to be almost there. This is Falcon Road. Turn left out the door and go to the corner. That's Falcon Way. The building you want used to be the ironmonger's. The bottom half's shut up. But you can get in through the side door to go upstairs to that private detective's place. That's where you're headed I take it?"

"Yes."

"In some sort of trouble are you, love?"

"Nothing like that," I said quickly. "I have to take something to a woman who works for him."

"Well, that's good." Clearly she wasn't sure whether to believe me. "A quiet sort of gent is Mr. Jugg. Comes in here once in a while for his lunch. Always has the cod and chips. Does mostly divorce work, as I understand it. Getting the dirt on husbands that are seeing someone on the side. Wives too I suppose. Marriage isn't what it used to be. And I blame the telly. There's not enough worth watching these days to keep people at home in the armchair. My own hubby started going out with the boys, so he said, Wednesday nights when they took off the snooker." Her chins wobbled disconsolately. "How about I get you a cup of tea before you turn back out into the rain?"

I thanked her, but said I was already late. No doubt she supposed that I had an appointment with Mr. Jugg that would set him on the trail of an errant spouse and a buxom blonde. As I went out the door, I noticed that the man at the table was still holding up the menu and had not touched his baked beans. Focusing on such trivia kept my unhappiness at bay for a few moments. Once back in the street I concentrated on regretting that in my haste to leave the house I hadn't had the sense to bring an umbrella. The pavement was as black and shiny as a freshly applied coat of tar. Rain-shrouded streetlights added a yellowish cast to the puddles that turned the road into a pond. Reaching the corner I turned into what in a more salubrious area might have been called a mews.

Here in Mucklesby, Falcon Way was merely an alley. Dustbins stood rusting next to the crumbling steps. Scarred doors and rotted windowsills added to the grimness of the warehouse-style buildings. And the brick-paved road was so narrow it barely allowed room to park a bicycle let alone a car. A scrawny cat crept up along side me, mewing plaintively in hopes that I had a couple of kippers in my pocket. I felt wicked ignoring it. My own Tobias would be comfortably ensconced in his favorite chair in the warm kitchen. But this one could also belong to someone, I told myself. On spotting number thirteen, I went down a few feet of cracked pathway toward the side door the woman in the café had mentioned. It opened with a melancholy creak onto a dingy flight of steps. A lightbulb dangled from the stairwell. I climbed to a narrow landing where a glass door faced me. This one swung inward without audible protest.

I was now in an office that looked remarkably like the sort I had seen in old movies featuring hard-drinking, hard-boiled private detectives. There were a couple of battered-looking filing cabinets against one wall, a coat stand in the corner sprouting a trilby hat and a desk bare of all essentials except a bottle of bourbon and an overflowing ashtray. Save for a couple of chairs, the room was otherwise empty. An inner door opened.

Coming toward me was a woman whose face and figure were as familiar to me as my own. She had, after all, been an important part of my life since the first days of my marriage. Since our last meeting, however, her appearance had undergone a dramatic change. Where once she had worn black taffeta frocks better suited to a nightclub than turning out the guest bedroom, she now sported a miniskirt and tight angora sweater. Her hair, which had always been dyed black, was now platinum blond. Only her makeup was the same. But the familiar neon-coated eyelids, false eyelashes, brick-colored rouge and magenta lipstick did little to lessen my shock.

"So what do you think, Mrs. H.?" She twirled about on her four-inch heels.

I was thinking that I couldn't say what I was thinking. Mrs. Malloy was a robustly built woman, and I suspected that she had to be wearing an iron ribbed corset under that skirt.

"Very nice," I managed.

"That don't sound overly enthusiastic." Planting her hands on her hips, she jutted out her imposing bosom. "But all's forgiven. I could tell you wasn't yourself when I phoned. For a moment I didn't think it was you speaking."

"Who else would it have been?" I responded bleakly.

"A burglar come to pinch all the silver. Would have been doing me a favor seeing as how I hate polishing the stuff."

"Oh, for heaven's sake, Mrs. Malloy! You've hardly been at Merlin's Court to polish anything since you started working here in the evenings. And I really can't see what there is here," I said, surveying the small room, "to keep you so busy."

"Trying to better meself, that's what I'm doing!" She parked herself in the desk chair, reached into a drawer for a battered packet of Lucky Strikes and lit up with a flourish. I was never more appalled. Mrs. M. was partial to a glass of gin, but I had never known her to smoke. "For your information, Mrs. H.," she continued with a determined look on her face, "I'm hoping that if I make meself a presence around here, Mr. Jugg will appoint me his Girl Friday. I've been teaching meself to type. Up to four words a minute, I am."

"Congratulations." I wandered over to the filing cabinets and back.

"You're put out, and I don't wonder!" She blew a couple of smoke rings. "I've been your right hand and no mistake. But much as I've enjoyed slaving away for you these past years, there hasn't been much in the way of mental stimulation, if you get my meaning. Which isn't to say," she stubbed out the cigarette in the hideous ashtray and adopted a more conciliatory tone, "that I'm handing in me notice. Once I get the hang of things around here, I'm sure I'll be able to fit you back in of a now and then."

"That's awfully kind." Not having been offered a chair, I stood unbuttoning and rebuttoning my raincoat.

"You could try and sound like you're broken hearted not to have me at your beck and call."

"One has to accept what life dishes out."

"I must say you don't sound at all yourself." Mrs. Malloy's voice shifted from peevishness to professionalism. "And you look something awful."

"Naturally," I snapped. "Your directions weren't first-rate, and I nearly drowned finding this place." To impress the point I lifted my hair, which had come undone from its chignon, out from under my raincoat collar and wrung it out briskly.

She waved a dismissive hand. "That's all by the by. Your

nose is red, your eyes is puffy, which means you've been crying. Also you've got one black shoe on and one brown. Clearly the situation is desperate."

"Please," I spluttered, "do stop talking as though you're already Mr. Jugg's Girl Friday."

My former ally furrowed her brow, closed her eyes, then snapped them open. "Speaking strictly professionally, the problem has to be Mr. H.! Gone and upset you, has he?"

"As a matter of fact . . ." I swallowed a sob along with a mouthful of secondhand smoke.

"Got himself a dolly on the side, I suppose." Mrs. Malloy oozed sympathy. "Well, I can't say as I'm surprised. Husbands are men when all's said and done. And yours is a good-looking bloke with that dark hair and those be-damned-to-you blue eyes."

"They're more green than blue." I sank down on the chair across from the desk. A feeling of lassitude enveloped me. Within seconds I would be hopelessly trapped in the persona of distraught client.

"Want to have him and the nasty little home-wrecker put under surveillance?" She reached for a lethally sharpened pencil. "That sort of thing is a big part of our business here at Jugg's Detective Agency. That and missing persons."

"There is no other woman," I said, endeavoring to square my shoulders. "Ben and I have had a minor tiff, that's all. I'm sure he didn't mean to be beastly and horribly ungrateful. And I don't doubt that by the time our golden wedding anniversary rolls around we will both have completely forgotten about it."

Mrs. Malloy's eyes narrowed. "Ticked off was he, that you went behind his back and did over his study?"

"He wasn't pleased."

"Well, I did try to warn you he wouldn't be thrilled." She tossed me a gun that had been on the desk next to the ashtray. For a blurred moment I thought she was offering me a way out of my misery. But when she handed me a cigarette I realized that what I had taken for a dainty pistol was in fact one of those gimmicky lighters. Without pausing to think, I lit up and at once felt vaguely cheered. Surely if one's own husband treated one like a fiend out of hell there wasn't much reason not to behave like one. To further substantiate the point I accepted the tumbler of bourbon Mrs. Malloy handed me.

"Won't Mr. Jugg mind?"

"Keeps it for clients. Never drinks on the job, he doesn't." She spoke apologetically, as if hoping this wouldn't make me think less of him.

"Down the hatch." I tossed off a gulp and felt my insides turn to molten ore.

"Course he'll probably make up for holding himself in check, now he's gone off on his holidays." Mrs. M. perched on the edge of the desk, her black miniskirt hitching up several more inches. When she crossed her legs I noticed between puffs of my cigarette that her stockings had seams down the back. Her face assumed a dreamy expression. "I expect Mr. Jugg will rent himself a room in some real dive and lay around half the day and most of the night on a bare mattress, when he isn't sitting on a barstool, thinking tortured thoughts of the blonde in the black Chanel suit that shot his partner, then wound herself around his heart, hoping he'd not realize she'd been working for the gang that stole the Green-Eyed God of Cat-Man-Chew. But being the clever dick he is, he saw through her. And had to send her up the river."

I couldn't imagine where Mr. Jugg would readily find a dive compared to this one in which to hole up. Accepting a second cigarette, I said that at least he consoled himself by smoking on the job. Mrs. Malloy's response was an apologetic shake of the head. I looked with alarm at the pile of butts in the ashtray. "Surely they're not all yours?"

"That was Mr. Jugg's 2:30 client. Smoked his head off, he

did. Suspected his wife of carrying on with his sister-in-law's cousin's uncle. I'd come in to practice me typing, like I told you I've been doing. The poor man was here for a couple of hours. Well, a complicated story like that takes time to tell, but I could see Mr. Jugg looking at his watch because he had a 6:00 coming in. And if that got off to a late start he'd likely miss his train. But as it happened the second client didn't show. And Mr. Jugg was away on time."

"I should get back home." I felt like a juggler with my cigarette in one hand and glass of bourbon in the other.

"Not coming out to have a drink with me?"

"I'm having one," I pointed out.

"So you are, Mrs. H." She topped up my glass. "But that's not the same as going down to the pub and having a knees-up with the locals."

"I'd just as soon avoid that." I reached for another cigarette. "I don't feel up to facing the madding crowd right now; now don't go looking put out. I'll loll around in my damp raincoat a bit longer and soak up this foray into wickedness."

"I hate it when you go talking posh." Mrs. Malloy's voice was somewhat slurred, and she was tilting sideways on the desk. "You did remember to bring my lipstick, didn't you?"

"It's the reason I came. You made it clear you couldn't live without it—which I don't quite understand."

"Well, it's not just the lipstick, although it is the perfect color with me delicate complexion. Neither nor is it the lovely black and gold case. Sentimental value. Finding it down the back of the couch in me living room was what got me convinced me third husband—or it could have been the fourth— had been carrying on with me neighbor Ethel while I was out Wednesday nights at Bingo. If it hadn't been for that lipstick I'd probably still be married to the man. Gullible as all get-out I was in me forties."

"Well, here it is." I stuck a hand in my raincoat pocket.

"What a relief." She tapped her replenished glass against mine.

"Un . . . for . . . tunate . . . ly," I had never realized before what a long word it was, "Rose found it first and wrote all over the walls with it. I thought I'd have to repaper, but sitting here thinking about it, I think those purple squiffles . . . squiggles may grow on me. She didn't use it all." I spoke into the mounting silence, "There's a nub left, but I'll buy you an . . . other one."

"They don't make that color no more."

"Oh, dear!"

While waiting for Mrs. M. to burst into sobs, I lit another cigarette. But she rallied nobly.

"There's no good blaming a two-year-old child. Course I've always said you spoil her 'cos she's the baby and you were so relieved when your cousin Vanessa finally signed the papers and you got to adopt her. Neither do I blame you for that matter, what with this rift between you and Mr. H. Couldn't be expected you'd be in any state to think of other people's hopes and dreams. I'd had this lovely fantasy, you see, of Mr. Jugg finishing with his difficult client, then laying eyes on me. I'd be emptying the ashtrays, and his eyes would be drawn like a magnet to me Purple Passion lips and it would hit him like a wallop that I was a real woman."

"Whereupon he'd ask you to marry him?"

"No," she spoke dreamily, "he'd tell me in ever such a masterful voice to sit down and take dictation." A pause. "What could be sexier than that, Mrs. H.?"

I didn't answer. Suddenly I was feeling extremely peculiar. The room was spinning, and Mrs. Malloy's face kept shrinking. Her voice seemed to come at me from the ceiling.

"Men being what they are, I'm sure Mr. H. will get over his snit," she was saying. "Probably what's upsetting him more than your getting rid of his stuff without his say so is all the money you spent fixing up the study the way you wanted it . . . for him, of course."

"The money was going to come out of my own earnings from a couple of design jobs," I explained. "But at the last moment both clients backed out. One woman decided to go on a cruise rather than redo her house, and the other took my ideas right down to one of the discount furniture places. And . . ." The desk was now floating across the room with Mrs. Malloy on board.

"Mr. H. can be hot tempered. Well, you do have to allow for the literary temperament, don't you? Him being a book writer when all is said and done. And cookery books no less. First-rate fiction most of them."

"What do you mean, fiction?" I put down my glass and pressed a hand to my clammy brow.

Her voice throbbed its way inside my head. "Have you ever had a recipe turn out like them cookery books promise? They tell you the Lancashire hotpot serves eight and there's not enough to feed you and the cat. And the cakes always as big and round as hatboxes. But more power to Mr. H., if he can earn a living making millions of women think they can get their egg whites to peak like Mount Everest."

"I feel awful." I wobbled to my feet.

"Well, now you say it, you do look a bit off. I wonder if it could be something you ate before coming here? But never mind that. Let's get you to the loo. Mrs. Malloy was marching me forward as she spoke. "If you're going to be sick I'd as soon it wasn't on this floor. Here we are Mrs. H., I'm opening the door for you and switching on the light. I'll be right outside if you should need me."

I would have preferred her to be in Timbuktu. There are times when one wants to be completely alone in the world. But after five minutes, having soaked my face in cold water and brushed my hair back from my forehead I felt somewhat recovered. Whatever had possessed me to smoke and drink like a sailor? Surely not the seaside ambience of Mucklesby?

Mrs. Malloy peeked in on me. "I was thinking about milk," she informed me as if this was of far greater importance than the state of my health.

I stared at her.

"Mr. Jugg. Milk is his nickname, given to him by an auntie when he was small."

"Really?" I trailed after her to lean against the big desk.

"There has to be a way to make him see that he can't do without me. I've got a fortnight, two whole weeks to work on becoming his Girl Friday. And," she smiled brightly, "I've decided to let you help me, even though you've shown you can't hold your liquor. It'll take your mind off your troubles."

"Help you? How?"

"We'll think of something," she said impatiently. "And it will have to be something more than doing up the place by putting a few potted plants on the windowsill."

She had barely finished speaking when a knock sounded at the door. Mrs. Malloy called: "Come in!" And in walked an elderly woman, regally clad in black, from her 1940s-style hat and flowing velvet cape to her buttoned boots.

Here, belatedly, was the 6:00 client.

Three

"Has to be her, don't it?" Mrs. Malloy stage whispered in my ear, while the woman in black took stock of the room. "Wouldn't be some gypsy come selling clothes peg; not at this hour, it wouldn't. Name's Lady Krumley. Got aristocracy written all over her long-nosed puss. But don't you go bobbing no curtsies, trying to get in thick, Mrs. H. We've no time for none of that. You and me, we've got to come up with a way to handle this here situation."

I wasn't at all sure I liked the sound of this. My insides still felt a bit unsure of themselves, and my head began revolving on its own axis several feet above my shoulders. Fortunately her ladyship did not appear to notice anything amiss. At her age—well into her seventies—she could be blessedly hard of hearing and worn out by her journey.

She might have been in the throes of hypnosis as she lowered herself onto a chair, rested her carpet-style handbag on her knees and drew the black velvet cape across the buttoned-up bosom of her decidedly dated frock. Were the odd clothes a misguided attempt at disguise, I wondered? I could almost see the thought drift off into the still lingering haze of tobacco smoke. Holding onto the edge of Milk Jugg's desk, I wavered a glance at Mrs. Malloy that I hoped would make it clear that Lady Krumley's arrival was none of my concern.

My place was at home with the husband who might at this

moment be planning to divorce me if I did not restore his study to what he considered its old world charm. The fact that I couldn't at that moment quite remember what he looked like did not stop me from deciding to telephone Kathleen Ambleforth, the vicar's wife, to ask her to return the items that she had assured me, with such grateful enthusiasm, would do very nicely for St. Anselm's annual charity drive. Kathleen I could picture all too well. She has a grimly controlled temper behind her brisk smile. Taking a firmer grip of the desk, it seemed to me the better part of cowardice to focus on returning Lady Krumley's blank stare.

She was, to put it as kindly as possible, a horse-faced woman beset with an oversized Roman nose, a sloping chin and hooded eyes, so dark as to be almost black. But perhaps when my head cleared she would improve. At the moment her hair was undoubtedly her best feature. It was was thick and coarse and either from art or nature mahogany in color, with only a touch of gray at the temples. She wore it wound in a thick coil topped by the 1940s-style hat.

Undoubtedly, Kathleen Ambleforth would have coveted that hat for the charity drive. I focused on it in an attempt to stop the walls revolving and prayed that Mrs. Malloy would do nothing to distract me. No use hoping for miracles. She wasn't about to fade gracefully into the woodwork. Not while wearing the pink angora sweater that looked as though it had been stolen from Marilyn Monroe, or the miniskirt that might once have been one leg of a pair of boy's shorts. The wretched woman was all bounce and enthusiasm as she informed her ladyship that it didn't matter a whit that it was now 9:00 and Mr. Jugg had left for the day.

"Better late than never," she batted her false eyelashes. At least you're here on your own two feet. Not in a bag with your arms being used for straps."

"Most kind!" came the quavering reply.

"And don't you go worrying your old head that there's only me and Mrs. Haskell to help sort out the problem that's got you into a state of fear and trembling, Lady Krumley." The obnoxiously bracing voice floated somewhere to my left.

"Mrs. Who?" Her ladyship opened her hooded lids a crack and surveyed me down the full length of that unfortunate nose. Her expression could have devoured at least three scullery maids, but her tone was bemused. She was coming back to life, slowly if surely.

"Haskell," chirped Mrs. Malloy, before I could get my lips unstuck.

"And she is?" The look directed my way registered the suspicion that I was tragically mute.

"Another of me lovely employers." A technically accurate but completely misleading reply delivered by Mrs. Malloy.

Lady Krumley straightened in her chair, her eyes suddenly snapping with inquiry. "This person," waving a gloved hand that missed me by inches, "is Mr. Jugg's business partner? But I had understood from the worthy source who suggested I seek assistance here that Mr. Jugg was a sole practitioner in the private detective business."

"Mrs. Haskell hasn't been on the scene long." Mrs. Malloy stood to my right on her high heels looking the picture of truth and rectitude. This was the moment for me to take a stand. Instead, as the floor began to tilt like the *Titanic*, I was forced to sit down and press a hand to my mouth.

"Looks a decent person. Nicely enough dressed for a woman of her stamp. Neat sort of hairstyle. Nothing too modern." Her ladyship was stripping off her gloves as she spoke and stowing them away in the handbag. "And who might you be, if it's not too complicated to explain?"

"Roxie Malloy, Mr. Jugg's Girl Friday."

Her ladyship appraised Mrs. M. in all her blonde-headed glory. "My pleasure. Although I must say that skirt's far too short and I have always believed pink to be a debutante's color. Still, I suppose one might justifiably suggest I am out of step with the modern generation."

Mrs. Malloy, who had abruptly stopped preening, brightened.

"My late husband, Sir Horace, occasionally cautioned me to moderate my opinions." Her ladyship shifted her carpet bag from her black-clad knees to the floor. "But we will however, come to him in due time. As I was saying I hadn't anticipated confiding in more than one pair of ears. To be frank, it never crossed my mind that Mr. Jugg would have a secretary or whatever they're called these days, let alone a partner." Lady Krumley looked around the office with its bare bones furnishings, uncurtained, night-darkened windows and the motley assortment of plants. Even my blurred vision took in the fact that the plastic ones looked as if they needed watering and the real ones appeared horribly fake. Clearly Lady Krumley, who undoubtedly had her own conservatory back at the ancestral hole, as my cousin Freddy would call it, was under no delusions that she was visiting Kew Gardens.

"The person who gave me the direction to this detective agency advised me that Mr. Jugg was very much a lone wolf," she continued in an increasingly robust voice. "But we never know all there is to know about anyone, do we, even when the relationship's of considerable duration?"

Mrs. M., for reasons I was unable to fathom, again looked put out. But she kept her voice affable. "Now don't you go being afraid, old ducks—meaning your ladyship—to spill the beans about what brings you here," She eyed the butts in the ashtray, but whether because she suddenly noticed they looked and smelled disgusting or because she was dying for a puff, I couldn't tell. "Discretion's the name of the game here at Jugg's Detective Agency. Always has been, always will be. Milk's been in the business a long time."

"Milk?" Her ladyship raised an inquiring eyebrow. "I wasn't given to understand he was also in the dairy business."

"It's his nickname." I cautiously supplied this tidbit.

"Ah, yes. I do see."

"Course only them closest to him use it regular like. But call him what you will. Doesn't mean the man don't know that one wrong word in the wrong ears could have some very nasty results." To illustrate her point, Mrs. Malloy drew a finger across her throat. A gesture wasted on her ladyship who directed her hooded gaze at me.

"I suppose it helps, in that regard, his partner being a mute."

Which of course completely took my voice away. Not so Mrs. Malloy. She tossed her blond locks, fluttered her heavily blackened lashes and giggled like a fifteen-year-old. "Got a sense of humor, haven't you, ducks? Course Mrs. Haskell can talk. Shell-shocked, that's what she is at this minute. Just come in from a nasty showdown between a husband and wife over some missing property. Very unpleasant these domestic situations can turn. I'll not say no more, but I'm sure you can picture it."

Clearly Lady Krumley could. The bullet holes in the library wainscoting, the bloodstains on the Persian carpet, the family dog covering its face with its paws in the corner, to say nothing of the body that would have to be temporarily put in the sideboard if the bridge game was to begin on time. I made the mistake of looking at the ashtray and another chance to speak up was lost.

"Horrible stuff we see in this business." Mrs. M. looked positively blissful. "Still, no disrespect to Milk, some jobs in this business are best left to women is what I say. Can't expect a man to really understand the female viewpoint, now can you?"

"You may be right." Her ladyship's eyelids narrowed. "Even my dear Horace was not always sensitive to my way of looking at things. Indeed, part of my reason for being late for my appointment was that I lost track of time wondering if Mr. Jugg would dismiss my fears as flights of feminine fantasy."

"There you are, then!" Mrs. Malloy was at her most triumphant. "All turned out for the best, didn't it? How about I fix you a good stiff drink before we get started? And don't be afraid to go ahead and smoke if you fancy a ciggy. Mrs. Haskell and me aren't ones to pass judgment. Would be the pot calling the kettle black, wouldn't it?"

It was all too much for me. Prying myself away from the desk I fled in what I hoped was the direction of the loo, somehow in the process managing to drag Mrs. Malloy along with me. She mumbled something over her shoulder, and I caught a glimpse of Her Ladyship's startled black gaze before I found myself again hanging over the washbasin. Oh, the blessed chill of the porcelain! For a moment I prayed for the guillotine to come slicing down on my neck, and then all at once—miraculously— I was whole and healthy again. Amazing! The floor didn't tilt. The room didn't spin. And even Mrs. Malloy's aggrieved voice did not make me wish to take a nosedive into the toilet and be flushed away into oblivion.

"Well, I hope you're proper ashamed of yourself, Mrs. H., giving that poor little old lady the silent treatment."

"I didn't feel well."

"Rubbish! You look proper blooming to me this minute. Never been so shown up in me life, I haven't! And after me going and promoting you too! Anyone else would have made you the secretary and me Mr. Jugg's partner. Unselfish to the core, that's always been me trouble. But there's no use standing here crying over spilt milk."

I didn't ask if there was any pun intended. "Lady Krumley isn't little," I said. She has to be five foot eight in her bare feet. And I doubt very much given the title that she's poor."

"There you go, picking me words apart like a sink full of lettuce! We've got to get back in there before she gets the wind up and disappears into the night." Mrs. Malloy stood like Justice on a pedestal, but I turned to straighten my hair in the dinky little mirror above the basin, feeling stronger by the minute. There was no way I was going to allow her to intimidate me into posing as a private detective—something I was sure would have nasty legal consequences. One petty criminal in the family was enough, thank you very much.

My cousin Freddy's mother, Aunt Lulu, had taken up shoplifting years ago when her women friends chose needlepoint or bridge as a hobby. To date she had not found herself in the dock facing a judge wearing a wig his wife had crocheted and who was not inclined to be moved by the fact that the accused claimed to give most of her "finds," as she termed them, to charitable organizations.

"So her ladyship's a tough-looking old bird living in a house with four hundred rooms—from the address I peeked at in Mr. Jugg's appointment book." Mrs. Malloy's blonde hair sat on her head like an ill-fitting halo. "Moldy Towers, I think that's the name of the place."

"Surely not!"

"I'm not here to argue with you, Mrs. H." Amazingly, Mrs. Malloy's nose did not grow with this brazen lie. "The point I'm making is that Lady Krumley wouldn't be here if she wasn't in some fearful sort of trouble, now would she?"

"People seek out private detectives for all sorts of reasons. She might suspect the butcher of overcharging her, for all we know."

"More like her very life's at stake. Otherwise why not send her man of business or someone of that sort?" She spoke with a long drawn-out hiss. "Her sort aren't used to doing for themselves. Not unless it's something they want kept hush-hush. Think on that!"

I didn't answer.

Mrs. Malloy wagged a finger under my nose. "What if she

was to walk out of here without us finding out what's up, and we was to read in the newspapers tomorrow that she'd been found stuffed in an attic trunk or dead from arsenic in the soup or pushed off one of them bloomin' towers? Course," Mrs. Malloy added to fend off any protests on my part, "could be there aren't no towers, for all you'd think that's how the place got its name."

"Really?"

"Too right! I once knew a woman as lived in a house called The Firs. And not so much as a Christmas tree front or back. You know the sort, always putting on airs, some people! But then again you did have to feel sorry for Doris, seeing as how she had a nephew that did her out of the money she'd saved up to buy the washing machine she'd been dreaming about for years."

"I'm sure Lady Krumley has plenty of washing machines. Enough to bequeath to the charity of her choice." I edged toward the door.

"And I'll bet you me second best fur coat, Mrs. H., she's also got a nasty nephew like they always have sneaking around in them Agatha Christie books."

"Who's desperate to inherit all the household appliances," I nodded.

"That's right!" Mrs. Malloy looked pleased as Punch that I was finally beginning to realize we were in the business of sniffing out evil. "And then of course they'll be the wicked step-daughter and the nasty chauffeur what's really a cousin from the wrong side of the blanket and the smiley-faced bank manager that's been embezzling the money Lady Krumley's hubby left when he died and . . ."

"A whole bunch of other good-for-nothings," I agreed smoothly, "anyone of whom could be itching to bump off her ladyship. I'm sure Mr. Jugg will have the time of his life sorting it all out when he returns. Although from what you've been telling me he's more interested in rooting out evil from the mean streets than the drawing room. Oh, well a change of pace never hurt anyone."

"I'm sure I don't know how you can be so callous!" Mrs. M. indicted. "What if you find out too late Lady Krumley was in mortal danger?"

She got me there.

"I should never have made you a partner in Jugg's Detective Agency." She folded her arms, thrusting her bosom ceiling-ward. "There's not many that gets promoted after fifteen minutes of drinking the company booze and smoking cigarettes like they was going up in price the next day. But there's no point in standing here breaking me heart over that poor woman in there. Thank goodness I bought meself that new winter coat. At least I'll be able to go to her funeral without fear of showing meself or Mr. Jugg up."

"Enough!" I was ready to capitulate. "I already feel like a villain out on parole after Ben's reaction tonight. It probably won't do any irrevocable harm to go back in there and hear what Lady Krumley has to say."

"Thanks for them kind words, Mrs. H."

"Think nothing of it."

"Well, they do say blondes have more fun, don't they?" Patting her hair complacently, Mrs. Malloy gave a final preen for luck in the mirror, before sailing ahead of me into the office, where our spirits were immediately dampened by a most unnerving sight: Lady Krumley slumped forward in her chair. At least we thought it was her ladyship. It was at first difficult to be one hundred percent certain, given that her hat was tipped down over her nose, which Milk Jugg, had he been here, might have documented in his notes as her most distinguishing feature.

Four

"How unforgivably rude of me to doze off." Lady Krumley raised her head and blinked in upper-crust distress. Only a nightmare could have brought her to this office with its plastic plants and inhospitable furniture. She sat rolling her gloves on her lap. "It has been months since my last heart attack, Mrs. Haskell, so one may not use that as an excuse. My home is in Biddlington-By-Water, not thirty miles from Mucklesby. Therefore, the journey was not the problem. It only seemed long because I haven't driven myself in years. My apologies to both of you," she said, directing her nose in Mrs. Malloy's direction, "for delaying you even longer after my late arrival."

"Don't give it a thought your ladyship ducks! But while you're on about it, what did keep you from your appointment with Mr. Jugg?" Mrs. Malloy nudged me toward Milk's chair and perched her miniskirted behind on a metal folding one, next to the dilapidated filing cabinet.

"Some vicious thugs took potshots as I drove past the Biddlington-By-Water police station."

"You were fired at?" I dropped the pencil I had just picked up.

"Thrown at!" Her ladyship's features narrowed, reducing her to a beaky-nosed silhouette. "They were sizeable flower pots, filled with bronze and yellow chrysanthemums." Such a sinful

waste of good flowers. "Not only was my front passenger window shattered, but I looked as though I had requested to be
buried in my car."

"And you wanting to look ever so nice for Mr. Jugg." Mrs.
Malloy was all womanly sympathy.

"You weren't hurt, Lady Krumley," I asked.

. "Shaken up and nerves all to pieces, nothing more."

"Do you think you were followed by someone who knew you
were on your way to consult with a private detective?"

"Not at all; I never said a word to anyone, except Mr. Featherstone, my friend and vicar, about where I was going."

"Then who?"

Her ladyship frowned with all the aristocratic command at
her disposal. "I very much fear that the assault was perpetrated
by someone aggrieved by my refusal to contribute to this year's
Police Benevolent Fund. One does have to watch one's pen-
nies these days. And I did see a heavyset man slinking off as
I rubbed the dirt out of my eyes. I suspect it was Constable
Thatcher without his helmet. But I may be doing the man an
injustice. He and his wife did send a wreath, rather a showy
one, for my sister-in-law Mildred's funeral last April."

"Nasty losing a family member." Mrs. Malloy would have set
her face at half-mast if possible.

"Mildred was my late husband Sir Horace's youngest sister.
A very spry eighty-year-old to the end, but I never questioned
her passing away in her sleep while on a fortnight's holiday in
Liverpool. After all, who can bear to spend more than a few
days in such a place? Even when the others began dying it
never occurred to me that an evil force might be at work." Lady
Krumley's voice faltered as she stared grimly into some distant
space.

"So that's why you're all got up in black." Mrs. Malloy
couldn't keep the excitement out of her voice. "Relatives dropping off the family twig willy nilly." She stood up with a good

display of leg and poured herself a shot of bourbon. I shook my head, but Lady Krumley accepted a glass.

"Sir Horace would have expected me to go into mourning, even though it isn't much done these days and he never had more than minimal contact with any of the recently departed, including Mildred."

"So there was others!" Mrs. Malloy beamed.

Her ladyship inclined her head. "Cousin Clement resided in Australia. He was mauled to death by a passing kangaroo in June. Uncle Dickie resided in one of the Channel Islands and met a mercifully swift end whilst celebrating his ninetieth birthday bungee jumping or whatever it is called. Aunt Theobalda was living in a loft in some newly trendy part of the East End and stepped into a lift that wasn't there." Her ladyship swigged down her bourbon. "All of them ancient and addled in their wits. One may not always like one's relatives. Yet only a fiend would sit back and watch them being systematically wiped off the map. Especially when knowing where the blame lies."

"Where is that Lady Krumley?" I inquired with what I hoped was the right amount of professional interest, although, to be honest, I couldn't see that this was going anywhere that mattered.

"With myself. I, Mrs. Haskell, am the villain of this piece!" She rose in a swoop of black to take a brisk walk to the outer office door and back. The hat trembled to one side, but her voice when she resumed speaking was calm. "I must say I now find it a relief that I was not in time to consult with Mr. Jugg. Men are too readily inclined to dismiss a woman's fears as hysterics. Sir Horace had a way of fidgeting with his thumbs when vexed by what he termed the excess of my imagination. No doubt he would insist that I am dramatizing the current situation."

"Husbands can be our sternest critics," I opined sadly.

"How right you are, Mrs. Haskell." Lady Krumley returned to

her chair. "Sir Horace was twenty years older than I. But it can hardly be said that I was a giddy young girl at age thirty-five, when I came as a bride to Moultty"—she spelled out the word—"Towers."

"I thought Mr. Jugg said Mouldy." Mrs. Malloy sounded justifiably aggrieved.

"That's the pronunciation. Has been for centuries. Nothing to do with our occasional problems with dry rot. Sir Horace was devoted to restoring the house to the way it had been before his father allowed it to fall into disrepair. Which makes it so particularly dreadful that it was I who sullied the family crest—Serve Well Thy Servitors—when close on forty years ago I sacked Flossie Jones."

"Who?" I asked, pencil poised above a dog-eared notepad.

"The parlor maid."

"Why did you get rid of her?"

"For stealing an emerald and diamond brooch."

"Well now, that was naughty!" Mrs. Malloy, as president of the Chitterton Fells Charwomen's Association, had her standards.

"You believe this incident has some bearing on the recent deaths you mentioned?" My glance at the uncurtained window showed it blacked out by night as if in wartime. Just how late was it now? How long before I would see home again? A tale dating back forty years was unlikely to be told in as many seconds. Would Ben think I had run away from home to destroy other marriages by revamping whole cities of unsuspecting husbands' studies?

"It has every bearing." Her ladyship slapped her knee with her gloves. "I now know Flossie Jones was falsely accused and, therefore, wrongfully dismissed. One week ago Laureen Phillips, my newly hired personal maid—very diligent in her duties—found the brooch between the skirting board and the wall in my bedroom, close to the dressing table from which it must have fallen all those years ago."

"You're saying?" I was at a loss to do more than resharpen my pencil.

"Isn't it as clear as the nose on her ladyship's face?" Mrs. Malloy was so excited she handed her ladyship another bourbon and sat down without bothering to pour herself one. "This Flossie woman is taking her revenge by bumping off all these members of the family! Well, one good thing. It shouldn't be hard to catch up with her. All we have to do is look for someone as fits her description that's been bobbing about on holiday all of a sudden to Australia and the like. Course she's probably aged a bit like we all do, but even so . . ."

"If bent on murder," I interposed, "why wait this long to get busy, and, if you'll forgive me, Lady Krumley, why not start with you?"

"I am not talking murder, Mrs. Haskell, at least not in the usual sense of the word." The bourbon disappeared in a gulp. "Flossie herself died within a year of leaving Moultty Towers. My contention is that she is wreaking havoc from beyond the grave. With her last breath Flossie Jones cursed the Krumley family."

"Gracious me!" Mrs. M. looked unsuitably thrilled.

"Are you absolutely sure the brooch your new maid discovered was the one that had gone missing?" The night wind moaned an echo and somewhere inside the building a floorboard creaked, but I didn't go and take a peak outside the office to see if anyone was lurking in the shadows. Her ladyship's dark tale, had yet to set my nerves jumping.

"Not a doubt in the world! That brooch was engraved on the back with his Sir Horace's maternal grandmother's initials and her birth date. He was seriously displeased at the time of its disappearance by what he asserted was my carelessness with a family heirloom. I had left it on the dressing table instead of locking it up in my jewelry box."

"Was it extremely valuable?"

"A mere trinket." She waved a gnarled hand. "It wasn't even insured. The stones weren't the finest, having been given to Sir Horace's grandmother when she was a young girl by an aunt in straitened circumstances."

"Shame! But have to cut your garment according to the cloth." Mrs. Malloy shook her head as if remembering all the second- or third-rate emeralds and diamonds she had accepted with feigned enthusiasm.

"My husband liked me to wear it. Alas, truth be told, it was not to my taste. Far too dainty and demure. It was never my desire to look like a determinedly youthful debutante. There were already enough people wondering why he had married a beanpole like me, when he might have had his choice among the great beauties of the day. Sir Horace was at that time an extremely handsome man in his mid-fifties; indeed his looks never left him. Upon his death ten years later he made a fine corpse." Lady Krumley stared into some distant place.

"Tell us how Flossie came into the matter?" I prodded gently, feeling an unexpectedly strong wave of sympathy for the autocratic old lady.

"Sir Horace and I had been married for three or four years when she came to work at Moultty Towers. Her Christian name was actually Florence. But as that was also the housekeeper Mrs. Snow's name, the senior members of the staff would have deemed it an impertinence for a parlor maid to share it. Hopkins the butler, after consulting with me, made the necessary adjustment. That should of course have been the end of the matter." Her ladyship's mouth tightened. But the girl protested to Sir Horace, not to Mrs. Snow or to me. I was annoyed. My husband amused. He laughed and said the girl had spunk and that we should make allowances. He reminded me that it had become increasingly difficult since wartime to keep any sort of help, good, bad or indifferent."

Mrs. Malloy opened her mouth. I thought she was about to state the main cannon of the Chitterton Fells Charwomen's Association, that employers needed to be kept firmly in their place. But she bit her lip remembering, no doubt, that if she really wanted to become Milk Jugg's Girl Friday, her first objective must be to keep the client talking.

"May I?" Lady Krumley reached out a hand for the half-empty packet of cigarettes on the desk. "I haven't touched the things in months. Doctor's orders." She lit up. "But what he doesn't know won't hurt him."

I wanted to say that it wasn't her doctor we needed to worry about. But who was I, after my recent stint with tobacco, to tell a seventy-plus titled woman she would be better off sucking her thumb? Cowardly of me. But I couldn't see into the future to know how bitterly I would regret not snatching that cigarette out of her mouth.

"Despite being amused by Flossie's cheek, as Mrs. Snow called it, Sir Horace told her that she would have to do as she was told about the name business, or find other employment." Her ladyship dangled her cigarette above the ashtray. "For several months she must have performed her duties adequately enough for I heard no more about her, until one morning Mrs. Snow reported to me that the girl was pregnant by the under gardner. And not evincing an ounce of shame! The young man was willing to make an honest woman of her, but seemingly Flossie wasn't sure that she wished to be married."

"Hanging out for a decent engagement ring, is my guess." Mrs. Malloy nodded her blonde head. "One with a proper diamond, not the sort you can't see even with a magnifying glass. Or perhaps the girl preferred emeralds. Taken a fancy to your brooch, had she? Is that why you thought she stole it?"

Her ladyship stubbed out her cigarette and lit up another.

"On the day the brooch disappeared Mrs. Snow informed me that she had seen the girl sneaking out of my bedroom, a place where a parlor maid had no business being. I had already, with the assistance of my personal maid, searched not only my bedroom and bathroom but also Sir Horace's adjoining suite, all to no avail."

"Because the brooch had dropped off the dressing table and was lodged between the skirting board and the wall?" I looked up from the scrawls I had been making on the notepad. "Meaning it wasn't found in Flossie's possession. Did you act entirely upon Mrs. Snow's information?"

"Well, you have to admit that made things look bad for the girl," tut-tutted Mrs. M., who would have taken the utmost offense if barred from any room at Merlin's Court and indeed would have taken up permanent residence in my wardrobe if she felt like it.

Her ladyship stared bleakly through a cloud of smoke. "Flossie didn't act the innocent when I sent for her. Her self-satisfied smirk was most annoying. She was pretty in a pert, snub-nosed sort of way. When I told her that the brooch was missing and that Mrs. Snow had seen her exiting my bedroom she tossed her head and was insolent, to put it mildly."

"What did she say, your ladyship ducks?" Mrs. Malloy leaned so far forward on her folding metal chair that she almost toppled into the wastepaper basket.

"To repeat her precise words: I was a spiteful old cow. Jealous that she was going to have a baby when I never would, because I was too old, along with being as plain as a flannel nightgown. She said the brooch was just a trumped-up excuse for my getting rid of her. If she had wanted it she would have taken it, but she hadn't. And Mrs. Snow was a snake in the grass."

"Hardly surprising that you sacked her." I didn't add that I thought Flossie might be right about Mrs. Snow.

"I told Flossie the room she shared with the kitchen maid

The Importance of Being Ernestine   35

was being searched as we spoke, but that didn't seem to bother her in the least. Indeed, she grinned more broadly than ever"— Lady Krumley was now onto her third cigarette—"making me sure she had hidden it elsewhere. So I wasn't surprised when it did not turn up. There was no doubt in my mind as to her guilt. Only anger when she said she would go to Sir Horace and hear what he would have to say about the matter. It was appallingly clear that she believed that being a man, however elevated above her lowly situation in life, he could be charmed into saving her from being dismissed. As it happened he was away from home that evening, and by the time he returned, Flossie Jones had already been escorted off the premises by Hopkins the butler, now also deceased. Her ladyship swallowed the inch of bourbon left in her glass and disposed of her cigarette in the ashtray.

"Flossie you said died shortly after leaving Moultty Towers." I was occupied in resharpening my pencil, while Mrs. Malloy looked on admiringly as if this were a secretarial skill she someday hoped to master.

"I heard about it from Mrs. Snow who received the information from the kitchen maid. Seemingly Flossie eked out an existence for several months in a dismal bed-sitter after giving birth to a girl she named Ernestine after the father."

"And what would his name have been?" inquired Mrs. Malloy.

"Ernest?" I suggested.

Lady Krumley inclined her head. Her black headgear shifted but did not fall off, thanks to a sizeable hatpin. "According to what I learned from Mrs. Snow, Flossie succumbed to pneumonia and the child . . ."

"Was left in a suitcase at a London railway station?" I asked before I could stop myself.

"Placed with a childless couple. I regret I cannot tell you more. Naturally, despite the handsome fee I am prepared to pay for your services, I would wish to make the business of locating Ernestine as straightforward as possible."

"So that's what you want from us. Exactly how much is handsome?" Mrs. Malloy teetered forward on her high heels, bourbon bottle in hand.

"That can be discussed later. It may not be a piece of cake to find a baby now approaching forty years of age." My wording might be muddled, but I anchored my elbows on the desk and twirled my pencil with professional precision. Inevitably I was thinking of Rose and wondering how Ernestine and her adoptive parents would handle the situation, should they be located.

Her ladyship picked up the carpet bag. "I wronged the mother and now must find some way to make the necessary reparations if the surviving members of the house of Krumley are not to crumble to dust in the churchyard. It is still my opinion that Flossie Jones was not a nice girl. All the more reason," she rose to her impressive height, "that you two women make haste to prevent her deathbed curse from being fulfilled."

"Curses are a specialty of ours at Jugg's Detective Agency." Mrs. Malloy laid a comforting hand on her arm, then added, as I knew she would, "But they do cost a bit extra."

Five

"Well, that's that for a night's work." Mrs. Malloy sagged against the office door after returning from seeing Lady Krumley down to her car. "Me feet is killing me, and I expect your fingers are worn to the bone after taking all them notes."

"It wasn't that bad." I stood up and stretched. "Every time her ladyship paused to light up another cigarette, I was able to go back and squiggle in the missing bits."

"Squiggle is right." Mrs. Malloy now hovered admiringly over the desk. "Clever of you to put it all down in code. Made it up as you went along, did you?"

"That's Pitman's shorthand." I shuffled the pages together. "While I was waiting to begin my design classes I took a course."

"Back in the dark ages," Mrs. M. smirked. "But that's all to the good, isn't it? Don't suppose too many people use is it nowadays with them modern gadgets you talk into with the bossy-sounding name."

"Dictating machines."

"Meaning your shorthand's as good as code, if it should fall into the wrong hands. Not that you won't be careful, Mrs. H., seeing that this is your big chance to prove yourself with Jugg's Detective Agency."

"I don't intend to prove anything," I stared her down, "other than that I can type as well as take shorthand. But not tonight. If it's all the same with you, I'll take these notes home with me and use Ben's typewriter in the morning." I was crossing to the coatrack to retrieve my raincoat when I was brought up short by a realization. Ben no longer had a typewriter. He was now the owner of a word processor, a piece of wizardry I wasn't sure how to turn on, let alone operate. Bother! There was no help for it. I would have to sit back down at the desk and set my fingers drumming on Milk Jugg's old manual, which looked to be in far worse shape than the one I had donated to the charity of Kathleen Ambleforth's choice. The thought of telephoning her the next day and explaining that I needed not only the typewriter but all the other items from Ben's study back caused me to feel quite glad to be stuck in the present moment.

"Changed your mind, have you? Can't wait to get everything her ladyship told us printed up?" Mrs. Malloy stood with arms folded as I sat back down. "If it's not too much trouble, better use some of that carbon paper stuff so's there's a copy for both of us. I'll go over mine when I get home. Should make for a nice read along with a cup of cocoa and a chip butty."

"But I'm not typing this for us." I began tapping away at the keys. "It's for Mr. Jugg. You can read it to him if he telephones or, if you can't get hold of him, put it away in a drawer until he gets back."

"Did I say cocoa?" Mrs. Malloy's musing voice drifted my way, "I meant to say another stiff bourbon. That's what Milk would advise, and as you're saying, we've got to keep him in the forefront as we get going on this case. Thrust into the thick of things through no fault of our own! A pity. But there it is. No rest for the wicked as the actress said to the bishop. You go ahead and forget I'm here, Mrs. H., I'll just sit here and think about that girl Flossie and the brooch. I wonder just what sort she was really?"

"I really don't care." I rolled paper into the typewriter. "I'm sorry she was falsely accused of theft and it was tragic her dying so young, but her date of birth and vital statistics do not interest me. All this stuff about the deathbed curse is complete rubbish. A product of Lady Krumley's guilty conscience. Aged family members die off without any unearthly interference."

"But that old geezer going balloon riding?" Mrs. Malloy screwed up the empty packet of cigarettes and tossed it into the wastepaper basket.

"Uncle Dickie in the Channel Islands?" I found him in my notes. "It was bungee jumping."

"Go on, correct me! The point is, Mrs. H., that's not the way most people end their days at ninety or whatever he was."

"The upper classes pride themselves on their eccentricities. True, it would have been safer for him to howl at the moon from the top of his tree house, but to each his own."

"And then there was the kangaroo."

"That got cousin Clement in Australia," I continued pounding away at the keys. "Perhaps he failed to read the notice that said, 'Please don't feed the animals or pull their tails.' And, Mrs. Malloy don't bring up Aunt Theobalda who fell down the lift shaft. Accidents happen. As for the sister-in-law," I typed in the name Mildred, "no one can make anything the least bit weird out of an old woman dying in her sleep."

"In other words you don't have an ounce of sympathy for poor Lady Krumley and her wanting to find this Ernestine person to try to make things right for what was done to her dear mum." Mrs. Malloy went to sit down on the metal chair, but her glare caused it to panic and skid into the wall. "Well, I must say I'm shocked, Mrs. H., shocked to me very core! I don't think I've felt this bad since me husband Leonard turned nasty and said I looked like I'd aged twenty years."

"But you had," I hit the carriage return. "He hadn't seen you in all that time, after going down to the shops to get a pound and a half of stewing steak for the meat pudding you wanted to make and forgetting to come back. You weren't all that thrilled if I remember rightly when he re-entered your life out of the blue"—I dabbed whiteout on a mis-typed word and looked up at her while waiting for it to dry—"just as Ernestine may not be especially thrilled at being hounded to ground. She's probably living a nice, fulfilled life somewhere. Possibly with children of her own. Why does she need to know that her mother died spewing vengeance on the Krumley family?"

"You forgot to ask what happened to Ernest, the dad?" asked Mrs. M. at her most uppity.

"Clearly he wasn't willing or able to take the baby, or she wouldn't have been adopted."

"If he wasn't married to Flossie he might not have been given the chance, not back in them days. Could be he was fair broke up and would give anything to finally meet up with his daughter."

"There is that. But it doesn't sound as though he was helping her mother out much financially, if Flossie was struggling to make ends meet in the miserable bed-sitter her ladyship described. Although, to be fair, I don't suppose under gardeners were paid more than a pittance in those days." I sat back from the typewriter. The clatter I had been making on the keys had drowned out the patter of rain on the windows. It made for a mournful sound. I wasn't as hard-hearted as Mrs. Malloy had claimed.

Flossie's was a sad story, and it could be that Lady Krumley's hope of finding the daughter would turn up some silver linings. She hadn't said how she planned to make reparation, but Ernestine might welcome a bank draft, along with a heartfelt apology. But there was no urgency to the matter. Mr. Jugg would return from his holiday and take care of the matter with the proficiency provided by training and experience. As an interior designer I could perhaps be of some help to Lady Krumley. Getting rid of the gargoyles in the Great Hall and repapering the dungeons in a nice bright plaid might do much to lift her spirits. But a detective I wasn't. I said as much to Mrs. Malloy and spent the next five minutes listening to her rant on about the number of bodies that would pile up while I sat twiddling my thumbs.

"And it's not like you've got any jobs lined up right now," she pointed out ruthlessly.

"True," I paperclipped my typed notes together, "but I do have to take care of the children, in addition to doing all my own housework now that you're spending so much time here. Although I do have to wonder why," I recapped the bottle of whiteout, "if you're really so keen on developing the necessary secretarial skills to become Mr. Jugg's Girl Friday you left me to do the clerical work this evening along with posing as his partner."

Mrs. Malloy heaved a sigh that shot out her bosom six inches. "I don't like to push meself forward. Let someone else steal the limelight, that's always been my way. Besides it wasn't like I was just sitting around looking like something Cary Grant would have died to hold in his arms for just one minute. I was taking it all in. Every single word as was said."

"I'm sure her ladyship would have thought the whole setup very odd if she hadn't been so intent on convincing us that dark forces were at work beyond the great divide. She failed with me, but don't let that stop you from being a true believer."

"What I believe is we ought to get busy finding Ernestine before Lady Krumley gives herself a ruddy nervous breakdown," retorted Mrs. Malloy at her most virtuous. "It's our Christian duty, besides being a chance for me to get a leg up in me new career. And I'll tell you another thing, Mrs. H., if I did know how to get hold of Milk, I'm not so sure I'd do it. He's entitled to some time off, holed up with his booze and his memories of the woman he had to send up the river. Wouldn't it be something if he was to come back all bleary eyed and unshaven—

my dream man come true—and I was able to put the spark back in him, just by saying, 'No need to upset you hangover about the Krumley case. It's all sorted out. A treat.'?"

I was silent. There is no reasoning with an infatuated sixty-year-old.

"Well, I never thought you'd let me down, Mrs. H." She brushed away an imaginary tear from her false eyelashes. "Not for all your funny little ways, I didn't. But if it means going it alone so be it! Tomorrow I'll head out for Moultty Towers on the bus. Going by car would have been more convenient, but it's not like I don't know where Biddlington-By-Water is. A proper dead-in-a-live-hole if ever there was one. Went there a few years back, I did, to play bingo at the Old Age Pensioners' Hall. Wasn't anyone in the room with their own teeth and most of them too deaf to hear the caller. Talk about a wasted evening. I remember this one geezer in particular that kept saying gambling was sin and he shouldn't be there and that if his wife, or it could have been his daughter, knew of it it'd break her heart. Never happy unless they're miserable some people, but that's neither here nor there to you, is it Mrs. H.?"

"What exactly do you hope to accomplish by going to Moultty Towers other than another chat with her ladyship?" I was putting on my coat and Mrs. Malloy proceeded to button hers.

"Talk to people, if there's any still around, that knew Flossie Jones. Like the kitchen maid. Could be someone will remember something being said . . . about her family, for instance . . . that will help me get started."

It wasn't a bad idea and for a weak moment I was tempted to go with her. Tracking down names and addresses, following up the most tenuous of leads would surely be preferable to facing up to Kathleen Ambleforth's voluble disappointment when I asked for the return of the vanload of items from Ben's study. Also, and far worse, was the possibility that Ben would remain angry with me. I had never seen him as he had been tonight, so cold and tight-lipped. His bouts of irritation with me tended to be vehement, with him stomping around, clutching his head and shouting an occasional lion's roar, a brief upset that rustled the curtains and shifted a couple of pictures out of alignment before he threw up his hands and suggested a cup of tea. This was different, and I both longed to be home and dreaded Ben's response when I came through the door.

"What's that?" Mrs. Malloy's voice bounced me back to the moment at hand.

"I didn't say anything."

"I know that! I'm not deaf!" It did not bode well that the second person in one evening to feel I had betrayed them was not ready to forgive and forget at a moment's notice. "I thought I heard something." She stood pulling on her gloves. "A creaking sound."

"I heard one earlier," I said. "Old buildings tend to make their own funny little noises. Or it could be a stray cat that's found it's way in from the alleyway. There was one hanging about when I came in." The words were no sooner out of my mouth than I heard the indisputable sound of a footstep.

"Cat! Me Aunt Fanny!" Mrs. M. gave the leopard toque, that matched her fur coat, a twitch. "There's someone out there. But there's no need to get your knickers in a twist. It'll be Lady Krumley come back to tell us something she forgot. Or Milk," she said, her voice trembling with emotion, "stumbling up the stairs to die at his desk with a cigarette between his lips and his very own bottle of booze in his hand after being shot in the back by some thug he was onto . . ."

She didn't get to paint a vivid word picture of her selflessly nursing Mr. Jugg back to health and vigor. The office door that neither of us had thought to lock after her ladyship's departure was thrust open and a man stood in the opening. He wore a raincoat and hat as befitted the weather and a pair of sunglasses that didn't. He also happened to be holding a gun, which he waved around in what seemed to me a random fashion while twitching on his feet like someone with a bad case of chilblains.

"Well, I must say! The least you could do was knock!" Mrs. Malloy glared at him.

"Where's the boss?" he snarled.

"Left for the evening." I glanced toward the desk hoping that some heavy object would leap off it into my hand.

"And who are you two?"

"A pair of waxwork dummies," snipped Mrs. M.

"Try not to annoy him." I gave her a nudge.

"That's right!" He waved the gun around some more. "I've got a real nasty temper and would as soon shoot your lights out as look at you."

"Be our guest," responded the comic in our midst, without so much as a quiver. "It's not like we pay the electricity bill. If you've got eyes in your head behind those stupid glasses one look around this place will show you that me and Mrs. H. . . . Hodgkins here are giving it to you straight. Mr. Jugg's not hiding under the desk or in the washbasin. He's off on his holidays. Can't say where he's gone or when he'll be back."

"Don't you neither of you move while I check out the joint." The man sidled toward the door leading to the loo and after a look inside opened the one to the broom cupboard. He was in his mid to late thirties. The brim of his hat was tipped down over his nose, and his shoulders hunched. A memory, a vague sense of familiarity, prodded at my mind. Was that why I wasn't trembling with terror. Because he made me think of a bad actor in an even worse movie. Or had I seen him somewhere, quite recently? This evening? I had the answer before he was fully facing us once more.

"You're the man in the café. You were sitting at a table by the window reading, or pretending to read a newspaper."

"So what if I was?"

"Just being chatty, that's always her way." Mrs. Malloy draped a comradely arm around my shoulder.

"You shut your gob, tiger lady, or I'll have you stuffed and hung on a wall." He had stopped twitching his feet and held the gun steady. "Now you two dames hear me good and clear. You're to get hold of your boss on the double and give him a message from me. He's to tell old Lady Crumb Cake she needs to stop making up stories or someone will see she's locked up in the loony bin and stays there. If he don't he'll be just one other P. I. that doesn't show up for business as usual."

"Could you give us your business card?" I was able to be flippant because I was sure now he wasn't going to kill us, unless we were stupid enough to follow him down the stairs and try to get the license plate number if he made off in a car. Although surely any self-respecting thug would know enough to melt into the shadows before hopping aboard public transportation or slipping into a waiting vehicle. I continued to muse along these lines when the door closed behind him and for several moments after his footsteps faded into silence. Of course I knew what Mrs. Malloy was about to say before she opened her mouth.

"That puts the case in a different light. Someone who isn't Flossie Jones seems to be up to tricks. And something's got to be done about it. You can't get away from that now, Mrs. H."

Six

The moon huddled behind a threadbare blanket of cloud. It was no longer raining, but the wind shook the trees as if intent on rattling some sense into their leafless heads. It was well after midnight when I dropped Mrs. Malloy off at her house in Herring Street close to the center of Chitterton Fells. And I did so without making any promises. Wasn't it enough that I had allowed her to talk me out of contacting the police in regard to the man we called Have Gun Will Travel, on the grounds that Mr. Jugg would not appreciate official interference? Her posture as she went up the path to her front door let me know in no uncertain terms what she thought of my saying I would sleep on the Lady Krumley situation. The wind slammed the front door behind her causing the forsythia bush to cower against the wall.

Feeling exhausted but strung up, I drove on home through the square with its tower clock and jostle of Tudor-style buildings. At the corner of Market Street and Spittle Lane I passed Abigail's. Shortly after Ben and I were married he had opened it as a restaurant serving fabulous French food. A year or so ago, when he decided he wanted to spend more time writing his cookery books, he had turned the ground floor into a coffee shop and let the upstairs to an elderly man in Edwardian dress with a dusty moustache who specialized in the sale of botanical and ornithological prints. The two businesses complemented each other nicely.

Driving up the Cliff Road I thought about Lady Krumley's obsession with Flossie Jones's deathbed curse. Was there some connecting piece of information her ladyship had withheld from Mrs. Malloy and me? Something that would explain the arrival of Have Gun Will Travel? Nudging around a bend in the road I thought about the flower pots thrown at her ladyship's car. In the new light of things it would seem someone had tried to prevent her from keeping her appointment with Milk Jugg. But Lady Krumley had not turned around and gone home as might have been hoped. Presumably, she had found a place to temporarily deal with her shattered window, making her several hours late in reaching Mucklesby. Was Have Gun responsible for that act of vandalism? Or had someone contacted him afterward to say that Plan A had failed and he was to proceed with Plan B?

The road grew darker as it climbed the cliffs. A spatter of rain hit the car windows and with the sound of the windscreen wipers going irritably into action I became suddenly aware that every bone and muscle in my body ached from the work I had done shifting furniture and lifting boxes in Ben's study.

Fortunately I was now almost home. St. Anselm's Church came into sight on my left. The vicarage looked cold and pinched-face in the drizzle. The veiled moon cast an eerie light on the graveyard. Its tombstones had life and movement to them as if they were staggering with excruciating slowness toward me through the tufted grass, which also moved in waves as if to suggest that beneath the ground old bones stirred and stretched and skeletal hands reached upward to claw their way to the surface. Where, I wondered, was Flossie Jones buried.

A moment later I was driving through the gates of Merlin's Court and parking the car in the old stables. I let myself in through the garden door. In the hall I took off my raincoat and tossed it onto the trestle table. There was, I thought, setting down my handbag, the distinct possibility that Ben would already be in bed and asleep, giving me the whole night to lie awake and worry myself sick rather than face up to our quarrel and get it behind us. If it could be put into the past? Remembering his face when he looked at the new computer I wasn't overly optimistic. Would Kathleen Ambleforth kill me if I rang her up at this late hour and explained my dilemma and the urgent need for the immediate return of my husband's old manual typewriter? At a pinch the rest of the stuff could wait until morning.

My hand reached for the phone, but the twin suits of armor standing against the staircase wall suggested by the very blankness of their expressions that I would be making a big mistake in dragging Kathleen away from her hot water bottle. Or worse, I might get the vicar himself on the phone and he—being the dear befuddled soul that he is—would get everything mixed up. A vanload of pews along with the church organ, and possibly the organist herself in flannel nightie and curlers, could show up at my door to be disposed of, causing Ben to accuse me of making a further mess of things.

The kitchen light, along with the ones in the hall, had been on when I came in, and narrow strips of light gleamed beneath the closed doors of the dining room and drawing room. I couldn't bring myself to look toward the study. But this excess of electricity did not necessarily mean that Ben was still up. He was inclined to be careless about switching off lights. A peek into the drawing room found it empty. When I came out I saw a man winding the grandfather clock that stood in an alcove facing the front door. He had his back to me, but there was no mistaking my cousin Freddy for a madman who broke into people's houses to make sure that they kept time with Big Ben under the illusion that any discrepancy would permanently disrupt Greenwich Mean Time. Freddy's straggly ponytail and dangling skull and crossbones earring were always a dead give-away.

"Hi coz!" He shifted his lanky six-foot frame in my direction and stuck his hands in his ragged jeans pockets. "Where did you spring from?"

"I spent the evening with Mrs. Malloy. Where's Ben?"

"In the study." Freddy stood tugging at his scroungy-looking beard. "Ellie, I think you've made a really big mistake this time."

"You mean," my voice trembled, "he's sitting in there . . . wallowing?"

"More a case of a man in a trance. I don't want to be overly pessimistic," Freddy said, shaking his head so that the earring rattled, "but I've got the feeling that it could be a long time before Ben comes out of this. I've been sitting with him for an hour or more and he didn't seem to know I was there."

"Oh, Freddy!"

"Maybe he'll snap out of it." He spoke with a complete absence of conviction. "Perhaps you could exert your feminine wiles, Ellie. Light some candles, put on some soft music, play the pitiful little woman to the hilt. It's a shame," Freddy flapped an arm around my shoulders, "that you don't have some alarming crisis to drop in his lap to make him realize that he can't let anything come between you."

"I suppose I could mention that a man pointed a gun at Mrs. Malloy and me," I responded despondently. "But would that be enough to do it? It's not as though he shot us. I'm not staggering around with a bullet in my head with the possibility of only fifteen minutes to live."

"A man with a gun?" Freddy looked as he had done when we were children and he had accused me of having all the fun when I came out with some weird rash and couldn't go to school until a medical name could be found for it.

"Forget it," I muttered. Ben had come out into the hall. Suddenly I was all at sixes and sevens about mentioning the incident to him. He'd be horribly alarmed and concerned for my future safety, which would push my revamping of his study into the background where it would molder and perhaps never be properly addressed, thus leaving a permanent scar. There was, it must be admitted, another reason for my keeping quiet. Knowing all, Ben would insist on my keeping my nose out of the Krumley affair. And I wasn't sure I could do that. Not because of how Mrs. Malloy would feel about my defection, but because I felt a certain responsibility to her ladyship. I wished now that I hadn't said anything to Freddy. But more than anything else I wished Ben would look as though he was thrilled out of his mind to see me.

"So you're back," he smiled at me. A pleasant enough smile. But one that reminded me of the vicar's benign bafflement at the sight of someone with whom he had been talking not five minutes before.

I could feel myself sinking waist deep into despondency. Freddy in an unusually tactful attempt to ease into the background went clanking up against one of the suits of armor. Ben didn't blink let alone glance in the direction of the ensuing cacophony. Neither did he relax that fixed smile. Which set me to babbling about not having expected to be gone so long and my need to check on the children.

"No need for you to worry. I looked in on them several times, Ellie."

I was consoling myself that he hadn't blocked me out to the point of forgetting my name when Freddy corrected him. "You talked about going up, but remember . . . I went instead?"

"So you did."

"It doesn't matter which one handled the spot checks," I responded heartily. "So long as they're snugly tucked in for the night."

"How about I make us all a cup of cocoa?" My cousin's helpfulness was truly heartwarming, but I wished very much that he would trot back down to his cottage and leave me to try put things right with Ben. It was no use. Upon his offer of a nightcap being declined he followed us into the drawing room and planted himself in a chair with every appearance of remaining there until a van showed up to collect him for one of Kathleen Ambleforth's charities.

It was, in my opinion, a lovely room with latticed windows at each end, a rose and turquoise carpet in the middle of the parquet floor and a pair of ivory damask sofas and several Queen Anne chairs grouped around the fireplace. Above the mantel hung a portrait of Abigail, who had been mistress of Merlin's Court almost a century ago. Her restful pose and serenity of expression added to the tranquility of the muted color scheme. Even when the children were fighting over a ball that bounced off the secretary desk onto the top of the glass-fronted bookcase or playing hide and seek under the coffee table or behind the brocade curtains I felt anchored in this room—to its history and my present life. This evening was different. I was cast adrift, buffeted by waves of unease, sinking ever deeper into a whirlpool of uncertainty. Ben was pacing up and down in front of the fireplace. Once or twice he glanced to where I sat on the edge of a chair, but he had yet to ask how my evening with Mrs. Malloy had gone. Nor had he said a word about the study.

Freddy shifted his feet onto a footstool, yawned hugely, scratched his beard and closed his eyes. I waited a few moments for him to start snoring and plunged into a garbled apology of the sort that would have brought a husband in a romance novel to his knees with a rose from the nearest flower vase between his teeth.

"I'm so sorry, Ben! I was completely out of line in bringing in all that new stuff and getting rid of the old. You were quite right in saying I was thinking about how I wanted your study to look. I didn't see that at the time, but I should have done if I'd taken the time to consider how you felt about that dear old typewriter and the easy chair and the . . ."

"Darling, don't give it another thought!" He interrupted his circuit to place a hand on my shoulder and kiss the air two inches above my head. "I went off the deep end without appreciating all the time and effort you put into surprising me. I'm a monster and I don't know how you put up with me."

"You really mean it?" I was enormously relieved by the throb of sincerity in his voice and the fact that he lingered beside me, even holding my hand for a moment or two before pacing off again.

"Absolutely!" He gave me a sideways smile. "How was Mrs. Malloy?"

"Intent on turning private detective."

"For that outfit where's she been working?"

"Her boss went on holiday this evening, and one of his clients showed up too late to see him. And you know, Ben, how Mrs. Malloy is inclined to take over. This time she's all fired up to impress Milk."

"Who?"

"Mr. Jugg. And because he wasn't there and I was . . . well, you can imagine how things went. I got roped into listening to the client—Lady Krumley's story and writing it all down in shorthand." I took a breath and made up my mind to tell him the rest, including the arrival of Have Gun. There must be no more secrets between us. If Ben told me to keep my nose out of the situation so be it. Feeling confident and virtuous I was about to expound when he stood stock still, before leaping a foot in the air and clutching at his head as if about to rip out every wavy black lock.

"What's the matter?" I shot off my chair.

"I forgot to turn off the computer." He was already halfway

out the door. "I spent the evening figuring out how to turn it on. And now what happens if it burns itself out? It's not like I have my typewriter to fall back on till we get it fixed. Just give me some quiet time, Ellie, to work through the manual." The door swung closed behind him, and I saw that Freddy's eyes were open and his ears on the flap.

"Men and their computers," he murmured consolingly.

I fell back in my chair. "That's why Ben was in the study all evening. He wasn't staring into space. He was scowling at the screen trying to blink it into life. I have to get his typewriter back."

"Not in the middle of the night, coz." Freddy wagged a remonstrating finger. "Neither," he added, as I inched forward, "should you go blundering into the study offering unwanted advice." He locked his hands behind his head, shifted his lanky legs to get a better foothold on the stool and leaned back. "Far better, Ellie, to tell me all about your evening with Mrs. Malloy leading up to the man with the gun."

"Perhaps you're right," I sighed. "A little lighthearted chatter to help me forget my troubles." Clearly there was no hope Freddy would remember that he had left the iron on or that he needed to leave a note for the milkman, so I rambled away about Lady Krumley. Tobias appeared out of nowhere to land on my lap as I was detailing Flossie Jones's deathbed curse. Freddy heard me out with only one or two gurgles of rude mirth and even wrinkled his brow in concentration when I spoke about having seen Have Gun in the café and his mercifully brief visit to Jugg's Detective Agency.

"Although it didn't seem all that short at the time. And perhaps it wasn't as comic as I've made it sound with him waving that gun around and talking like someone . . ."

"In a bad play?" Freddy shifted out of position so suddenly that Tobias let out an infuriated meow and disappeared under the bookcase.

"It was rather like that," I conceded. "He seemed to grow more confident as he went along."

"Getting into his part."

"You could say that." For the moment I had forgotten Ben.

"What sort of a gun?"

"I don't know. I'm not up on the different kinds. But, now that you ask," I stood up and sat back down, "it was rather like the one you had when we were children and played cowboys and Indians. But it could have been a real gun. It must have been . . ." I sat biting my lip, remembering how for a moment in time I had been taken in by the gun-shaped cigarette lighter Mrs. Malloy had tossed at me. It had been that sort of evening.

"Explain something to me, Ellie." Freddy's eyes narrowed, just as they had done when he was a ten-year-old Wyatt Earp pacing toward me with his hand at his holster. "Why would this bloke in the sunglasses try to frighten you into giving up on a case that no one in their right minds would have given the time of day if he hadn't shown up?"

"Not a bad question."

It was one that had been nagging at the back of my mind as I drove home.

Seven

I awoke to find another question staring me in the face: What about Ernest, the under gardener who fathered Flossie Jones's baby girl? There had been no mention of him when Lady Krumley talked about Flossie living out her last days in a miserable bed-sitter. Was he a rotter who had bunked off rather than face up to his responsibilities? Or had Flossie shut him out of her life? Did he even know that the baby had been put up for adoption?

A moment later I lost interest in these speculations. Ben was not in bed beside me. A distant bonging of the grandfather clock let me know that it was 8:00 and that I had overslept by an hour. There was no reason for me to panic. He would be downstairs giving the children their breakfast after getting them up and dressed. We usually did this together and had become quite good at speeding things along without making anyone feel rushed. But if I didn't wake with the alarm clock, he would let me sleep on before bringing me up a cup of tea. Usually on those days he would take Abbey and Tam to school and Rose to her playgroup. Even so, as I dragged on my dressing gown and headed barefoot for the stairs, I couldn't stop myself from feeling abandoned. I had dozed off in the drawing room the previous night while still talking to Freddy. He was gone when I came drowsily back to my surroundings at 3:00 in the morning. And Ben was in bed and asleep when I climbed under the covers. The sensible thing would be to take him at his word that he had forgiven me, but I couldn't. The mad idea crossed my mind that if I looked in the study I would find a note propped up on the mantelpiece, saying that he had gone away for a while because he needed time to think, the classic words to end a doomed relationship. I reminded myself, even as I pushed open the door, that Ben loved me, that our marriage was solid and he would never abandon his children, especially over something so trivial. The study was exactly as it had been when I showed it to him last night, except for a cold cup of tea sitting beside the computer. Really, I did need to get a grip on myself. But to be fair a lot of women might go to pieces after having a gun pointed at them, real or not. Shaking my head so that my hair, which I hadn't combed, tumbled out of its pins, I entered the kitchen, which didn't look as inviting as usual.

On chill, gray mornings such as this it helped to have a small blaze going in the red brick fireplace, but Ben hadn't got one started. Nor was he there. Freddy was the one wandering around the table urging the children to eat up their cereal.

"I want porridge," Tam had his elbows on the green and white check cloth and was blowing bubbles in his juice glass.

"Daddy always makes us porridge," Abbey contributed wistfully.

"Love Daddy." Rose dropped her spoon in her cornflakes and giggled with delight when milk splashed everywhere. Tobias sat happily licking his whiskers while Freddy appeared ready to tear his out. Indeed his beard already looked extra mangy.

"We all love Daddy," I said, stepping up to the table, "but it seems we've got to manage without him this morning."

"Mummy! Mummy!" squealed Rose.

"Your hair is so pretty." Abbey reached up to stroke it. "Will I have to be all grown up before mine gets long down my back?"

"Can I have a boiled egg?" Tam asked. " With the army?"

"He means he wants his bread and butter cut up into soldiers," I explained to Freddy while getting down a saucepan from the hanging rack above the Aga. "Where is Ben?"

"Gone down to Abigail's. He said that if he stayed here he'd waste the whole morning at the computer. Obviously, he would have waited until you got up if I hadn't done my cousinly duty in showing up to forage through the fridge. I've nothing in mine except a bottle of tomato sauce."

"There are such places as supermarkets," I replied, popping eggs into the boiling water.

"I've heard they charge money"—Freddy stood eating cereal out of the box—"and I don't think that sort of thing should be encouraged. Call me an idealist, but someone has to make a stand." He elbowed past me to munch on the slice of bread I had buttered for Tam.

"I suppose it's a matter of principle with your mother," I said before I could stop myself. "Enjoying getting things for free, I mean."

"You mean pinching stuff?"

"It was wrong of me to bring it up."

"A girl at school pinched me," Abbey's mouth trembled.

"She'll go to hell for that." Tam was gobbling up his egg, and Rose was looking around for hers. Abbey did not eat eggs. She said they gave her indigestion just like they did Mrs. Malloy. All three children were devoted to Mrs. Malloy, cheerfully believing that she had magic potions in her bag and flew around on the Hoover when they were in school to speed up the cleaning.

"Your mother's a dear," I said, handing Freddy a cup of tea. "And we all have our little foibles. I know you worry about her, but look on the bright side. She doesn't smoke or drink. . . ."

"People that smoke go to hell." Tam licked egg off his face. "Who told you that?"

"A boy in my class. His father says he hopes they all fry. Like a pan of chips. And choke on the smoke."

"Did you ever smoke, Mummy?" Abbey clutched my hand in blue-eyed terror.

Freddy saved me from answering. "Some ghoul, that father! Puts the point across that there are worse things in life than dear old Mum's little problem. Although I've got to admit, coz, that I do occasionally worry that it'll all catch up with her, and she'll end up in the clink." He sighed heavily. "The thought of Dad cooking Christmas dinner for the next thirty years is not a happy one. I'll be lucky to get a poached egg. He was fixing himself one last night when I phoned. And was in a very nasty temper about it. You'd have thought Mum had left him to fight the Battle of Waterloo all on his little lonesome."

"Where was she?" I was gathering up plates and putting them in the sink.

"Down at some pub."

"She's entitled to a little outing."

"Dad said she'd been there for three days."

"That's odd, considering as I was just saying that she doesn't drink." I spoke lightly, hoping Freddy wouldn't see that I was worried. I was fond of Aunt Lulu and couldn't believe Uncle Maurice hadn't got off his rump to go and look for her. She could have taken a knock on the head during a brawl and be wandering the London streets senseless or gone off with the Guinness deliveryman. Or something worse, too terrible to contemplate, might have happened. "What exactly did your father say, Freddy?"

"Not much. He was in a state trying to get the poached egg out of the saucepan. To hear him shouting, you'd have thought it was a fish that kept leaping back into the water. I told him to calm down, and he said that if I couldn't stop making silly suggestions I could hang up. The thing is, Mum doesn't know how to cook, but she knows how to send out for a curry. So I imagine he was taking her absence harder than he was prepared to admit. All I got out of him was the name of the pub."

"And what was it?" I was wiping Rose's face and hands.

"That's just it!" Freddy thumped his forehead with a fist, sending his skull-and-crossbones earring into a wild spiral. "I can't remember. For some reason I keep thinking Long-fellows . . . but that's not it."

"Phone again and ask your father."

"I did this morning, risking getting an earful about my lack of fiscal responsibility—two of his favorite words—in making back-to-back calls. But there was no answer."

"Try his office."

"He told me he was taking a few days off to get his shirts washed and ironed. Mum always pinches a couple of new ones for him each week. So it's understandable that he's at sixes and sevens without her."

"I expect she got tired of spoiling him and has gone some-where to relax." It was a logical explanation, and I reminded myself that Aunt Lulu had proved well able to take care of her-self in the past.

"Mummy we're going to be late for school." Tam eyed me sternly.

"Oh, my goodness!" I looked at the clock on the mantel-piece above the kitchen fireplace. "So you are! And I'm not even dressed. But I promise you no one goes to hell for arriving two minutes after the bell rings."

"I'll take them if you'll let me use your car," offered Freddy, whose only vehicle was a motorbike.

"Are you sure you don't mind, with this business . . ."

"Of the missing Mum?" He grinned at me. "She'll turn up. Come to think of it this isn't the first time she's done a bunk. A spirited lass, my mother. Dad isn't easy to live with. Remember how I was forced to run away when he stopped my pocket money after finding me playing 'doctor' with that girl next door?"

"Freddy you were twenty five at the time. And she was married."

"Picky! Picky! Come on gang!" He marshaled the children toward the alcove, where their coats and schoolbags hung, and had them out the door before I had completed my second round of hugs. "Back in half an hour, Ellie."

Usually I enjoyed a little time on my own, but the house seemed too quiet after they had gone. Almost as though it had taken Ben's side and was giving me the silent treatment. Tobias, who usually came slinking out of hiding when it was just the two of us, was conspicuous by his absence. Even the twin suits of armor appeared to avoid my gaze as I headed for the stairs. Telling myself that I had to snap out of this silly mood, I took a quick hot shower, washed my hair and after blowing it dry got dressed in a pair of brown corduroy slacks and an olive green sweater. There, that was better! Rather than waste time pinning my hair into a chignon I tied it back with a rubber band. A dash of lipstick, a brush of mascara, and I would be ready to march down to the vicarage and beard Kathleen Ambleforth in her den.

Freddy wasn't back with the car when I left the house, but I didn't mind walking even though it was pouring down rain. My umbrella sprang a leak before I reached the end of our drive. All to the good. It couldn't hurt my cause to arrive looking pathetically drenched. Kathleen, I reminded myself as I rang the bell, had a kind heart under her forthright manner. She took a few moments to answer the door and usher me into the dark hall, crammed with enough cupboards, chests and sideboards to hide a dozen members of the clergy escaping persecution in foreign parts. Donations to her charity drive, I concluded. But although I peered into every corner I couldn't spot any of the items from Ben's study. Hope leaped in my damp breast. Perhaps Kathleen had decided they weren't worthy of being delivered even to the most needy, and they were already on their way back to Merlin's Court with a sensitive little note of apology.

"Sorry to barge in without phoning first," I said, as she took my umbrella and shook it out the door before propping it up against a chair with three legs.

"Don't give it a thought, dear. You know I'm always glad to see you, even when I'm just walking out the door."

"Oh, are you?" It was a stupid thing to say given the fact that she was wearing a rain hat in addition to her coat and a long wooly scarf. But Kathleen had a way of rattling me. She was an imposing figure of a woman, with a commanding voice and brown eyes that missed very little. Freddy said she scared him most when she was being jolly, but I would have been thrilled at that moment to see a glimmer of a smile. "I promise not to keep you more than a few moments." My voice came out in a pitiful stammer. "It's just that I've got this little problem."

At that her eyes did light up. Kathleen thrived on setting people's lives to rights. All she asked was that they take her advice to the letter and not waste her time dithering on about what someone else had to say on the subject.

"You'd better come into the sitting room." She maneuvered her way toward a door to our right, and I skinned both legs climbing over a chest of drawers in her wake.

"I hate to delay you."

"First things first, I always say, Ellie." She waved me toward an elderly sofa with a couple of cushions that looked as though a six-year-old child might have embroidered them. It was a shabby room with oatmeal-colored wallpaper and faded red curtains. Books and magazines were scattered over almost every surface, an old cardigan and a floral apron were tossed over the back of a chair and the mirror above the fireplace needed resilvering. Kathleen wasn't the house-proud sort. She didn't have the time, or the interest. I shifted my feet, so as not to knock over a cup and saucer that had been left on the floor, and sat back and admired the cozy muddle. I couldn't have lived with it, but I envied Kathleen's ability to do so.

She sat opposite me in a chair with mismatched arm covers. "No call to worry, Ellie, I'll explain to the parishioner I'm to visit that I was unavoidably delayed."

"That is kind."

"Now tell me about this problem."

Before I could do so, the Reverend Dudley Ambleforth wandered into the room by way of the French doors that opened onto the back garden. The white hair that normally stuck up around his head like a dandelion clock was flattened to his head by the rain. He wasn't wearing a jacket, let alone a coat—just a thin gray cardigan. Impervious to his drenched state he had his nose in a book—probably one he had written himself of the life of the venerable St. Ethelwort, founder of a monastery whose ruins were located a few miles along the coast. The vicar was his own favorite author, which was a good thing because most people had trouble wading through even one of the thirteen volumes he had produced on his beloved subject.

"Dudley!" His wife got out of her chair to fume over him. "You really are naughty going outside in this weather. With all I have to do must I be worrying about your catching one of your nasty colds? And all your handkerchiefs already in the wash. It simply is too vexing. If I weren't so fond of you," she said, wiping the rain drips off his neck with her scarf, "I would be very much put out."

"So sorry, my dear." The vicar dragged his mild blue eyes away from his book. "Such a trial I am to everyone. As was St. Ethelwort from time to time. His bishop had to admonish him on several occasions for allowing his monks to sunbathe on the beach in their birthday suits while groups of nuns were picnicking nearby. He was, as I have so often written, a saint ahead of his time."

"That's all very nice, Dudley."

"Good morning, vicar," I piped up from the sofa, and he responded with a blink before taking a couple blundering steps toward me. In this room one must always be wary of stumbling over some object left lying in the middle of the floor.

"So you've arrived." He extended a hand pried away from the book. "We received your letter and are delighted to have you pay us a visit. I didn't think," he turned a bemused face to his wife, "that we weren't expecting her until next Tuesday."

"Dear," Kathleen responded with obvious restraint. "This isn't cousin Alice. She came and spent four days with us and only left this morning."

"So she did." Reverend Ambleforth shook his head, causing his white hair to fluff out. "Then who, my dear, is this lady?"

"Ellie Haskell."

"Ah!"

"From Merlin's Court."

"The," he spoke into Kathleen's ear, "the psychiatric place? Did they let her go, or has she escaped?"

There were some of my acquaintance who suspected that the vicar had himself escaped by way of a knotted bedsheet from some such facility, but as clergy were difficult to come by in small parishes they thought it best not to make a big thing about it.

"Always one of your little jokes, Dudley!" Kathleen produced an unconvincing chortle. "You're talking about that place at Melton Kings, where they put criminals who can't help doing what they do—like Peeping Toms and kleptomaniacs."

I thought about Aunt Lulu, Freddy's mother. How terrible if she was to end up in such a place.

"Merlin's Court." Reverend Ambleforth closed his book and stowed it tenderly in his trouser pocket. "I remember now. It's the house that looks like a castle just past the bus stop." He did, as even his detractors admitted, have his brief moments of lucidity. "And this lady is married to," he hesitated, furrowing his brow, "her . . . well, it would be her husband, wouldn't it? No need to help me on that one, my dear."

"Dudley, you have caught a cold," Kathleen bundled him into a chair. "They always go straight to your head."

"I can see him as we speak." The vicar flashed us both a triumphant smile. "A dark-haired, good-looking young man. By the name of Jones. I'm almost sure that's what he said. Or maybe it was Smith. One of those common names. He was here this morning. Wanted a word with me about books approved by the church on the subject of divorce. Said he had a friend . . . or it could have been a relative who was considering leaving his wife. One of those overbearing women from the sound of it." His abstracted look had returned. "Dear me, we do live in unsettled times."

"It wouldn't have been Ben." Kathleen threw up her hands. "Why on earth would he come here pretending to be someone else?"

"He wouldn't." I smiled because it gave me something to do with my face. The vicar got up, patted his pocket, took out his book and crossed the room to the door. A moment later we heard a couple of thumps as he encountered some obstacle out in the hall. Then all was silent save for the ticking of the clock on the mantelpiece.

"Dudley's always the same when he gets wrapped up in St. Ethelwort." Kathleen sat back down. "If there was a man here this morning he was probably fair-haired and never said a word about a friend or divorce. No need for you to look so upset, my dear. Unless," she said, eyeing me intently, "that problem you mentioned has to do with your marriage?"

"Ben and I had an argument last night." I stared down at my hands. "He was very angry that I had given away all the stuff in his study. I hadn't consulted him, you see, and I realize it was upper-handed of me. That's why I'm here . . . oh, not because Ben is considering a divorce . . . it's not that serious," I squeaked out a laugh, "but I am really hoping that you will let me have everything back. You have every reason to be annoyed with me, but I am in this awful predicament."

"You did explain to Ben that all donations go to highly worthy causes?" Kathleen could look her most fierce when not moving an inch.

Despite quaking on the inside, I answered boldly: "He knows that, but he's pining. And I don't want him miserable. The study is both his personal space and his workplace. I'm not sure he will be able to get anything done the way things are. He particularly hates the computer. The point, as I should have realized, is that stuff isn't just . . . stuff. That old typewriter was his friend . . . his partner . . . his . . ." I floundered to a halt.

"I suppose I do understand," Kathleen responded with a little more warmth in her voice. "How could I not, being married to Dudley with his obsession with St. Ethelwort. I'll do what I can, Ellie, but I didn't handle all the incoming and outgoing of the donations. That's why cousin Alice was here, to help me with a job that became too much for one person. There are so many organizations in need. Some old, many of them fairly new. I couldn't begin to list them off the top of my head. I'll have to check through my records and Alice's. She's a most efficient woman."

"That's good."

"Perhaps not given your situation. She may well have sent your stuff on its way without wasting time having it first unloaded here. We get very specific requests for items, and if yours fit the bill, well . . . you do see what I'm getting at, Ellie?"

"Could you let me know something, fairly soon?" I got dole-

fully to my feet. "If I had an address I could perhaps track the
things down and offer to buy them back."

"Let's hope for the best." Kathleen ushered me into the hall
and hurried me into my raincoat. "They could well be in the
church hall. We only have the overflow in the house. Now off
you go," she said, handing me my umbrella, "and try not to
worry. Say a little prayer. But not to St. Ethelwort; from what
I've read of his journals the man was frightfully long-winded,
and might keep you talking all day."

With this small sally she closed the vicarage door. Glad to
see the back of me and be off to her appointment. Who could
blame the poor overworked woman? I walked back along the
Cliff Road heedless of the rain to enter the hall at Merlin's
Court, where Freddy appeared like a wraith at my elbow to
announce that Mrs. Malloy was on the phone, sounding as
though someone had just died.

Eight

"What's wrong?" I held the receiver with one hand while struggling to get out of my raincoat with the other. I was chilled to the bone, but there was no one to notice except the twin suits of armor and neither one of them looked ready to clank across the Turkish rug with offers of a cup of tea. Freddy had disappeared into the kitchen. Seasoned eavesdropper that he was he didn't have to be standing next to me to get the gist of my conversation with Mrs. Malloy. Whistling kettles and doors left open the merest wedge would be no deterrents if he chose to snoop. But it could be that he wasn't in the mood to involve himself with my trials and tribulations, given his worries about his Mum.

"Never mind me." Mrs. Malloy's voice blasted in my ear. "What's wrong with you? Don't tell me that gunman found out where you live and is there this minute, threatening to shoot your head full of enough holes to turn it into a colander, if you don't keep your trap shut? It's alright," she said, misinterpreting my silence, "I understand you can't talk. Give one scream for 'yes' and two for 'no'."

"Please!" I finally managed. "Let's not go taking last night too seriously. After talking to Freddy I'm convinced our visitor played us for a couple of idiots."

"So that wasn't a gun he shoved under our noses?" She laughed sarcastically. "What was it then, Mrs. H., a banana?"

"A toy one."

"A toy banana?"

"No!" I tossed my raincoat on the floor and barely restrained myself from kicking it the length of the hall. "A toy gun."

"Well, that makes a lot of sense, that does! But if Mr. Freddy Flatts says that's the way things was who'm I to argue? Course, it could be said I was there and he weren't, and it would be nice to think that you and me stood together as a team, especially now that things have taken such a nasty turn. But why should anyone consider my feelings? I'm just the woman that's worked her fingers to the bone for you all these years, scrubbing and polishing on me poor worn-out knees."

I didn't remind her that she had always strictly adhered to the Chitterton Fells Charwomen's charter (commonly referred to as the Magna-Char), which prohibited its members from performing any tasks above or below eye level. This was no time for petty bickering. "What sort of nasty turn?"

"Well, it's like this," she said, dropping her snotty tone, "I came down here to the office to water the plants and practice up on me typing and I wasn't through the door when the phone rang. I picked it up all of a tremble, thinking it would be Milk ringing up to say he'd been stabbed coming out a bar."

"And his wallet pinched by a one-legged jogger?"

"I'll let that pass, Mrs. H., seeing it's clear you're having a bad day. Not made up with the hubby from the sound of it. But you're about to feel downright ashamed of yourself."

"I am?"

"That phone call was from the old Cottage Hospital in Mucklesby. Seems," Mrs. M. continued with relish, "Lady Krumley was brought in last night after a car accident. I couldn't get the gist of how bad she was because the woman phoning, some nurse I suppose, had one of those posh voices like someone talking Shakespeare."

"What sort of an accident?" I asked stupidly.

"I just told you."

"I mean did her ladyship collide with another vehicle or did she crash into a lamppost after being forced off the road? What I'm getting at is . . . was it really an accident or attempted murder?"

"So now you're admitting it wasn't all fun and games with that bloke last night? Change with the wind you do, Mrs. H., but I can't stand here fussing with you all day. We've got to get down to that hospital. Don't want the old girl sinking into a coma before we arrive, now do we?"

"She wants to see us?" I was struggling back into my raincoat.

"No, that nurse phoned for the weather report." Mrs. Malloy's sarcasm dripped through the receiver. "Her ladyship had told her to phone Jugg's Detective Agency and keep ringing until someone answered. Poor soul! Sounds as though she'd worked herself up into a terrible state. Don't suppose she's meant to have visitors except for the immediate family."

"Who might not be such a good idea under the circumstances."

"Well, I must say it's about time you came round to my way of thinking, Mrs. H., 'cos my name's not Roxie Malloy if there isn't a nasty nephew or sneaky sister-in-law at the bottom of this." The woman could be unbearably smug, but I reminded myself that one had to keep Lady Krumley front and center.

"I'm merely keeping an open mind. No more, no less. You can fill me in on any other information you've acquired when I pick you up." I not only had my raincoat back on but also was wearing Tobias around my neck as a scarf. That cat was worse than the children for demanding attention the minute I got on the phone. He would drop off a wardrobe onto my head or, as on this occasion, leap from the table onto my arm and shin the rest of the way with a steel-clawed determination worthy of an assault of the Alps. By the time I had disentangled him, Freddy had stuck his head around the kitchen door to say that he had a lovely pot of tea ready. And if I was in the mood to turn a loaf of bread into a plateful of sandwiches we could have an early lunch. I hated to see the light go out in his eyes. It's a tough business being a housewife pretending to be a P.I. I told him, while draining half a cup of tea, that there was sliced ham, lettuce and tomatoes in the fridge, but he would have to assemble them on a plate without any help from me because I had to meet up with Mrs. Malloy.

"Ah!" He stroked his beard, eyes gleaming. "So the Krumley case thickens."

"Freddy," I rammed a rain hat on my head, "do not be melodramatic."

"What? Me? Make mountains out of molehills?" He staggered backward until he rammed up against the sink. "Her ladyship has merely been in a near fatal car accident that may or may not be the result of foul play. She's lying in The Cottage Hospital at Mucklesby, clutching her oxygen mask, clawing at all the tubes while waiting for you and Mrs. Malloy to arrive so she can impart some vital piece of the puzzle before she gasps her last."

"Good marks for listening."

"No need to thank me," he said with a winsome smile, "someone has to look out for you. And Ben's not here to do it."

"I'm sure there's plenty to keep him occupied at Abigail's," I replied with superb nonchalance. "Not that you don't do a great job, Freddy, but he always likes to catch up after being away on a trip. He didn't happen to phone while I was at the vicarage?"

"It so chances that he did. Said to tell you he would collect Rose from her play group at 1:00 and go back for the twins at 3:30."

"Oh, splendid!"

And so it was, because now I wouldn't have to shift my attention away from Lady Krumley every five minutes to check my watch. Driving down the Cliff Road I heroically banished Ben, between one sniff and the next, from my mind. I was wondering just how badly Lady Krumley had been injured when I drew level with Abigail's. Ben's car was neither out front nor visible in the side parking lot. Nothing to that of course, although at 11:30 he would not have set off to collect Rose. There were dozens of places he might have gone. I just couldn't think of any for the moment. I had the car heater going full blast, and my head was fuzzy. A moment later I was given my answer. While passing the Chitterton Fells Library I saw a man who was unmistakably my husband exiting by the side door with an armload of books balanced precariously under his chin. To honk at him would have been disaster for he would undoubtedly have dropped the lot. So I proceeded on my way, wedged in between a lorry and a woman wobbling along on a bicycle, feeling vaguely comforted. Ben and I were both avid readers. Not much for television, we enjoyed many an evening—especially in wintertime—locked in our own separate worlds yet linked by that special silence that can be better than any amount of talking.

It was no longer raining, but the roads had the black gloss of night and ragged clouds whipped across the sky like clothes blown off a line. What had been a scattering of cottages became rows of tight-faced houses with front doors opening directly onto the street and shops that looked as though they should have signs in the windows warning customers that they entered at their own risk. I drew level with a greengrocer's. It had boxes of drowned fruit and vege set out front, being sniffed at by a mongrel dog. Catching my eyes he cocked his leg in a desultory fashion and disappeared around a corner. Mucklesby, I decided, was no more attractive by day than at night, a thought shared by Mrs. Malloy when I stopped in the alleyway outside Jugg's Detective Agency and she climbed into the car.

"What a rat hole of a town!" she said, buckling her safety belt around her middle. She removed her headscarf and patted her blonde hair back into shape. "Course it suits Milk a treat, and us too, Mrs. H., in our line of business. But you couldn't pay me to live here. Pigeon muck everywhere you step, and the whole place smelling of cat's pee. Drive on do." She gave me a nudge that shot the car forward. "Before we catch something and end up in the hospital along with Lady Krumley."

I started to say that I was not in any line of business other than being a wife, mother and part-time interior designer, but a glance at her set profile let me know I would be wasting my breath. So I stuck to the issue at hand.

"How critical is Lady Krumley's condition?"

"Oh, you know them nurses, they can spend ten minutes putting the wind up you just saying 'the patient is doing as well as can be expected.'" Mrs. Malloy took a compact out of her handbag and waved it at me before powder puffing her nose with enough abandon to cause me to gasp and choke.

"Could you put that thing away," I said testily. "It has to be every bit as hazardous as secondhand smoke."

"Well, you're a fine one to talk! But you know what they say about them holier than thou reformed types."

I ignored this thrust. "Did the nurse who phoned say if her ladyship was in ICU?"

"What?

"The Intensive Care Unit."

"No, she didn't, and watch where you're driving. You almost went up the back of that van and now me lipstick's all smeared." Mrs. Malloy eyed herself in the compact mirror before dropping it back with an irritated plop into her handbag. "And me wanting to look my best for all them handsome young doctors that's bound to be lining the corridors. Some of the happiest days of me life was watching *Emergency Ward 10* on the telly and now that I'm going to live it you have to go and spoil things."

"That's not a van?"

"What isn't?" Mrs. Malloy was dabbing at her purple lips with both pinkies.

"The one you just said I almost hit." I rounded a corner and drove under a short brick tunnel and emerged into a parking lot. "It's an ambulance. And this is the Cottage Hospital."

"Well, I could have told you that! There's the door to out-patients. Don't see as we can go too far wrong if we go in that way."

It sounded sensible. But after fifteen minutes of wandering green hallways that hadn't been updated since the 1940s and not having spotted one handsome young man in a white coat with a stethoscope dangling around his neck, the fact that we were hopelessly lost became my fault.

"Thanks a lot, Mrs. H.! Me feet are killing me. In the time we've been here I could have had me insides taken out and put back in again. That's five times, as I've counted, we've been around this way. Even them pictures on the wall are beginning to look at us funny."

She had a point. The expressions on the faces of the illustrious personages who had served this hospital over the past hundred years appeared to have grown increasingly stern. The directions given to us at the information desk had seemed straightforward at the time. We had taken the lift to the second floor as instructed and turned left at the maternity unit. After that it was pretty much all a blur. But it wasn't my fault that Mrs. M. was wearing her customary four-inch heels. Neither was I to blame because her miniskirted powder pink raincoat now reeked of disinfectant, or so she claimed. I was about to explain that I wasn't happy at the prospect of wandering these labyrinths for all eternity, when a man in hospital attire came up behind us wheeling a gurney. Mrs. Malloy immediately brightened. The man wasn't bad looking and the gurney was unoccupied. Stepping away from the wall she stretched her butterfly lips into her most engaging smile and hooked up a thumb. Hadn't her mother ever told her she was liable to end up in the morgue if she hitchhiked lifts from strange men in hospital corridors?

Luckily his mother must have warned him about the sort of women he was liable to encounter in the course of a day's work. Or maybe he had a bad back and couldn't risk hoisting Mrs. Malloy onto the gurney and making off with her into the sluice room. (From what she had told me sluice rooms had figured prominently in *Emergency Ward 10*.) At any rate he chuckled in appreciation of what he obviously took to be her little joke and escorted us a short distance to where personnel were occupied behind a desk area talking into telephones, bustling about with notepads or issuing instructions in a kind of verbal shorthand. Feeling like a lion singling out one deer from the herd to pounce upon I caught the eye of a woman in a floral cotton jacket that seemed to indicate she might be a nurse or possibly a member of the housekeeping staff. She came toward me, while Mrs. M. was still muttering in my ear.

"It's not like I was ready to go off with a perfect stranger. His name was Joe; it was right there on his jacket pocket. And whatever you're thinking I know he was dying for a moment alone with me so he could tell me all about his bunions. It was there in his eyes—the deep quiet knowledge of a man who has just met the woman of his dreams. But it was all ruined because you had to insist on tagging along. The very least you could have done was stay behind and pretend you was looking out the windows."

Clearly in addition to her enthusiasm for *Emergency Ward 10*, Mrs. Malloy had been reading too many of those nurse doctor books. I little doubted that in next to no time Joe would be transformed into a well-built, well-heeled senior consultant—probably a titled one at that—and instead of wanting to talk about his bunions he would be casually mentioning his three ancestral homes and his silver gray Rolls Royce. I was wondering what sort of car Lady Krumley had been driving, while explaining to the woman in the floral jacket that we had received a phone message requesting we visit her ladyship.

"Let me see what I can find out for you, Mrs. Haskell." She gave me a brisk smile before going into a huddle with the other assorted jackets and coats. After what seemed ages she came around the counter to escort me and Mrs. Malloy the length of the corridor. "You're to be allowed ten minutes. The doctors are due back to examine her ladyship shortly. I'm sure I don't need to caution you that our object is to keep her calm, so please restrict the conversation to general chitchat—nothing to get her the least bit worked up." A beep sounded and with an exclamation of apology that she was needed elsewhere, the woman pointed a finger to our left and made off at a fast walk.

"Go on." Mrs. Malloy nudged me. "I'm right behind you."

"Okay." I pushed open the closest door and tiptoed into a small square room with a generic landscape print on the wall. Otherwise it was all beige and gray. The figure in the hospital bed did not move. The folded hands appeared glued to the sheet. An oxygen mask covered a good part of her face, and everywhere there were tubes, hooked up to machines that flashed and beeped as if carrying on personal conversations.

"Oh, the poor duck!" Mrs. M. inched her nose over my shoulder. "Why, it don't even look like her."

"That's because it isn't."

"What?"

"Isn't Lady Krumley. We're in the wrong room."

"Now you tell me!"

We were backing out, hopefully before the machines set off the alarm and several very large men arrived to cart us away in straitjackets, when we collided with someone. Turning, we faced a man of medium height and middle years, with a receding hairline and eyes set rather too close together above a long thin nose.

"So sorry," I said, "we're looking for Lady Krumley's room." My nervousness was heightened by the fact that he was staring at us as if we were a pair of German shepherds, readying to leap at his throat if he tried to edge past us. But perhaps he was a man who always looked frightened. His voice when he spoke sounded as though it might be habitually timid.

"Pardon me for asking, Are you the social workers?"

"What's that to you?" Mrs. Malloy barked back at him.

Had anyone been passing he would have jumped into his or her arms. "I assumed . . . under the circumstances . . . that they might be sending some up. After all, poor Aunt Maude's rather been through it."

"Aunt who?"

"Sorry! I'm making a real hash of explaining." He didn't sound as though he expected any argument on this. "I'm talking about Lady Krumley. I'm her nephew by marriage. Niles Edmonds."

"Well, isn't that interesting!" Mrs. Malloy gave a sigh of pure satisfaction. "I was sure you'd show up sooner or later. And here you are looking just like I pictured you. Now tell me, just for the record like, do you happen to know if your dear kind Auntie has left you a nice lot of money in her will?"

Nine

"What my colleague means to say," I got in before Mrs. Malloy could spout off another word, "is that we hope her ladyship's condition will not create any financial problems for you. That's what social workers are for." I squeezed out a laugh. "To try and sort through these potential difficulties."

"Oh, quite!" He looked as though he yearned to fade into the paintwork.

"Good!" I brightly smiled. "Then I hope we'll talk later, Mr. Edmonds. In the meantime we do," I continued, latching on to Mrs. Malloy's arm, "need to see Lady Krumley before the doctors do another round."

"Absolutely." He stood working his hands together. "Must put Aunt Maude first. She's in the next room to this. Please tell her I've just arrived and will be in to see her as soon as is convenient. Cynthia, my wife, is with me, or will be when she finishes parking the car. I don't drive. Regrettably I never could get the hang of it."

"We all have our individual gifts," responded Mrs. Malloy with a girlish giggle that was meant to go with the powder pink raincoat and the false eyelashes, one of which had come slightly askew.

"Yes, well . . . off we go," I prodded her forward.

"My dearest love to Aunt Maude," Mr. Edmonds murmured

faintly in our wake. "And tell her not to upset herself over Vincent, just think of him as off on another adventure."

"Who? What?" I turned to ask, but he was already halfway down the corridor. Life, I thought sourly, got more complicated by the minute. Here I was pretending to be a private detective pretending to be a social worker, when all I wanted was to have a make-up session with my husband. It was all getting to be rather too much. And I hadn't even had lunch. There was one person who was primarily to blame, and if I'd had a mean bone in my body I would have said something really snippy.

"There's no need for all that nasty breathing down my neck," Mrs. M. complained. "Course I understand you being jealous because of how I was the one what figured out from the start there'd be a nasty nephew somewhere in the picture. But look at it this way, Mrs. H., you still get to play Milk's partner and my boss."

"Thanks a lot."

"I should think so, seeing that means you're the one what gets to open that door and take a peek inside to see just how horrible her ladyship looks before giving me the okay. All them machines and tubes hooked up to that other old girl made me insides go all queer."

"Very well, you stay out here and keep guard in case Mr. Edmonds comes creeping back to have a listen at the door."

"Not on your Nelly!" she fumed, and was on my heels as I went into the room that was the right one this time. To say I was shocked by Lady Krumley's appearance is putting it mildly. No one looks their best in a hospital bed under lighting that is worse than that found in department store changing rooms, but even so the woman I had been visualizing clinging to a life raft bobbing its way toward death's portals looked remarkably . . . bobbish. She wasn't flat on her back; she was sitting up with a crocheted shawl around her shoulders and her mahogany hair, far from hanging drearily around her shoulders, was tidily pulled back in a coil. As for her hooded black eyes, they had lost little of their intensity as they turned toward the door.

"So you came." She beckoned Mrs. Malloy and me over to a pair of stiff-looking armchairs positioned at the side of the bed. "The circumstances are not what I expected for our second meeting. You did make sure that door is closed? Good! One wouldn't wish to invite passers-by to listen in on our conversation, given how very odd it would all sound. And yet if there was anything needed to convince the skeptical of the validity of my fears concerning Flossie Jones, I would think it must be this new tragedy."

"Nasty things, car accidents." Mrs. M. took the more comfortable looking of the chairs and sat with legs crossed at the ankles for the best display of her fishnet hose. "But it don't look like you took too bad a pasting."

"I am not talking about myself. I'm sure I would have been perfectly fine if I hadn't allowed myself to become so upset, which I wouldn't have done under other circumstances. After all, not wishing to be callous, I hadn't seen Vincent in twenty years. Not until he showed up at Moultty Towers so unexpectedly the night before last. However, blood being thicker than water, one could do no less than make him welcome, and I encouraged him to stay for a few days. Regrettably, he had not been in the house two minutes before he offended Watkins's, the butler, sensibilities by being too familiar." Her ladyship drew the shawl up around her chin. "Watkins is not cut from the same cloth as his predecessor Hopkins. But even so, servants do not care for that sort of thing. My late husband Sir Horace did not approve of Vincent. Went to Eton together. Thought him a blot on the old school tie. Unfortunate, considering they were first cousins, but there it is and now . . . he has been added to Flossie's list of casualties."

"You mean he's . . . ?" I began.

Mrs. Malloy finished for me: "Dropped off the family twig?"

Lady Krumley folded her hands. "I had just begun the drive home last night when I heard a ringing from somewhere under the dashboard. I had forgotten there was a phone in the car. I am rarely in the vehicle these days. Watkins drives it two or three times a week when I have some commission for him. Otherwise, for the most part, it remains garaged. At all events, I was sufficiently startled to almost go off the road. When I did locate the receiver, it was to hear my nephew Niles Edmonds's, informing me in his sad little voice that Vincent had met with a fatal accident."

"Oooh! Nasty!" Mrs. Malloy batted her eyelashes in horror. "What sort of accident?"

"He had fallen into a well. . . ."

"What? One of them fancy wishing well types? With a bucket hanging from its little wooden roof?" Mrs. M. looked most unsuitably entranced. "Me and me first husband met at one of them. I was wishing he'd stop looking up me skirt as I bent over to drop in a penny for luck and . . ." on catching my eye she continued smoothly, "just thought we should know for the record like."

"The well is as you describe, although it is not located in a public place." Lady Krumley shivered despite the fierce central heating. "It is in the garden of a cottage on the Moultty Towers property. They are kept for longtime family retainers. A Mrs. Hasty, who was the kitchen maid in Flossie's time, lives in it. If she is deceased by the time Watkins retires he will be offered it. As I told you yesterday, it has long been viewed a duty by the Krumleys to honor the promise inscribed on the family crest."

"I'm sorry I don't have my notes with me," I hedged. "What is the exact wording?"

"Serve Well Thy Servitors." Her ladyship leaned back on her pillow, looking all at once like a woman who needed a nurse with a syringe at her side. "It dates back to the early thirteenth century when Hugh de Krumley took a blow on the head in a skirmish against King John. He wandered about the country for a year thinking he was a peasant, until rescued by his ever-faithful jester, a fellow by the name of Lumpkin who brought him back to his senses with another blow by way of a juggling skittle that went astray. Overjoyed, Hugh rewarded Lumpkin by not having his hands cut off. Upon his return to the manor, after taking a long hot bath one would hope, Hugh swore upon his sword and his father's beard—or it may have been his mother's (the Krumleys all tend to be hirsute)—to deal mercifully with those who served him. He also vowed that should this pledge not be kept, by himself or future generations, the house of Krumley would fall. One may assume that none failed in their duty until"—her ladyship's dark eyes seemed to sink into her head—"I so cruelly wronged Flossie Jones."

"Is it known how your cousin Vincent came to fall into the well?" I asked.

"He had gone out into the grounds in search of his dog, a Maltese terrier that he had brought down with him and had insisted be allowed to dine at the table. It was discovered missing from the house shortly after I left for Mucklesby. A tiresome, yapping creature. One would think no one could regret its absence. But Vincent was quite besotted. Credited it with having helped him stop drinking, by threatening to walk out if he ever touched another drop. One could never tell if Vincent was serious or joking. And I suspected upon this visit that he had grown addled in his wits."

"Was he very elderly?" I inquired.

"In his nineties, close in age to what Sir Horace would have been." Her ladyship lay plucking at her shawl. "So I suppose there is some excuse. He kept saying Niles's wife looked like a go-go dancer and something about Daisy Meeks, another relation who was present on the evening of his arrival, having a twin. He'd chortle in a silly way. It was all extremely tedious. And I must say I was happy to get out of the house."

"Family!" Mrs. Malloy sat looking soulful. "It's never all it's cracked up to be, is it, your ladyship ducks? Still, I'm sure you wasn't pleased to hear he'd kicked the bucket . . . on the way down the well."

"When I put down the phone after receiving the news from Niles I must have gone into shock. The realization that the deathbed curse of Flossie Jones had been again at work was too much for me. For I have no doubt that it was my breaking the family code of honor that empowered her. The doctors here suspected I had suffered another heart attack, but I knew such was not the case. I had merely fainted—something I had never done before in my life—thus precipitating the crash."

"That's all it was?" Mrs. M. looked seriously aggrieved. "No one had done nothing nasty to the brakes, or run you off the road."

"I merely lost consciousness for a few moments." Her ladyship sat back up with a surprising bounce. "I should have been allowed to go home instead of being kept imprisoned in this most uncomfortable bed and woken up in the night to be made to take a sleeping pill. And this morning they were talking about having me examined by a cardiologist to be brought down from London. So much nonsense. I detest having poor, sensitive Niles. . . ."

"We met him," I said, looking toward Mrs. Malloy, "just now outside in the corridor. He thought we were social workers and agreed to let us come in and see you first. He said he would go back to meet up with his wife who had parked the car. You didn't mention yesterday, your ladyship, that they live with you at Moultty Towers."

The black eyes darted my way. "I was distracted after being so late for my appointment, distressed over those flower pots

being thrown at the car, uncertain as to the advisability of
dealing with Mr. Jugg's associates. My head was in something
of a muddle."

"Understandably you were agitated. It is why you smoked
those cigarettes." There was a hollow feeling in the pit of my
stomach. I hadn't stopped her even after she mentioned those
heart attacks. And what if, despite her protests, she had suffered another? How much of the fault lay at my door? The
question was enough to make me vow silently that I would take
on her case, however madcap it seemed, and see it through to
what I hoped would not be the bitter end. There was Ernestine
to be located and perhaps a villain to unmask. I still had serious doubts of the latter's existence. The advent of Have Gun
might mean nothing. He could have been a mad prankster, out
for a night's fun at her ladyship's expense. But how could it hurt
me to spend a few days helping an ill and troubled old woman?

Lady Krumley shifted a leg, and I'm sure that only by exert-
ing her formidable will did she restrain herself from getting out
of bed and marching up and down the room. There were no
tubes to restrain her, no crisply starched nurse rustling forward
to instruct her to be a good girl.

"Did Niles Edmonds inherit the title?" I got up and poured
her a glass of water.

"I could do with a brandy." The black eyes flashed.

"Well, it just so happens . . ." Mrs. Malloy reached into her
bag but susbsided on meeting my scowl. "I was only going to offer her a lemon drop," she muttered.

"No, Niles is the son of Horace's youngest brother. The title
went to another nephew, Alfonse Krumley, whose father was
next in line to my husband." Lady Krumley straightened her
leg and sipped at the glass of water. "Niles came to live at
Moultty Towers when he was ten-years-old and Sir Horace and
I were newly married. He has been all but a son to me."

Mrs. Malloy and I made appropriate noises.

"His parents had died in a freak accident. Sadly, his electric train set blew up and completely gutted the nursery one night when they went in to hear him say his prayers."

"And the poor little lamb wasn't hurt?" Mrs. Malloy gave a knowing smirk that I itched to wipe off her face.

"He had suffered an asthma attack and gone down to the kitchen to be cosseted by the cook. Understandably, the incident affected poor Niles deeply. He was afraid to sleep alone for years after he came to Moultty Towers. Sometimes I think he married Cynthia to have someone in his bed."

"Well, that is odd," Mrs. Malloy said in an effort to straighten her face.

"Always so afraid of the bogeyman coming to get him." There was a suggestive glisten of tears in Lady Krumley's eyes. "And Cynthia, whatever else might be said against her, isn't afraid of anything or anyone. My husband wasn't particularly sympathetic to Niles even when it came to his asthma. Sir Horace insisted that Niles used his attacks to get me to spoil him. And it must be said that at age fifty he is still very much a small boy in long trousers. He began to wheeze yesterday when I said I was going out in the car and would not be back for several hours. I did not feel comfortable leaving him until Cynthia came in from her riding lesson, especially as Daisy Meeks who would agitate anyone, was present. A foolish, nattering woman. Another family connection of my husband, living in the village. She has the most irritating yap, like that dog of Vincent's."

"Was it found?" I asked.

"Pipsie or Wipsie or whatever it was called? Niles didn't say, nor did I think to ask. All that can be assumed is that Vincent must have gone looking for it in the cottage garden and got it into his panicky head that the animal had fallen in the well, and in peering down to take a look, himself fell in."

"And who found Vincent?"

"Again Niles didn't say."

"And all because the dog got out," Mrs. Malloy said. "A door left open by mistake. Easy enough done." Mrs. Malloy didn't fool me. She had already worked it out in her mind that the dog had been removed from the house so that Vincent would go looking for it and end up being dropped down that well.

"Lady Krumley," I said, "matters have taken a most regrettable turn since last night. I understand your wish to bring Mrs. Malloy and myself current with the situation, but is there any other reason why you wished to see us so urgently today? Is there perhaps something you consider to be of significance that you forgot to mention? For instance," I rattled on as she stared silently back at me, "I have been wondering if you know what became of Ernestine's father."

"Her father?"

"Ernest the under gardener. Was he around when she was born, or had he deserted Flossie by that time? From the way you described her living arrangements during her illness it doesn't sound as though she was receiving any significant financial support." Receiving no reply I kept going: "Of course the young man may not have been making much money."

Lady Krumley stared down her eagle nose at the bed covers.

"Or was he given the sack for getting her pregnant? This all happened nearly forty years ago, and I do realize that times were different then." I sat still, thinking that thank goodness society was less condemning now, at least to the point of not routinely referring to children born out of wedlock as illegitimate. Mrs. Malloy started to say something at the moment when Lady Krumley spoke, her voice coming out so deep-throated that I shot sideways in my chair to collide with Mrs. Malloy.

"What I told you yesterday was true. The rumor went around the house that Flossie was pregnant by this young man Ernest. Mrs. Snow, the housekeeper, apprised me of the fact that he was making quite a nuisance of himself coming indoors under any pretext in hope of seeing the girl and also waylaying her in the garden. And when her condition was revealed he offered to marry her. One may assume that he loved her. But he wasn't the father."

"Then who was?" I asked, surmising the answer.

"My husband. Sir Horace."

"Rotten bugger!" Mrs. M. proffered a lemon drop, which seemed somewhat inadequate under the circumstances. "Don't tell me he wanted to up and marry the flighty piece."

"He wouldn't have done that, even had Flossie been of his social standing." Her ladyship's mouth curved in a bitter smile. "He was fond of me. I never doubted that even then. But it was a quiet affection, of shared interests and common background. There was never any passion on his part. No fire in his loins where I was concerned. How could it have been expected? I was ever a plain woman. Without feminine whiles. What I did have—being an only child—was a fortune inherited from my family. Sir Horace was badly in need of money when he married me. Without what I brought with me he would have been unable to hold onto Moultty Towers. And the place was everything to him."

"Until Miss Flossie showed up on the scene." Mrs. Malloy who'd had her own trouble with errant husbands glowered in sympathy.

"As I told you she was a pretty girl, and clever with it in a pert cockney sort of way, as Mrs. Snow told me."

"That woman seems to have been a fount of information," I said.

"She was a loyal employee, doing her duty as she saw it. But even without her input I would have had my suspicions. I twice observed him kissing her in the conservatory."

"Did you say anything to Sir Horace?"

"It was difficult but I was determined to take the pragmatic approach—turn a blind eye and hope that when the hunting season began the silliness would end. He was after all a man in his late fifties, wanting to think of himself as still in his prime. I told myself that any giddy young girl's coy ways and flattering adulation would have done to boost his male ego. So I focused my attention on Niles. A mistake. I see that now. It only added a source of irritation to our marriage. When I heard that Flossie was pregnant I clung to the hope she would marry the gardener boy and that they would make a life for themselves elsewhere. On the day that the emerald and diamond brooch disappeared matters came to a head. When Mrs. Snow informed me that she had seen Flossie coming out of my bedroom that morning, I knew the truth. She had been with Sir Horace in his connecting dressing room while I was away from the house at a luncheon. Being confronted by Mrs. Snow's knowing look was the utmost in humiliation. And when I discovered the brooch to be missing, I lost all control, storming at my husband and threatening to leave him. He retaliated at first by accusing me of pretending to lose his grandmother's brooch. But I could see in his eyes that he did not believe it. He knew that I was not a liar." Lady Krumley's face closed in to even greater hauteur. "You may doubt that, with justification, since I withheld part of the story from you yesterday. But whatever my state of mind I would not stoop to a downright untruth. Sir Horace then insisted that I had misplaced the brooch and in my spite was intent on fixing its loss upon Flossie. He went to battle for her, asserting that she would never attempt to turn his world upside down, especially with the baby on the way. It was then," her ladyship continued, slumping back on the pillow, "that I knew two things: that he was in love with her—in the sadly desperate way of an older man for a young girl."

I moved to the bedside, but resisted the inclination to stroke her hair back from her brow. There wouldn't be much I could do for her if she ordered my hands to be cut off. "Was there no possibility that it was Ernest's?"

"My husband retreated behind a wall of silence that condemned him utterly."

"Did it cross your mind, Lady Krumley, that Flossie might have been playing both men to her own ends?"

"How could it not? But if Sir Horace doubted he was the father, why did he not say so? All I could wrench out of him was that the child must be his, and he would see it suitably provided for when the time came. It was, as even I knew, the right and honorable thing to do. But hatred had entered my soul, Mrs. . . ."

"Haskell," I provided, and she actually reached out and touched my hand.

"I told my husband that the girl would be dismissed for stealing and if he so much attempted get in touch with her, let alone see her, I would divorce him and take every penny of my money with me. He tried to bluster. But I knew I had won." The hand that gripped mine tightened painfully. "Flossie was sent packing, and I became a murderess in the making. I allowed her to die in that bed-sitter by depriving her of the support to which she was entitled. Now do you understand why I am so desperate to find Ernestine? She is my husband's daughter, and I am convinced that only by making the fullest reparation possible can I prevent Flossie's vengeance from whittling away at every branch of the family tree."

"And just how do you plan to put things right?" Mrs. Malloy teetered onto her high heels.

"By leaving her the bulk of my fortune."

Which provided, I conceded silently, an interesting twist to the situation. I could tell by the glint in her eye that Mrs. Malloy was thinking the same. Or was she pondering just how much money her ladyship would be willing to pay for our services? She named an amount and Mrs. Malloy was turning her gasp into a cough when a courtly, silver-haired gentleman stepped into the room. He wasn't a doctor. He was introduced to us as Lady Krumley's friend and Vicar, Mr. Featherstone. The one person, as she had told us last night, which whom she had discussed her appointment with Mr. Jugg. Mrs. Malloy looked at him with deep suspicion while he took Lady Krumley's gnarled hands in his and stood looking down at her without speaking. Words—mere words would have been superfluous. The expression in his eyes betrayed him. Or so I would have thought. Her ladyship regarded him in the mildly affectionate manner that takes for granted the rights afforded by long acquaintance.

"Do sit down, Cyril," she said. "These women are about to take their leave; so I depend on you to scare away any doctor with the temerity to sidle around the door. For it has been brought home to me that I am not ready to be reunited with Horace at the pearly gates. Dying at this moment would be tantamount to running away, and what ever my failings, I was never a coward."

"My dear Maude," replied Mr. Featherstone, "What am I going to do with you?"

Ten

"Five thousand pounds!" Mrs. Malloy folded her arms and looked up at the ceiling with a beatific smile on her face. We were seated in a café halfway between Mucklesby and Chitterton Fells. There were bottles of tomato sauce on the tables and a menu scrawled on a chalkboard behind the counter. This was definitely not the Sistene Chapel, but I could understand why she felt heaven was within our grasp.

"That's only if we find Ernestine within the week," I pointed out as the waitress bustled our way with plates of baked beans on toast and a pot of tea for two.

"And why shouldn't we, if we set our minds to it? The point is, Mrs. H., that Lady Krumley wouldn't have offered us a tenth as much if that Vincent bloke hadn't taken a nosedive. No getting round it. His misfortune, not to sound callous, is our good luck. Her ladyship's panicking, the poor duck. Probably thinking it won't be any time at all before the curse gets her too. Leastway, that's the way I see it."

"Do you?" I bit thoughtfully into a forkful of beans.

"What's that supposed to mean?" Mrs. M. eyed me as if I were a genie who had just popped out of the bottle of tomato sauce. "That funny look on your face is what I'm talking about."

"I was just thinking."

"About what?" She picked up the teapot.

"Mr. Featherstone."

"So?"

"He looked rather nice."

"Being a vicar; that's his job." Mrs. Malloy dabbed irritably away at a drip of tea that had landed on the bosom of her powder pink raincoat.

"Somehow I don't think he just came to minister."

"Am I getting this right? You think he's involved with the bad guys and you just walked me all light and breezy out of that there room, leaving him to strangle her sweet little old ladyship in her hospital bed? Well, I think you should be downright ashamed of yourself Mrs. H.! The least you could've done was hand her a bedpan so she could hit him over the head." Clearly, Mrs. Malloy could see the five thousand pounds vanishing as we spoke.

I laid my knife and fork down on my empty plate. "What I am saying, and it is only a feeling, is that I wouldn't be surprised to discover that Mr. Featherstone is very fond of Lady Krumley."

"What sort of fond?"

"Come on, Mrs. Malloy! Didn't you notice the way he looked at her when he took her hand? Didn't that faint tremor in his voice make you think that here was a man fighting desperately to control his emotions?"

"Could be you're right. But it's kind of hard to grasp right off the bat, seeing that her ladyship, through no fault of her own," she spoke piously, "isn't what anyone could call passable, let alone a raving beauty. And then there's her age."

"Mr. Featherstone may be younger," I said, "but I doubt by much. Not that it matters if he's thirty-five to her seventy odd, if she has none but friendly feelings for him. And I didn't see anything in her manner to suggest that her heart was throbbing a mile a minute at the sight of him. When we left she seemed to be more concerned about why her nephew Niles was taking so long to show up. Besides, Mr. Featherstone could be married, and Lady Krumley may be the sort of woman for whom there is only one man."

"Go on!" scoffed Mrs. M. "She'd have to be a fool if you're talking about that hubby of hers. She as good as said he married her for her money and then off he goes and gets another woman pregnant right under her nose. Think on the humiliation! That Mrs. Snow, the sneaky housekeeper, rubbing salt in the wound for all she was worth. And all them other tongues clacking. If I'd been that Sir Horace I'd have run for me bloody life."

"And Lady Krumley could be a woman who knows how to hold onto a grudge." I poured myself another cup of tea and looked longingly at the toasted teacake being handed to a woman at a nearby table.

"Out with it, Mrs. H., what is it you've got ticking away inside that clock of yours?"

"I'm just trying to look at the situation from another point of view."

"Meaning?"

"That maybe we shouldn't be so quick to take Lady Krumley at her word when she talks about wanting to locate Ernestine to make up for the wrongs done to her. What if there's another reason? A darker one, born of old hate and a desire to protect the interests of someone near and dear to her?" The waitress passed by, and I ordered a toasted teacake.

"Spell it out, Mrs. H., before me nerves give out."

"What if her ladyship has twisted the facts to suit her story? What if Sir Horace had plenty of money in his own right? What if he left a will bequeathing his estate upon his wife's death—and in the event of there being no other living relations—to his out-of-wedlock daughter Ernestine?"

"What, including the house?"

"It may be entailed, just as her ladyship said, to that other nephew, Alfonse Krumley. And no great loss. A house of the size I imagine it to be must be enormously costly to maintain and horribly inconvenient to live in. Niles, with his asthma, might be a lot more comfortable living in a modern flat without big overstuffed sofas and voluminous curtains harboring a century's worth of dust. Besides, if my idea is correct, it won't matter that Alfonse is to inherit Moultty Towers, because he will shortly go the way of Vincent Krumley—the victim of another unfortunate accident."

"Arranged by Lady Krumley is what you're saying?" My toasted teacake arrived on the table, and Mrs. Malloy reached for the plate. "Just like she had all them others—like the old geezer in Australia that got mauled by a kangaroo and the woman that fell down a lift—bumped off."

"I'm not accusing her ladyship of mass murder," I responded coldly to Mrs. Malloy's snicker. "What I am suggesting is that when she learned of those deaths, most of them the result of freak accidents that no one questioned because the victims were all old and possibly not in full possession of their faculties, it may have got her thinking."

"Takes some thinking about." Mrs. Malloy polished off the teacake.

"Just being a dear old auntie getting rid of the remaining family members so that Niles, whom she described as the closest thing to a son, could inherit a fortune."

"But how many would she have to do in? That's the question, Mrs. H. We're talking about an old woman that you'd expect to be parked in the rocking chair most of the day. Murdering people's got to take up a lot of time and energy, which would make for skipped meals. Maybe we should check with her doctor to see if she's recently been in asking for a prescription for iron and vitamin pills."

"Perhaps only Alfonse and possibly that woman Lady Krumley mentioned—Daisy something—now stand between Niles and what she considers his rightful inheritance. Apart from Ernestine that is."

"Oh, good! Because I wouldn't want to think of her overdoing things!" Mrs. Malloy sat back in her chair replete with baked beans, teacake and the wink received from a man on his way out of the café. "I suppose what you're telling me is she dropped Vincent down that well before leaving for Mucklesby and she's only pretending to be poorly enough to be in hospital. There wasn't no car crash. No one threw no flower pots at her and all that business about Flossie Jones and the deathbed curse was just a load of malarkey? So who was it what sent the man with the gun to scare us off the case?"

"Or into taking it."

Mrs. M. gave one of her most condescending smirks. "The way I sees it, sitting this side of the table, is that if her ladyship is up to no bloody good, wanting to find Ernestine to make sure she's got rid of permanent, there'd be no need for all that stuff about deathbed curses and such. Now I'm a believer in such things, but I'm not fool enough to think most people, including yourself feels the same. So why make it up? Wouldn't it have done better for her to keep things simple—tell us what happened between Sir Horace and Flossie Jones and how she kept him from helping the girl out?"

"You're right," I admitted.

"You don't have to sound so snippy."

"Why not? You just ate my teacake."

"Oh, go on! Have the crumbs." Mrs. Malloy pushed the plate my way and eyed me kindly. "There's no need to sit there feeling silly. What you've got to realize is you're a newcomer to this business. I've a whole three weeks experience on you working for Milk. And let me say this, I've nothing against the upper classes so long as they knows their place and keeps to it, but I can't fault you for being cautious where her ladyship is concerned. It wouldn't be right for us to go looking for Ernestine if we thought we was handing her over to be murdered. I'm sure there's a rule somewhere in the private detective's code book about that sort of thing. Now how do you suggest we set about this job?" It was clear she was asking mainly to help give my morale a lift, and I almost forgave her for eating the teacake.

"We'd better start by going to Moultty Towers to see what we can sniff out. We might even find someone that was there at the same time as Flossie Jones who might give us a tip as to who handled Ernestine's adoption."

"Just what I was going to suggest meself. Like that woman as lives in the cottage by the well. Give me a minute, her name's coming to me . . . Mrs. Hurry."

"Hasty."

"Right. But will she or anyone else be falling over their selves to talk to a pair of private detectives? Even them as have nothing to hide, Mrs. H., could shut up tight as the shops on early closing day the minute we open our mouths."

"Also, Lady Krumley will undoubtedly wish us to be as discreet as possible, which means we need to go in undercover."

"Now you're talking." Mrs. Malloy positively beamed at me. "Who should we pretend to be? How about electrical inspectors? I rather fancy meself in a pair of overalls with a cap on me head."

"I thought, and it's only a suggestion, that the simplest thing would be to say we were interior designers, hired by her ladyship to redecorate Moultty Towers."

Mrs. M. stopped looking thrilled. "That's all well and good, seeing as how that's your line of work. A nice chance for you to show off. And boost your ego back up after that upset with Mr. H. over his study. But what am I supposed to do while you're preening about? Stand around holding the tape measure?"

"We'll be the firm of Malloy and Haskell. You'll be the expert in wall and window treatments."

"Treatments?"

"That's one of the buzzwords in the business. You'll also need to talk a lot about maintaining the integrity of the structure."

"You did say Malloy and Haskell?"

"You think it might sound better the other way round?"

Mrs. Malloy picked up the bill the waitress had deposited on the table and made a pretense of opening her handbag. "Look, I'm not daft. I can tell when you're trying to butter me up. My question is what if someone got suspicious and went and looked us up in the telephone directory, or checked with some independent business group?"

"That's what's so good about the idea. I am listed and all I have to say is that I've recently taken you on as a partner and that Lady Krumley consulted with us yesterday. As for Niles seeing us at the hospital today and our allowing him to think we were social workers, we can get around that by saying we didn't feel free to discuss her ladyship's plans for redecorating without her permission."

"No rest is there in this business? Still, it's hard to complain when there's that five thousand pounds."

"Think how grateful Mr. Jugg will be when he returns—if we're successful, that is."

"Fancy! I'd forgotten all about him." Mrs. Malloy looked suitably shamefaced. "Course, I'm sure he'll be all broken up with gratitude. And if he don't make me his Girl Friday on the spot it'll shock me back to me old hair color, sure as my name is Roxie Malloy." She was so moved by this image that she left a twenty pence tip on the table, insisting I was doing my share by paying the bill.

Upon venturing out into the gray chill of the afternoon she looked up and down the street, saying that we needed to get to a telephone kiosk in order to give Lady Krumley a ring and explain the setup before we set out for Moultty Towers.

"We can't go now," I said. "I don't have a notebook or my measuring equipment in the car. More importantly the best part of the day is gone, and we don't want to be urged off the premises before we've got properly started wheedling information out of people. We'll go early tomorrow morning."

Mrs. Malloy continued to look miffed as we drove home under stormy skies. It was with the promise of picking her up at 8:30 the next morning that I dropped her off at her house in Herring Street and breathed a sigh of relief. I was eager to get home. By now Ben would have collected the children from school and would very likely have dinner started. Perhaps it would be possible for us to sit down with cups of tea and have a good talk that would banish the lingering atmosphere of constraint between us.

When I reached St. Anselm's I spotted Kathleen Ambleforth crossing the gravel space between the church hall and the vicarage. Rolling down the car window, I waved at her and saw her start toward me with a beckoning gesture. A moment later I was parked alongside her and sticking my head out into a wind that blew my hair around my face.

"I won't keep you." She stood tugging the brim of her hat down over her brow, with her coat flapping about her legs. "Looks like we're about to get another downpour and, unfortunately, I don't have much to report about your furniture. I did find cousin Alice's dispatch list, but as there were a number of duplicated items, it's impossible to be sure which ones were yours, or if they all went to the same place. Let's hope Alice will remember, but she's not always easy to get hold of; she plays a lot of bridge. I never could understand why people get so worked up about card games. But to each his own."

"You weren't able to narrow it down"—the wind tore the words out of my mouth—"to a few charitable organizations where the stuff might have gone?"

"There are half-a-dozen possibilities."

"Look," I said, "I'll pay—more than it's worth—to buy it all back. Don't you think that would soothe any ruffled feathers? If you give me a list of the places, I could start ringing them up?"

"I think that could make a great deal of unnecessary work for a lot of people. My dear," Kathleen, who tended to throw those two words in when her patience was wearing thin, said, "try to be patient. I may have the information you want by tomorrow." With that she waved me off in a resolute fashion, and I watched her battling her way through the wind to the vicarage before I reversed the car out onto the Cliff Road and drove the short distance home.

Ben wasn't in the kitchen when I entered through the garden door. Neither were the children nor Freddy for that matter. They could, of course, have been anywhere in the house. It was foolish of me to take it as a bad sign that there was not a whiff of dinner in the air. Stripping off my raincoat and hanging it on a hook in the alcove by the door, I allowed myself the luxury of self-pity. In the course of the day I had gone from being a housewife and interior designer, pretending to be a private detective and social worker, to end up pretending to be my very own self. Was it too much to expect to be greeted at the door by a husband who had been counting the minutes until my return?

Ben came into the kitchen when I was in the middle of telling him just what I thought of his ability to harbor a grudge. He didn't hear a word because the entire conversation had taken place inside my head, but it was heartening to see that he looked suitably shamefaced.

"Sweetheart," he said, standing and rumpling his fingers through his dark curly hair, "are you back already? I took it from what Freddy said that you would be gone until late afternoon. The children, all three of them are at the Thompson house playing with young Julian and Trevor." His blue green eyes, always his strongest weapon in making me want to let him off the hook, stared at the wall clock. "Good grief! It's gone 5:00. I don't know where the time's gone." He came toward me with the quick stride of an impatient lover and drew me into his arms. The rasp of his bristly cheek against mine made me suspect that he had hurried shaving that morning. But then all other thought was lost in his kiss, which was long and deep and made me forget all about the cup of tea I had been aching for a moment ago.

"Oh, darling." I gazed lovingly into those eyes. "You have forgiven me!"

"For what?" He sounded completely at sea.

"The study, of course. My insensitivity to your feelings. My manic desire to make the house over into my ideal, ignoring the fact that you loved that lumpy old chair and that dear little typewriter."

"Hush!" He kissed me again. "Did I really make you feel that wretched about it? God help me, I'm becoming my father! Irascible and set in my ways. Have you been worrying about this all day?"

"I know it's silly," I said, cuddling in even closer, "but I let my imagination run away with me to the point where I wondered if our marriage was on the rocks."

"Over some furniture?"

"I know. But when I was at the vicarage this morning to speak to Kathleen about the . . . upcoming meeting of the Hearthside Guild, Reverend Ambleforth came in and began talking about how you had been to see him, wanting advice on reading materials dealing with divorce. He said that you wanted it for a friend who had a controlling wife. Someone called Smith or Jones . . . one of those really common names.

Or maybe he thought that was you. I should have realized that he had the whole thing wrong. He gets so hopelessly muddled when he's got a nose in one of his books about St. Ethelwort."

"I did go to see him."

"Him being the vicar?" It was crucial to be absolutely clear on this.

"The one and only Reverend Ambleforth."

"But not to ask for books on divorce?"

Ben cupped my chin in his hand so that his tender smile was just a breath away from my lips. "I'm afraid so, Ellie."

My heart slowed to a dull painful thud. "What are you telling me?"

"Are you sure you're up to hearing this?"

I could only gaze at him mutely.

"Sweetheart, don't take it too hard." His voice had deepened to a throb. "These things happen sometimes to people who once loved each other very much, and I'm close to certain that Ralph Brown does still love his wife. It's her need to check up on him every fifteen minutes to make sure that he hasn't stepped outside without his coat or forgotten to eat his packed lunch that he has begun to find intolerable."

"Ralph Brown?" If there had been a rolling pin handy, I would have clobbered the husband now gazing soulfully into my eyes. I showed my remorse by making a pot of tea and sitting down to a roast beef sandwich with plenty of horseradish. "The upstairs tenant at Abigail's. The man in Edwardian dress with the art shop."

"It could be that his wife has to do something to keep from being frightened to death by his pictures of nasty-looking owls. You know the old saying: never trust a bird with eyes that are too close together."

I stood for a moment mulling things over before saying, "I hope Mr. Brown appreciates all the trouble you've taken on his behalf. I suppose those books I saw you hauling out of the library when I drove past this morning were for him."

"No, Ellie, they were for me."

There was nothing in this reply to unsettle me. And I would have asked Ben why he had that guilty look on his face if Freddy hadn't chosen that moment to walk into the kitchen with the children in tow.

Eleven

After dropping Abbey and Tam off at school and Rose at her play group, I picked up Mrs. Malloy at one minute past the time arranged and then headed toward Biddlington-By-Water, which Mrs. Malloy proceeded to remind me was a proper dead-in-a-live-hole.

"But you were only there once to play bingo," I pointed out.

"So?" She sat looking the picture of some Hollywood costume designer's idea of an interior decorator in a black velvet toque trimmed with faux leopard to match her coat and a pair of doorknob-sized earrings. "As I've been known to say time out of mind, the people you sees at bingo is a micro-cousin of what the rest of the place is like."

"You did get in touch with Lady Krumley? And explain our plan?"

"Course I did. And she said she didn't mind what sort of cover we used if it helped us pick up some clues about how to find Ernestine. Poor duck! Can't be easy lying on that hospital bed, hoping and praying that she'll live to see the day she can put things right with her hubby's love child after all these years." Mrs. Malloy heaved a sentimental sigh before telling me I was driving in circles.

"I'm on the roundabout."

"You've been round it three bloody times."

This was true, but I was having trouble figuring out which exit would get me to Biddlington-By-Water. Pressed into making a decision by Mrs. Malloy's nudge in my ribs, I took the sign to Swayford, because it sounded vaguely familiar, and relaxed into my seat. It wasn't as though we were in a rush to arrive at an appointed time, but I did hope that her ladyship had warned her nephew Niles or his wife to expect us sometime during the morning.

"She said she'd phone the moment she hung up after we'd done talking." Mrs. Malloy opened her handbag and popped a lemon drop into her mouth. "Now let's get ourselves clear, Mrs. H., about what we're really up to in going to Moultty Towers. Is it just about Ernestine? Or are we going to have a nose round and see what we can't sniff out about all them deaths in the family, including the fellow that just got murdered down that well? Now what was his name?"

"Vincent Krumley. And for all we know it was an accident, plain and simple."

"And I'm the Queen Mother!"

"All right!" I said. "We have our suspicions. But we're not the police. We're not even proper private detectives. And I'm not all that keen on being tossed over the cliffs for sticking my nose in where it isn't wanted."

"There aren't any cliffs at Biddlington-By-Water." Mrs. M. could nitpick with the best when she chose. "It's not a seaside place. Got nothing going for it, as I told you."

I had to agree when we reached High Street that Biddlington-By-Water did not abound with charm. The buildings mostly looked as though they had been erected in the 1950s. There were a couple of banks, a cinema and what appeared to be a local department store. Even the cakes in the bakery window might have been there for half a century, with the cherries on top being replaced periodically as the proprietor saw fit. The

Pizza Hut and McDonald's on opposite corners looked as though they had been put up in the night when nobody was looking.

"There!" Mrs. Malloy pointed at a block of concrete with a door stuck in the middle. "That's the hall where I played bingo. And if I remember Lady Krumley's directions rightly, we need to turn left at the next traffic light, go down to the post office and take a right. That should bring us onto a road that narrows into a lane about half a mile down. Right after we come to a field with a sign saying 'Free Range Eggs,' we'll round a corner and see Moultty Towers on our left, or it could be right." She continued to vacillate on this point for the next two-and-a-half miles, at which point we could see the house, for surely there could not be two of such size in close proximity.

"Looks the right sort of place for a murder!" Mrs. Malloy had her nose pressed to the windscreen.

"What a monstrosity!" I was truly appalled. "All those towers stuck up on the roof like a bunch of cannons, and the whole thing looking like a boys' reformatory school in some black and white film from the 1920s. Probably at some point in its history it was a perfectly charming house—until some fiend decided to modernize it and then not being happy with the results glued the towers back on and hammered big iron nails in the front door."

"Okay! Okay!" Mrs. Malloy climbed out of the car to stand beside me. "I can see for meself it needs to be knocked down and put out of its misery. Now tell me again," she was looking uncharacteristically nervous, "what sort of things I'm to say to show I knows what I'm talking about."

"You could suggest that the fireplace needs merchandising."

"Meaning they should sell it?"

"That," I said, hoisting the bag containing furniture catalogues and fabric samples onto the curve of my arm, "it should make a decorating statement. Look, follow my lead and you'll be fine."

"That's right, let you queen it while I walk three places behind like poor Prince Phillip!" She was still grumbling as we
mounted the broad sweep of steps to the front door, and would
undoubtedly have gone on indefinitely if it had not been
opened almost immediately by a man in a dark jacket and sober
tie. He was short and almost completely bald. His age appeared
to be in the sixties. His expression intimated nothing more
than a mild inquiry.

"Good morning." One of his eyebrows shifted a hair or two.

"Haskell and Malloy, interior designers." I tapped the bag
and beamed at him. "Lady Krumley did say to expect us?"

"I know nothing of the matter, madam." He stepped aside
for us to enter and closed the door behind us. "If you will wait
here"—indicating the large and intensely gloomy hall—"I will
apprise Mr. and Mrs. Edmonds of your arrival." His was the sort
of face that one sees on dozens of buses, neither good looking
nor ugly and impossible to describe five minutes later. But Mrs.
Malloy was eyeing him coyly.

"Have you and me met somewhere?"

"Not that I recall, madam?"

She giggled. "Then it's on to the next line, isn't it? Do you
come here often?"

"Frequently. I'm Watkins, Lady Krumley's butler." He turned
and entered a door to our left, leaving Mrs. Malloy with a sigh
on her lips and a dreamy look in her eyes. "I'd have sworn, but
I suppose it could be as how he reminds me of Cary Grant."

"Have you had your eyesight checked recently?"

"It's the voice." She now stood admiring herself in a mirror,
carved with bunches of gigantic fruit, hung above a table
topped with a bilious shade of green marble. "All lovely and
posh, but with a hint of earthiness underneath. Give me a man
of mystery any day. So long as he's not the sort to look down his
nose at bingo."

"Slip him a note before you leave. Just don't suggest meeting him at moonlight by ye old wishing well. Remember it's usually the butler who did it in these situations."

"You're right!" Mrs. Malloy froze in place. "How could I have been so taken in? Now you say it, there is something about his eyes—sort of shifty like—and that nasty cruel twist to his mouth. I've been missing Milk, that's my trouble. Now there's a real man if ever there was one."

"You haven't heard from him?"

"Not a dickie bird."

I was staring at the black oak staircase that, in conjuction with a fireplace suitable for roasting an ox, dominated the far end of the hall, when Watkins reappeared.

"If you will be so good as to follow me, Mr. Edmonds will see you now. Mrs. Edmonds is out, but is expected back shortly."

"If we might leave our coats?"

"Certainly." He waited patiently for Mrs. Malloy to finish unbuttoning hers, laid them across a chair, sprouting more carved fruit, and led us into the room that he had just vacated. "The decorators, sir," he informed Niles Edmonds who was hovering in the center of the room looking as if he had wandered into the women's loo by mistake and was about to have half-a-dozen rolls of toilet paper hurled at him.

"Thank you, Watkins." His bleating voice matched his sheepish look.

"If you should require me, sir, to have the furniture draped in sheets and the floors covered with plastic cloths, I will arrange for it to be done with all due speed. I am sure that Mrs. Hasty would be happy to oblige by coming up from the cottage to lend a hand."

"Yes, quite! Absolutely! Good idea." Niles Edmonds retreated back a few paces under Mrs. Malloy's frowning stare.

"We're not them kind of decorators—the ones with paint pots and brushes." She set about putting him straight before

Watkins was out the door. "Me and my partner, Mrs. Haskell here, are a high-cost operation. I'd have thought as you'd have been able to tell that by this hat I've got on me head. A model it is, bought at one of them fancy boutiques, like I expect your own wife shops at. But of course there's them that can wear hats and them that looks like they've got a colander on their head. You can put people in big houses I always say, but you can't always make them look the part."

"Very true. Your point is well made. Couldn't be better expressed." The man appeared ready to collapse on the carpet that looked as though it might have seen better days, perhaps in the time of Henry VIII, although the room wasn't of the Tudor style. It was a game room. Not the billiard table, chess set sort, but the other . . . wild animal kind. Almost every inch of wall was covered with furry heads. Everywhere I looked there were glass eyes gazing at me with deepest reproach. Unbidden, the tune to "Old Macdonald Had a Farm" wormed its way into my head, and I caught myself humming "here a moose head, there a moose head, everywhere a moose moose." Before I could burst into song, Mrs. Malloy kindly trod on my foot with her four-inch heel, and I was able to meet Niles Edmonds's eyes without a song in my heart.

"Didn't we meet at the hospital?" He adjusted his glasses for a better look. His frown etched lines on his forehead all the way up to his receding hairline. Here I suspected was a man living permanently in a state of perplexity. It was cruel to keep him on pins and needles for a moment longer than necessary. Seemingly, it was all up to me. Mrs. Malloy was prowling the room, inspecting the cushions on the half-a-dozen armchairs that, in addition to two sofas, encircled the fireplace with an eight-foot tapestry rotting away above it.

"That's right, Mr. Edmonds, we spoke in the corridor outside Lady Krumley's room at the hospital. You mistook us for social workers, and neither Mrs. Malloy nor I felt in a position to correct you, because her ladyship had told us that she wanted to surprise you and your wife with her plans to redecorate."

"Yes, quite! A very difficult position for you." He waved a limp hand. "Won't you please be seated?"

"Thrilled!" Mrs. Malloy gingerly lowered herself onto a wooden chair, of the sort that might conceal a chamber pot for use in emergencies, while I perched on a sofa.

"I do understand Aunt Maude's wanting to keep it a secret until the last minute," Niles murmured with doleful resignation.

"Likes her little surprises, does she?" Mrs. Malloy elevated a penciled eyebrow.

"Dear Auntie! She's very sensitive to my feelings, knowing that change of any sort can bring on one of my attacks." He demonstrated with a wheeze, but rallied after thumping his chest and grasping the arms of his chair. "I suppose she thought it best to say nothing until she had brought you on board ship. Indeed I do see that there are things needing doing to the house. Things have rather been allowed to slide since Uncle Horace's death. And Watkins is not the butler Hopkins was," he said through another pathetic wheeze, "but he's done his best these past five years while managing with shortage of staff. We've been without a housekeeper since Mrs. Snow retired. It's all been very hard on my wife. Cynthia married me hoping for better things."

"Indeed!" I said.

"She anticipated that I would be out of the house most of the time. But I had to take early retirement from my work as an accountant."

Mrs. Malloy made sympathetic clucking sounds while sitting as if about to lay an egg.

"I do keep my hand in managing Aunt Maude's business affairs. Everything except the housekeeping accounts. Watkins sees to those. It gives him an outing once or twice a week to go

to the bank. Did Aunt Maude say how you would be paid?"
Niles flicked a glance between Mrs. Malloy and me. "How big
an expenditure are we talking about? A couple of tables and
chairs . . ." He blinked behind his glasses. "Or something more
drastic? You won't be tearing down any walls, will you?"

"Lady Krumley has given us carte blanche." I opened my bag
and produced my paint chart and fabric samples. "So we may
be in and out of here for a few days before making any final de-
cisions. Please don't let us upset your routine. We'll be as un-
obtrusive as possible and, of course, we are hoping that her
ladyship will be out of hospital very soon."

"It don't bear thinking about that she could be laid up there
for weeks being jabbed with needles, every time one of them
nurses gets bored, until her poor old bum's like a pincushion."
Mrs. M. exuded gloom. "Terrible shock it must have been her
hearing about that relative of yours dying so unexpected like."

"Vincent?" Niles wheezed out the name. "Frightful cheek is
the way Cynthia viewed it. His showing up here out of the
blue. I mean we hadn't seen or heard of him in years."

"And then to go and make free of that well, without a by-
you-leave." Mrs. Malloy adjusted her hat to a more business-
like angle. "Talk about taking liberties! But mustn't speak ill of
the newly departed, must we now? From what Lady Krumley
had to say, me and Mrs. H. here got the idea he could have
been going a bit potty in his old age. Wasn't there something
about him saying as how he thought your wife had been a go-
go dancer before you was married? And that some other relative had a twin? That was news to Lady K."

"That would be Daisy Meeks. Lives in the village. She was
here the night Vincent showed up and the following day. An
annoying woman, but definitely an only child." Niles stirred
restlessly in his chair. "Drink, that was Vincent's problem, although he made a big point of saying that he'd not touched a
drop in years. Taken the cure at one of those places, where one

gets to see that one's life up till that point has been nothing but wickedness and sin. Heard him going on to Watkins about it out in the hall, causing dinner to be delayed half an hour. And if there's one thing Aunt Maude dislikes it's not having meals to time. It was some sort of beef stew." He shook his head fretfully. "Mrs. Beetle, the cook, called it a ragout, but to me a stew by any other name is still the same."

A pity he had to mention food. I had been feeling decidedly peckish for the past five minutes and had little hope of the butler materializing with a silver tray on which would repose a teapot, cups and saucers and a large plate of buttered crumpets. It couldn't be expected with so many disruptions to the household routine.

"Very upsetting, Vincent's death," Niles continued.

"Let's just be glad he didn't linger," said Mrs. M., who then had to go and add, "that's if he didn't teeter on the edge of that well, fighting to save himself while his whole life flashed before his eyes and him crying out for that little dog of his, just wanting to hold it in his arms one more time . . ."

"Mrs. Malloy," I patted the paint charts and fabrics on my knee, "we're here to do a job, not to take up Mr. Edmonds's time with our expressions of sympathy."

"No, no! It's good for me to talk. If Aunt Maude were here she would insist I not bottle up my emotions. You see," he removed his glasses and polished them against his sleeve, "I was orphaned as a child of ten and, as with Vincent, my parents died in an accident. Perhaps it may be said, as my wife often does, that I have never recovered from that experience."

"You poor lamb." Mrs. Malloy dabbed at her eyes, leaving mascara smudges on her cheeks. "Loved your Mum and Dad to bits, did you?"

Niles returned his glasses to his nose. "Sometimes. Mummy had been awfully cross with me that day when I brought home a note from school saying I had cheated on the spelling test and Daddy took her side that I shouldn't be allowed any ice cream for a week. Then," his voice dropped to a whispering wheeze, "my electric train set blew up with fatal consequences."

"And I suppose you went to pieces." Mrs. Malloy winced in sympathy.

"No, Mummy and Daddy did."

"Tragic," I said.

"But then I came to live here, which would have been perfect but for the fact that Uncle Horace never liked me. The only person who ever really did like me was Aunt Maude. And even she . . . just recently seems to have been focusing her attention on someone else. Someone named Ernestine."

A silence added its somber weight to the room, but only for a moment. The door was flung open and a tall, slim woman stormed into the room. She had shoulder-length blonde hair and was dressed in black leather trousers and a cashmere sweater with a flutter of feathers around the neck.

"My wife, Cynthia," Niles said, struggling to his feet, "back from an appointment with her hairdresser."

"Who are these people?" His better half flung a look at Mrs. Malloy and me that should by rights have sent us flat on our backs. "Don't tell me you're from the undertakers? Is this the coffin brochure?" she asked, snatching the paint chart out of my hand as I stood up. "Please tell me, Niles, that you haven't gone nuts and picked the most expensive one? Didn't we agree to economize this month, what with the charges for stabling Charlie going up to almost double."

"Charlie is my wife's horse," he explained.

"We are the interior decorators hired by Lady Krumley." I returned Cynthia Edmonds's scowl with a crisp smile.

"See any colors you like in them paint charts?" Mrs. Malloy chirruped.

"I certainly do!" The blue-eyed vixen shot out her arm full

length while moving toward the window for a better inspection. "This one: platinum mink! It's exactly the shade I told that wretched man I wanted my hair tinted. But what he's given me is," she said, flinging the chart across the room, "champagne pearl."

"And what's your hairdresser's name?" Mrs. Malloy appeared to forget that we were pretending not to be private detectives. "Just for the record like." Cynthia Edmonds was so incensed she didn't balk at answering.

"Jorge!" She spelled it out. "And to think I've given that man sixteen of the best years of my life. But I'll get even! I'll cut my own damn hair! And you," she said, pointing a scarlet-nailed finger at me, "can redecorate to your heart's content. It won't matter to me if you bury Vincent under the floorboards, because I don't plan to be here much longer. Not if my little business venture bears fruit!"

Twelve

"Well, I must say," Mrs. Malloy confided into my ear when we were out into the hall, "you're coming along a treat. I think Milk will be pleased when I put in my report, but don't expect him to gush all over you, Mrs. H., because he's not that sort of man. Keeps his emotions to himself, he does, on account of being let down hard by that blonde he had to send up the river."

"You don't suppose she could have been Cynthia and that some senseless clod of a prison warden set her loose on society again?" I had not taken to Mrs. Edmonds in a big way and had cut short the chitchat by telling a little white lie.

"That was a good one," Mrs. Malloy continued to whisper, "telling them two lovebirds in there as how Lady Krumley had asked you to look for some old pieces of furniture that might still be stored in the house. Gives us a good excuse for poking around from cellar to attic."

"And for talking to that Mrs. Hasty who lives in the cottage with the well in the garden and was here at the same time as Ernestine. Of course it's hoping for a lot that she'll be able to tell us anything very useful. But we won't start with her. I think we should first take a look at that skirting board in Lady Krumley's bedroom where the brooch was so conveniently rediscovered."

"Right you are, Mrs. H.," Mrs. Malloy replied with a meekness that demanded a suspicious glance. The staircase loomed to our left, a stuffed bird under a glass dome eyed us speculatively and Watkins the butler stood in an open doorway with a silver candlestick in one hand and a polishing cloth in the other.

"May I be of help?" The hall echoed with his oncoming footsteps. He was looking at my bag as if suspecting that I had somehow managed to stuff the rest of the family silver in it.

"Aren't you a handy one to have around." Mrs. Malloy moistened her lips and twitched a hip. "We didn't even have to tinkle."

"Even so you may wish to know the powder room is to your left."

Mrs. Malloy's response was a Shirley Temple giggle that set my teeth on edge, but produced no change of expression on Watkins's face. "I was talking about one of them little brass bells. But I expect they do things on a bigger scale here and use a bell rope. Quite the country estate, this place with cottages at the bottom of the garden and all. I'll bet you're on the go from morn till night, never giving your poor tootsies a rest."

"I was seated, madam, when I heard you talking with this other lady out in the hall." He eyed me with a wariness made understandable given that Mrs. Malloy, and I were standing shoulder to shoulder. "I wondered if you might require directions to one or more of the rooms."

"Exactly right," I replied. "We would like to take a look at her ladyship's bedroom. During our consultation with her the other day, my partner and I suggested it might be the place to begin the redecorating."

"Her own personal space, setting the tone for all the rest, if you see what we're getting at Mr. Watkins." Mrs. Malloy still sounded unbearably girlish. "And after what happened to that poor gentleman, the one what came and left so abruptly, well, it does seem likely Lady Krumley would tend to find the room she used a bit gloomy were it to stay the same. So we'll take a look at that one too, and see if we can't cheer it up with some bright curtains and new hot water bottle cover."

"Mr. Vincent Krumley slept in the room that is the second to the left at the top of the stairs. Her ladyship's is two doors to the right. Would you wish me to escort you?" Watkins creaked another few steps toward us.

"Please don't trouble yourself," I said.

"You just go and enjoy yourself polishing that candlestick." Mrs. Malloy beamed at him.

"I just finished polishing it, madam."

"The light," I murmured. "It's not good. We'll make a note," I said, taking Mrs. Malloy by the arm, "about a new hall chandelier." Upon Watkins's retreat into the room from whence he had come I led the way upstairs for about half a mile before pausing to pant on a small landing. It was provided with a bench, where one could sit and adjust to the altitude or admire the view below.

"So I put me foot in it." Mrs. Malloy wheezed while bending over and clutching at a wooden arm. "But how was I to know what with all that tarnish he'd left."

"Her ladyship did say he wasn't up to the standard of her former butler."

"It slipped me mind."

"It might not have done, if you hadn't been so busy dimpling at the man." I staggered upward, shifting the bag from one arm to the other, "But I have to give you points for finding out where Vincent slept. It's a stretch, but you might find something in his suitcase or a drawer that could provide us with a hint as to why someone decided he needed to be got out of the way." We had reached the top and were leaning against the banister railing. All was dark brown varnish, dimness and shadow, the only window being the stained glass one behind us at the final bend in the stairs.

"So you want me to check out Vincent's final resting place so to speak, while you do Lady Krumley's bedroom?" Mrs. Malloy sounded as if she wasn't sure whether or not to take umbrage.

"You're far more experienced, having had more than one husband, at going through men's pockets and knowing where they hide things when they want to be sneaky, than I am."

"Every little piece of expertise helps in this line of work." She was clearly appeased. "Well, off we go! Me left and you right. And let's make it snappy. We've a lot of ground to cover while we're here. Have to hope there's lightbulbs in the bedrooms, not just candles—seems her ladyship likes to keep to the old ways."

"It's daylight."

"You could have fooled me, Mrs. H.!"

"There'll be windows."

"Ha!"

There were indeed several windows in Lady Krumley's bedroom. Unfortunately, they were so heavily draped with curtains of undeterminable color that only narrow strips of glass were exposed. A few faint slivers of light managed to creep around the enormous four-poster bed that was itself swathed, from ceiling to floor, in some tapestry material. I felt very much like Pip groping his way toward Miss Haversham. It would not have surprised me if a family of mice had run over my feet or my searching hands had become entangled in a tattered veil of cobwebs. Fortunately one of them located the light switch instead, and the room became fairly decently illuminated. Nothing, short of hauling out all the furniture, could have made it cheerful. But it was neither cobwebby nor dusty. I forgot that I wasn't really here to redecorate and, after setting down my bag on a table under a portrait of a woman who looked as though she had died before it was painted, wandered about the room, sizing it up. It was large and well-proportioned. And if the hideous marble was removed from the fireplace and replaced with a mellow brick or tile it would make a world of difference. I was picturing a peachy faux finish on the walls and copper wall lights on either side of the bed, which perhaps could be made to do to the point of becoming a magnificent focal point if stripped of its dreary tester and hangings. My mood was turning quite dreamy—a soft-colored whirl of Irish linens, plaids and toiles. No chintz. It would be quite out of character for Lady Krumley. I came back to the real task at hand when I stood in front of her dressing table, where she claimed to have left the emerald brooch before it disappeared. It was now crowded with framed photographs, many of Niles, and an assortment of boxes and bud vases that, knowing her ladyship, I guessed she had been given and felt obliged to keep and display. The mirror that needed resilvering cast a distorted reflection back at me. My eyes looked haunted, my nose off center. Behind me the furniture—a wardrobe and several tallboys—seemed to be crowding in on me, growing taller and wider until they became one giant barrier to the world outside this room. My heart started to hammer. I leaned forward to rest my hands on the dressing table. I thought I heard something. A shifting of position . . . a scratching . . . a rustling. Then mental clarity returned. I wondered why the bed had been positioned where it was instead of on the long wall facing the fireplace and closer to the door. A moment later my head was literally in a whirl—a terrifying, screeching, wing-beating darkness grew around me. I don't like birds, not indoors. Not even so much as a trapped sparrow. And now they surrounded me. Bolts of feathered fury, diving at my head, slamming into windows, walls and furniture. Everything they hit made its own sound. Even though I covered my ears while cowering on the floor, there was no muffling that piercing cacophony. I thought if I could reach the bed, I might be able to get under it. But they seemed to sense what I was about. They pecked at my shoes as I crawled. They were on my back, in my hair. At this point of utmost terror I felt a hand close around my neck. I couldn't scream. My voice had been beaten deep inside me, but I struggled upright on my knees and lashed out with my arms. I felt rather than heard whoever it was retreat. And a calm descended on me. I recognized the birds for what they were: not some gothic horror, but a weapon unleashed upon me by the human villain of Moultty Towers. As I struggled to my feet the birds thinned out. Their mind-tearing sound began to fade, and only the occasional flutter disturbed the air. The rectangle of solidified darkness that had to be the wardrobe momentarily displayed a crack of light, and I rushed toward it, pawing for the door. I had it open, and someone sprang, pushing me back so that I was again down on my knees, but only for a second. I was back up and blundering in what I hoped was the direction of the door. If I reached it I could find the light switch. I needed the clarity of electric light. I was there. My hand made contact at the instant my legs were grabbed. But before pitching forward I swung around and grabbed at a hank of hair.

"Got you!" I hung on for dear life.

"Ouch!" It was a familiar voice, and I dropped my hand like a rock.

A flutter of wings punctuated the ensuing silence. And then one of us—I wasn't sure which—turned on the light. Mrs. Malloy and I faced each other. Her hat was gone and her eyelashes were both askew. Otherwise she appeared not too much the worse for wear.

"You've got feathers in your hair." She eyed me as if this were some ghastly breach of etiquette. "But at least you're you. Although I'm not so sure I should be pleased. We'd be a lot closer to that five thousand pounds if I'd been about to capture Vincent Krumley's murderer like I thought."

"You hid in the wardrobe." I was looking around the room.

There were plenty of feathers and white splotches on the furniture, but not a blackbird in sight.

"I was plotting me next move."

"Very sensible." I dropped down on a chair, suddenly overwhelmed by exhaustion.

"Just what happened here, Mrs. H.?"

"Birds."

"I know that." She stood over me, looking severe. "They were bloody well everywhere when I opened the door. They converged when I reached for the light switch, like they knew what I was up to and weren't going to let me. I got down on me knees and was floundering around when I bumped into you. If you'd screamed like someone sensible I'd have known it was you, and we wouldn't have ended up chasing each other around like two cats."

"I'm sorry."

"Proper shook up aren't you, and no wonder. I only wish I had some brandy to give you. But there, there, Mrs. H., Roxie's here for you." She did the unthinkable for her—bent down and kissed me on the cheek. "Think they came in through the windows? It's how they got out. I saw the last one go."

"I didn't realize with all that curtaining that any of them were open." I got to my feet. "But no, I don't think that's how they came in. Why would they? We're not talking about a swarm of killer bees. Someone set them loose. A whole cage full of them I would imagine. Someone who wanted us to believe that Flossie's deathbed cruse was again at work."

"To scare us away from Moultty Towers." Mrs. Malloy picked up her hat and set it back on her blonde hair.

"To give us something to report to Lady Krumley. To keep her shivering in her hospital bed. The original plan may have been to enact the performance when she was in this room, wakened perhaps out of a deep nighttime sleep."

"A good way to give her another heart attack."

"True, but adjustments have to be made. And we provide a credible pair of witnesses."

"So how do you think they got into the room, Mrs. H.? Through the door? It could have been opened a crack. . . ."

"Too risky." I had been walking in circles and now turned to face her. "I've got another idea. It struck me that the bed is in the wrong place. And there is something else. Sir Horace's dressing room adjoined this one, which means there has to be another door. But where is it? What if after his death Lady Krumley could not bear looking at it and had the bed moved to conceal it? Look at all those hangings, not just at the sides but along the back. It would have been the simplest thing in the world for someone to enter Sir Horace's room with the bird-cage, open the connecting door and release the birds through the folds of fabric."

"Hold on a tick." Mrs. Malloy's rump became the room's focal point as she crawled over the bed. "Let's see if you've got it right." Her head momentarily disappeared into a flurry of tapestry, before she returned whole and triumphantly to view. "Just like you said." She bounded onto the floor, which was quite an accomplishment given the four-inch heels. "Now I suppose you'll want to try and figure out how whoever it was trapped them dratted birds."

"Any ideas?" I was standing at the dressing table mirror plucking black fluff and feathers out of my hair.

"Well, it seems to me, Mrs. H., the easiest way would be if they was in the house to begin with. Where would they most likely get in is the question, and seems to me it would be through some gap or missing tile in the roof. And what's under the roof is the attic. Put some birdseed in a couple of cages, and somehow rig the door to close once a nice group of them was inside. Wouldn't require more than time and patience. Think we ought to take a look at them attic?"

"Absolutely, Mrs. Malloy. But first I should take a look at the skirting board where Lady Krumley's maid found the brooch. It's why I came in here." I was still looking in the dressing table mirror, plucking at my hair. "Did you have any luck in Vincent Krumley's room?"

"Not really. That little dog of his—it was a Maltese terrier—was lying on the bed looking all mournful like and it made me feel a bit awkward, like I was out to rob the dead. I kept trying to explain meself and apologizing. There was a suitcase on a chair, but that didn't offer anything up—just a pair of trousers, a couple of shirts and a cardigan. I did find his wallet in a shoe that the dog had its head on, poor mite. Didn't snarl at me, just whimpered a bit when I reached for it. But all that was inside was a five pound note, an expired driver's license and one of them little address cards for restaurants and the like. This one was for some place called The Waysiders. Could be a pub. Remember Vincent Krumley had a drinking problem at one time."

"So he did." I heard what she was saying without really listening. Upon kneeling down to check the infamous skirting board my hand had encountered something small, flat and round. And when I stood up I was holding a brooch. An emerald and diamond brooch. Had it been on the dressing table, unseen among the clutter or photographs and ornaments, to be knocked onto the floor by the swoop of birds?

At my exclamation Mrs. M. came over to take a look. And we moved together to stand directly under the ceiling light fixture, eager to more closely inspect the source of so much trouble. "It's pretty," I said, moving it around in my hand, "but I think that Lady Krumley was right in saying that it isn't of great value."

"It'd look better after a good cleaning." Mrs. Malloy had taken the brooch from me and turned it over to inspect the back. It was engraved with initials and a date. "Look at all that dirt trapped in the setting. It's proper caked with crud." She held up a blackened finger. "You'd think some kiddy had taken it outside and buried it in the back garden. My cousin did that with her Mum's engagement ring. She was playing at pirates and treasure troves, you know how they do at that age. And oh, what a spanking she got!" Her voice dwindled away to a thread, and her eyes widened under the penciled brows. "Are you thinking what I'm thinking, Mrs. H.?"

"That maybe Flossie Jones did steal the brooch after all?" The horror of the birds receded to a distant memory.

"And she buried it out there in the grounds, so that it wouldn't be found if she or her room was searched." Mrs. Malloy looked primed to jump up and down on her four-inch heels. "Then all these years later someone dug it up, either by mistake or on purpose, and set about stirring up the deathbed curse."

"All we have to do is find out who and why." I had just placed the brooch on the dressing table, well in the center where it couldn't be easily knocked off, when the door opened and a dumpy woman with badly permed hair entered the room, causing Mrs. Malloy to finally jump several inches off the ground.

"You'll be the decorators." The woman in addition to her other dubious attributes had staring eyes and an expressionless voice. "I'm Daisy Meeks. I came over to spend the morning with Niles and Cynthia. Under the circumstances they can do with some cheering up. We heard noises from downstairs. Niles said you would be moving the furniture, seeing how it looks best. The vicar, Mr. Featherstone, was also here. He left shortly after I arrived. He's not always as chatty as one would like, except with Maude. That's Lady Krumley. He is very fond of her."

"And are you fond of birds?" Mrs. Malloy asked with a slick magenta smile.

The expressionless face didn't alter. "Oh, yes. Dear, sweet-singing things. I can't think of anything nicer than to be surrounded by a lovely soft flutter of wings, can you?"

It was as much as I could do not to hit her. And the thought came to me that it was a great blessing that she didn't have a twin, evil or otherwise.

Thirteen

Mrs. Malloy and I were forced to scotch our idea of immediately searching the attic after leaving Lady Krumley's bedroom. Daisy Meeks said she was going up there to look for a black hat, which she thought she remembered having seen in a trunk, that she could wear to Vincent Krumley's funeral.

"More likely she intends getting rid of them birdcages," Mrs. Malloy muttered as we plodded downstairs to the hall. I longed desperately for a cup of tea and even the smallest biscuit. Immediately ahead of us, half obscured in shadow, was a baize door. I pushed it open and, closely followed by Mrs. Malloy, entered a large and surprisingly cheerful-looking kitchen—very old world in general appearance, but with an up-to-date cooker and fridge. A tabby cat dozed on a chair by the brick fireplace and standing at the scrubbed wood table in the center of the room was a comfortably built woman, swathed in a white apron. Her age could have been anywhere between thirty-five and fifty. She had a couple of chins and bundled-up hair, escaping in wisps around her red face, and she was occupied in slapping a circle of pastry into a pudding basin.

"Come on in," she wagged an elbow in our general direction. "No need to stand there like you're waiting to go into the confession box."

"Thank you," Mrs. Malloy and I responded together.

"You'll be the decorators I take it from what Watkins was saying. And about blooming time, if you ask me, that someone was brought in to bring this place out of the dark ages. Oh, the kitchen's not too bad. I wouldn't have come to work here if it had been, although I did insist on the new appliances and the stainless steel sink. There's no point in being a Muggins I always say and letting your employers treat you like dirt."

"How right you are!" Mrs. Malloy shot me a meaningful look.

"Not that Lady Krumley's all that difficult. Likes her meals to time, but that suits me fine, and she gives me a free hand with the menus. Why not sit yourselves down while I finish up this steak and kidney pudding and get it into the steamer?" The woman had picked up a rolling pin and was rolling out another circle of pastry. "Then I'll brew us up a pot of tea."

"That sounds lovely." I set down my bag, perched on a stool and watched Mrs. Malloy do likewise. "Have you worked here long?"

"A little over four years. I came about a twelve-month after Watkins, which worked out well. Never lorded it over me, he hasn't. In fact, I've had to set him straight about a few things: laying the table for special dinners, that sort of thing. Mrs. Edmonds can be nasty if all the wineglasses aren't lined up just right. Comes from not being used to much before she married His Wheezyness. Read all she knows about etiquette in books; you know the type. I'm Mrs. Beetle, by the way, and in goes the pudding." She cleared away the pastry scraps and wiped off the table before bustling over to the sink to fill the kettle and get down cups and saucers from an overhead cupboard.

"My partner here is married to a chef." Mrs. Malloy proffered this piece of information with her nose stuck up so high it hit the brim of her hat. "You may have heard of him, seeing as how he writes cookery books."

"Well, I don't know." Mrs. Beetle did not look ready to swoon with excitement. "What's his name?"

"Ben Haskell," I told her.

"Not . . . not Bentley T. Haskell?" Now she did clutch a hand to her bosom and, at my nod, her eyes widened to the size of the saucers she was setting down on the table. "Why I've got all his books! Wouldn't be without them! Every one of my favorite recipes come from . . . oh, I don't know if I'm on my head or my heels. Who would have thought it? To be standing here talking to his wife. Just wait till I tell my husband."

Mrs. Malloy was beginning to look somewhat miffed under the fancy hat. "I may not be married to him, Mrs. H. here having met him first you understand, but there's not much I couldn't tell you about the way he whips his egg whites and tosses his pancakes. And it could be, if you hurry up with that tea and come up with a slice of fruitcake, that I'll get his autograph for you."

"You think he might? Oh, I would be thrilled!" Mrs. Beetle put both feet forward, producing not only the cake but also a plate of potato scones. The tea was hot and strong. A blue and white striped sugar bowl and milk jug appeared in the middle of the table, and I sat contentedly listening to her sing my husband's culinary praises.

"What a way that man has with ingredients! And his measurements! Exact to the quarter teaspoonful. When he says the recipe makes four dozen biscuits that's what you get. No going round pinching off bits of dough to eke out two or three more. The other night when that Mr. Vincent Krumley showed up I'd made the ragout on page 336 of *The Edwardian Lady's Cookery Book*." Mrs. Beetle's face glowed a deep shiny red. "Two and a half hours in a moderate oven and the Queen herself couldn't have asked for better. It comforts me to think," she said, again passing me the scones, "that the poor man had a thumping good dinner his last night on earth. You'll have heard what happened to him, I suppose?"

Mrs. Malloy and I nodded in unison.

"Went out looking for his little doggie the next afternoon, soon after Lady Krumley went off in the car."

"To keep an appointment with my partner and me," I said.

"About the decorating." A certain person, with the initials R. M., was eyeing my scone, presumably to see if it was bigger than the one on her plate.

"Poor Mr. Krumley! Not Vincent the Invincible, was he?" Mrs. Beetle crossed herself. "And no one to give him the last rites. Well, they couldn't do, could they? Not with him stuck down that well, and no one knowing. Mrs. Hasty from the cottage being away for the afternoon like she always is on a Tuesday. But then maybe he wasn't Roman Catholic like me. And the other churches don't give much of a send-off, do they?" Mrs. Beetle went on to explain that she had been happy to convert to her husband's religion, seeing that her parents hadn't brought her up in a faith and she had always felt there was something missing in her life, to which Mrs. Malloy responded that she was deeply religious herself, never missing Wednesday night bingo at the church hall.

"When did you get news of the accident, Mrs. Beetle?" I asked.

"It was in the evening around 8 or 9:00, give or take. There hadn't been any big excitement about him being missing. Mrs. Edmonds isn't the type to worry about other people, and I imagine Mr. Edmonds was busy pining for his Auntie. Terrible dependent on her he is. Daisy Meeks, some sort of cousin, was here for dinner."

"We just met her upstairs," supplied Mrs. Malloy. But Mrs. Beetle was still thinking about that dinner. "A lovely lamb roast if I do say so myself—another of your husband's recipes, Mrs. Haskell. Miss Meeks is always in some dreamworld of her own. Probably quite clever, but looks and sounds daft, if you understand me. I was just sitting down after finishing the washing up when the doorbell went and Watkins went to answer it.

It was Constable Thatcher on the doorstep, but whatever he'd come for couldn't have had anything to do with the accident because just then the phone rang. And he was as surprised as anyone. Watkins said you could see it in his face, when it turned out to be a call from the police station. Seems Mrs. Hasty had reported seeing a foot sticking out of the well when she got home and would Constable Thatcher go down and investigate."

"Horrible to be a policeman." Mrs. M. reached for a slice of cake. "Or to do any sort of crime work—like them private detectives, for instance." She pensively sighed. "But then it takes all kinds, don't it?"

"Constable Thatcher's a decent sort. A bit strict with his nine-year-old son, Ronald, but that's better than being too lenient, some would say, and then having the lad grow up to be a disappointment." Mrs. Beetle wiped her floury hands on her apron. "Which from what I've heard is the case with Mr. Featherstone, the vicar's nephew. Seems he refused point blank to go up to university because he'd set his mind on being an actor and when nothing came of that had to settle for any job he could get." She got up to refill the teapot.

"When did the little dog turn up?" I asked, wondering if anyone had much cared.

"Showed up that evening or the next morning. Poor little orphan!" Mrs. Beetle looked misty eyed, but that could have been the steam coming out of the kettle. "Now where's he got to? It crept in here about fifteen minutes ago, and I didn't see it go back into the hall. I wonder if it could have got shut up in the cellar when Watkins went down with the bottles of wine we didn't use for last night's dinner." She looked toward a door to the left of the fireplace and had crossed the room to place her hand on the knob when Watkins came in from the hall. "Oh, good, you're here!" She nodded at him. "We need to check and see if the dog's locked in the cellar."

"I think that doubtful, Mrs. Beetle. I am sure I would have seen if he had slipped in behind me when I went down just now, but if it will ease your mind I will make the necessary search." Producing a key from his jacket pocket, Watkins unlocked the door and could be heard descending the stairs.

"I was offended when I came to work here and was told the cellar door was always kept locked." Mrs. Beetle refilled our teacups. "I thought it was because Lady Krumley didn't want the help getting into the wine. A waste of time where I'm concerned because I never touch alcohol, except for cooking. My parents drank more than was good for them, and it put me right off. But it give her ladyship her due, I've come to think she's mostly worried about the steps being steep. Watkins knows better than to run up and down them, but the young girls that come up to help in the house a couple of days a week don't have his sense. It's Mrs. Edmonds that gets upset when she can't get hold of Watkins to borrow the key so she can go down and get a couple of apples if we don't have any up here."

"Apples?" I said.

"We usually have a store of them down there."

"And Mrs. Edmonds is particularly fond of apples?"

"She likes to take them to Charlie, her horse. Passionate about that animal, she is. And I've got my suspicions that Lady Krumley quite enjoys putting her nose out of joint. The two women don't get on, not that I want to gossip."

"Of course not," Mrs. Malloy and I responded in unison.

"It'll be interesting to find out what Madam Cynthia thinks about this redecorating scheme." Mrs. Beetle mopped her damp brow with her sleeve and began gathering up the crockery and putting it in the sink.

"I hope she'll be pleased with the results," I responded with my best professional smile and began to wander around the kitchen. "You won't mind if I take some measurements? I had just produced my tape from my bag when Watkins emerged from the cellar to announce that the dog was not down there. After relocking the door he returned the key to his pocket, removed his jacket and hung it on a peg inside an alcove, very like the one by the garden door at Merlin's Court.

"A cup of tea, Mrs. Beetle, if you will be so good and then I will retreat into the butler's pantry to straighten up the newly polished silver; unless," he eyed Mrs. Malloy and me in quite a kindly manner, "you two ladies require any immediate assistance from me."

"We are finding our way around, thank you," I told him.

"Don't let us keep you from your work, not that we wouldn't enjoy watching you flexing them muscles of yours." Mrs. Malloy peaked coquettishly up at him from under the brim of her hat, her expression becoming thoughtful upon watching his stately retreat. It seemed the time to allow Mrs. Beetle to return to her cooking. After thanking her for the tea, cake and scones I eyed the kitchen up and down in my most professional manner and said that my partner and I would discuss our vision for the necessary improvements before returning to take further measurements.

"We believe in maintaining the integrity of the structure," Mrs. M. piped in with all the aplomb of having coined the phrase rather than parroting a bit of my coaxing. She was saved from getting carried away by Mrs. Beetle's response that she wasn't any too sure that there was all that much integrity on the parts of some people at Moultty Towers.

"Well now," intoned my partner, practically smacking her lips, "a good thing you mentioned that, seeing as how it could make a big difference to the paint colors and . . . the curtains we was to choose. Isn't that right, Mrs. H.? There's some shades of red and some fabrics, especially satin, that can bring out the beast in people. I remember one of my ex-husbands . . ." Her eyes took on a dreamy glow, and I wasn't any better. I was picturing Freddy's mother, Aunt Lulu, in a soft shade of pink; she said it always put her in the mood for a successful day's shoplifting. The golden opportunity was lost. We had given Mrs. Beetle the necessary few seconds to remember that gossiping was frowned upon by the Catholic Church, as was bribery. But without a qualm of conscience I promised her, with what I hoped was a winning smile, that I would bring her a first edition copy of *The Edwardian Lady's Cookery Book* on my next visit.

"Oh, that is good of you!" Her face was wreathed in smiles. "Would he . . . do you think you could ask your husband to autograph it?"

"He'd be delighted."

"And would he . . . not just write his name . . . but put 'To Tina'?"

I assured her that this would be no problem before asking if it would be best for us to go out the kitchen door to get to Mrs. Hasty's cottage.

"It's at the bottom of the garden, but that's not as close as it sounds. The grounds are large, and there's a copse you have to go through. But at least it's not raining at the moment, although it looks like it's trying." Mrs. Beetle escorted us outside with a good deal of waving about, still apparently in a fluster. "We need some information about some pieces of furniture, the ones that Lady Krumley recalled having been in the house when she first came to Moultty Towers. She thought Mrs. Hasty, having been working here at that time, might remember if they were disposed of, or stored in one of the attics." This fib rolled off my tongue convincingly, something which the Church of England would have frowned upon in full accord with the Catholics. I pictured Kathleen Ambleforth having a chat with God on the subject, saying that in her humble opinion, I didn't deserve to get back the items I had donated from Ben's study. Not that she was trying to do his job for him, but as a vicar's wife she knew better than most that he was overworked and once in a while needed a sound woman to keep him organized.

"Mrs. Hasty's the chatty sort. There's not much she won't tell you for a bag of sweets." Mrs. Beetle laughed and went back into the kitchen, leaving me with the lowering feeling that we were about to prey upon a lonely old lady well into her second childhood. I said as much to Mrs. Malloy as we walked down a shallow flight of stone steps into the extensive garden, where statues of nymphs shivered in lifeless flowerbeds under the bare branches of the trees. Her response was to tell me that I would never harden myself to the life of a private investigator if I didn't stop thinking soppy. I apologized meekly, and we trudged on along meandering paths, among gently undulating lawns that would have made for a fairly decent golf course.

My mind shifted to Ernest the under gardener, who had been thought to be the father of Flossie's baby girl, without bringing him into focus. He remained a shadowy figure on his haunches plucking up weeds with his back to us, and it suddenly seemed vital to the investigation that he be fleshed out. We had reached the copse, dark and somewhat ominous looking under the overcast sky. Through the shift and shadow of its branches could be glimpsed the cottage, and I wondered if Mrs. Malloy feared as I did that we were Hansel and Gretel about to knock on a door that would open onto unforeseen dangers, where evil hid under chintz covers and sugar-coated words would send us skipping away down one wrong path after another until the truth was hopelessly trodden underfoot like breadcrumbs tossed by an unseen hand.

Fourteen

Seeing the wishing well in the cottage garden heightened the feeling that Mrs. Malloy and I were trapped in a fairy tale with all its attendant horrors. My mind squeezed shut when it veered toward the horrific moment when Vincent Krumley met his end. But Mrs. Malloy was not so squeamish.

She stood, shaking her head vigorously. With the wind picking up it would not have surprised me had her hat started to spin around to the accompaniment of merry-go-round music. "The only way as I can see for him to have fallen in by accident is if he'd been kneeling on that wooden ledge peering way over to see if the dog was down there. And he couldn't've been pushed because then he'd have gone sprawling over the top. It's quite a big well, but we're not talking the size of a swimming pool. Meaning Mrs. H., that if it was murder someone had to wrestle with the poor old blighter and shove him in headfirst."

"Or," I said, turning away to face the cottage, "someone pretending to help him look for the dog encouraged Vincent Krumley to kneel down and peer into the well and then toppled him in."

"There you go, taking the words out of me mouth!"

"And did the dog get outdoors by accident, or was he removed as a key part of the plan?"

"As if I wasn't just about to say that!"

"Did the murderer tie him up somewhere, where he could be heard frantically barking but not be easily found? Somewhere close to here so that Mr. Krumley could be maneuvered this way."

"Again what I was thinking!" Mrs. M., still sounding peevish, followed me up the short path with its little lawn on either side to the cottage door. It was a charming place, with cobbled stone walls and tiny latticed windows overhung by a thatched roof. But Mrs. Malloy could be counted on to keep the Grim Reaper scything away in the shadows. "Led like a lamb to the slaughter, was Vincent Krumley. Poor old gent!"

She might have gone on at length if the door hadn't opened before I could lift the doorknocker, and we found ourselves confronted by a tall slim woman with thick coppery hair plaited around her head. She was in her mid to late thirties, I decided, and unlikely to be Mrs. Hasty unless she had participated in a test study of rejuvenating tablets. It was apparent from her expression that she took us for a couple of Jehovah's Witnesses or door-to-door salespeople. Her expression remained doubtful, as I explained why we wished to see Mrs. Hasty. But after a prolonged stare, she edged back into the narrow hall and instructed us to come in.

"When was it you last spoke with Lady Krumley?" She still struck me as liable to take an umbrella from the brass stand by the staircase and dish out a series of pokes if either Mrs. Malloy or I so much as looked as though we might make a false move.

"Yesterday, at the hospital during a consultation about the redecorating."

"How did she seem to you?" The woman's hazel eyes probed my face.

"Not too bad," I replied cautiously, "and insistent on keeping her appointment with us."

"Depressing places, hospitals. Worst sort of place to be when you're feeling poorly." Mrs. Malloy got in before I could hog more of the conversation. "We saw Lady Krumley's nephew, Mr. Edmonds, there. His wife was parking the car, so we didn't have the thrill of meeting her until today. And her ladyship's vicar—he showed up to see her too. So you mustn't go thinking," she added comfortingly, "her ladyship was left sitting on her bedpan all day with no one to talk to." Feeling perhaps that she had dropped a clanger, Mrs. Malloy flexed her butterfly lips and said, "And very dignified I'm sure she would look, even under them circumstances. Good posture. It's drummed into the aristocracy, and very handy when it counts."

The woman's face assumed an expressionless mask. "The vicar has the highest regard for Lady Krumley. I'm sure she found his visit comforting. Did she tell you about what happened the night before last right outside this door?"

Mrs. Malloy and I, in talking over each other, managed to get the point across that we had heard about the tragic death. "Some relation on her husband's side of the family. Just arrived on a visit, wasn't it?"

"A cousin. Mr. Vincent Krumley."

"And you'll be another member of the family?" Mrs. Malloy was eyeing a narrow table set against the staircase wall as if it and its vase of chrysanthemums might be persuaded to provide some useful titbit of information.

"I'm Laureen Phillips, her ladyship's maid," she said, still unsmiling and with her arms folded across the gray blouse and cardigan that topped her charcoal skirt, an outfit that could have been a uniform or her personal choice of daily wear. "New to the job, but not the village. I've lived here most of my life."

"So you're the one that found the missing brooch!" Mrs. Malloy wouldn't have looked quite so thrilled if I'd managed to tread on her foot in time, and I did my best to retrieve the situation.

"Lady Krumley was inclined to ramble during the hour or so we spent with her. . . . The shock of the accident I imagine . . .

and the medication she was given. Probably we were talking about redecorating her bedroom at the time. It was there, wasn't it, that the brooch turned up? Much of the time her ladyship was completely coherent. Such as when she asked us to talk with Mrs. Hasty about certain pieces of furniture she would like put back into use."

"Then it's not for me to say you can't, but I do hope you won't go pestering her to the point where she gets upset." Laureen's handsome features softened. "She's a dear old soul. Worked hard all her life and been like an auntie to me, which means a lot seeing that I was moved from pillar to post as a child. Come on, I'll take you in to her." Opening the door to our right, she ushered us into a room with windows at both ends and a fire burning in the small grate under a mantelpiece lined end to end with cheerfully inexpensive figurines. It was altogether a pleasant little space—overfurnished but comfortable as a cat's basket. There was indeed a cat, a large tabby that was possibly a relative of the one we had seen in the kitchen of Moultty Towers. It was curled up on the crocheted blanket covering the knees of the elderly woman seated on the old-fashioned settee. It was a scene of picture-perfect contentment. No one could have looked less like the witch in "Hansel and Gretel" than the snowy-haired little personage with the child-like sparkle to her bright blue eyes.

"Well now, Laureen," her voice trilled with excitement, "who's this you've brought to see me? A pair of reporters come to ask me about finding the body? And me with my hair not properly combed. But I don't suppose they'll be taking pictures," she added wistfully.

"Nothing like that, Mrs. Hasty." The younger woman walked over and adjusted the crocheted blanket. "These ladies are decorators Lady Krumley has hired to do up the main house. And they're wanting to ask you some questions about pieces of furniture you may remember having been there years ago. Her ladyship has a fancy to put some of them back into use if they're still on the premises. Although it does seem to me"— the hazel eyes now struck me as both reflective and shrewd— "the simplest thing would be to take a look at what's up there in the attics."

"Sometimes asking a few questions of the right person helps speed up the process." If my response sounded a bit lame to my ears it did not appear to strike Mrs. Hasty as such. Her face creased into a beaming smile, and she said that if this wasn't a day brightener she didn't know what was. At her age it was nice to have a chance to chat about the old days.

"Now what did you ladies say your names was?"

Mrs. Malloy and I duly introduced ourselves and upon her urging sat down in easy chairs across from her. Still looking somewhat dubious Laureen Phillips announced that she would go upstairs and do a little straightening up before returning to the main house.

"A nice girl. Don't know why she isn't off working in some office." Mrs. Hasty sat stroking the cat after the door closed. "There's not that many that wants to go into service these days. Even in my young days it wasn't most people's first choice. But it was different for me. I grew up in the village. And I didn't see much sense in shelling out bus fare and cutting an hour at least out of me day going back and forth to Mucklesby or some other town to stand on my feet in a shop. Not when I could walk to Moultty Towers in five minutes and end up with same amount of money in me pocket at the end of the week? And, as me old Mum always used to say, there's never been no shame in housework."

"Truer words was never spoken," Mrs. Malloy said with the vehemence befitting the chairwoman of the Chitterton Fells Charwomen's Association, but caught herself to add craftily, "Lady Krumley gave us to understand that you started work at the house as the parlour maid."

"Not me, ducks." Mrs. Hasty shook her head. "I was the kitchen maid."

"That's right," I hesitated, suddenly feeling a strong distaste at the idea of leading this nice old lady down the garden path. This was different from spinning a web of deceit to elicit information from Niles and Cynthia Edmonds, or even Mrs. Beetle. This pansy-faced old lady could be somebody's grandmother. It didn't much help telling myself that the end justified the means, but I forced myself to continue: "I remember Lady Krumley mentioning another girl . . . someone named Flossie. . . . I think that was it."

"That's right! Flossie Jones! It was her that was the parlour maid." Mrs. Hasty beamed a smile. "One of you nice ladies wouldn't happen to have a sweet on you, would you now? Ever such a sweet tooth I've got. Not so much for chocolates, but those nice old-fashioned boiled ones."

"As a matter of fact, you're in luck." Mrs. Malloy reached into her handbag and produced with a conjuror's flourish the lemon drops she had been dipping into in the car. Teetering onto her high heels, she handed the bag to the old lady, who rummaged around inside before popping one into her mouth. The rustle of paper had disturbed the cat; it sat up to stretch and yawn in a hard-done-by sort of way, before settling back down on her crocheted lap rug. There was a 1940s-style clock on a curio cabinet, and Mrs. Hasty sat sucking contentedly away in time to its rhythmic ticktock. Mrs. Malloy returning to her chair, crossed and recrossed her legs, her false eyelashes flickering with impatience, but I felt it would be a mistake to try and hurry things. Mrs. Hasty helped herself to another sweet before picking up the threads of our conversation.

"Flossie came to work at Moultty Towers shortly before I got married. I was coming up for thirty and she'd have been about twenty-five. It surprised me that she didn't have a ring on her finger, her being as pretty as a picture. But she'd laugh and say she was waiting for a man with one hand on his wallet and one foot in the grave. Always one for a quick answer, was Flossie."

"And does she still live in the area?" I asked, feeling like the worst kind of slippery slug.

Mrs. Hasty shook her head.

"Oh, what a shame!" Mrs. Malloy sounded convincingly downcast. "Here was us hoping that if you don't know what happened to them pieces of furniture Lady Krumley's so worked up about, this other woman might just possibly have helped us out."

"Flossie Jones." Mrs. Hasty sucked away on her lemon drop. "I hadn't went and thought about her in years."

"One loses touch." I wondered if I sounded uncomfortable or completely vacuous, and, ignoring Mrs. Malloy's irritated expression, ploughed into a description of the imaginary pieces of furniture that we were supposedly anxious to locate. But my partner need not have got her knickers in a twist. Mrs. Hasty was clearly eager to stick to the subject of her former coworker.

"Died donkey's years ago, did poor Flossie."

"You don't say!" Mrs. Malloy studied the rings flashing on both her hands. "And her name cropping up over and over again when we saw Lady Krumley in the hospital."

"It really wasn't the time or place to talk about the redecorating." I could at least say this with some conviction. "But her ladyship had telephoned to insist on the consultation. It isn't surprising if her mind wandered, causing her to ramble from time to time during our conversation."

"But why have this Flossie Jones on her mind?" Mrs. Malloy's innocent expression merited an Academy Award.

"There was something about a brooch," I paused, feeling more treacherous by the moment, and heard a creek outside in the hall. Was Laureen listening at the door? Or was someone else in the cottage? I told myself that I was being silly, that old houses talked to themselves all the time. But even so I shivered at the thought that someone—someone who had already committed murder—was not convinced that Mrs. Malloy and I were who we claimed to be.

Luckily it did not appear that Mrs. Hasty had a suspicious nature. "I'm not surprised Lady Krumley had that brooch on her mind. You see it showed up again a few days ago, near on forty years after it went missing. It was Laureen that found it, stuck behind the skirting board in her ladyship's room."

"What a nice surprise!" Mrs. Malloy echoed my exclamation.

"Well in one way it was and in another it wasn't." Mrs. Hasty was sucking on another lemon drop. "Nice for her ladyship to have it back in the family, but too late for her to put matters right with poor Flossie, who she dismissed for stealing it! And her dying like that not long afterward, it doesn't bear thinking about. No wonder her ladyship had that heart attack and went off the road in her car. She must be blaming herself something awful. Although if you ask me it was that snake in the grass Mrs. Snow that fueled the fire! Had it in for Flossie from the word go, she did."

"Mrs. Snow?" I sat listening for further sounds out in the hall, but heard nothing.

"Her that was the housekeeper back in them days." Mrs. Hasty stroked the cat. "A big bustling figure of a woman, she was, all got up in black. How she ever got a man to marry her I don't know! If there ever was a Mr. Snow, I never heard mention of him. It was her nephew she would go on about: Arthur or Archibald—something like that—away at some boarding school she was paying for. I remember feeling sorry for the lad, thinking about what he'd have to give in return over the years. But it did get sickening listening to how clever he was, doing sums a page long. Flossie and me, we'd have a bit of a snicker about it. Mrs. Snow did that, brought out the worst in you. And she got to Lady Krumley with her nasty insinuations, made her suspicious of Flossie about . . . this, that and the other." Mrs. Hasty sighed. Some of the sparkle had gone out of her blue eyes.

"Before the brooch went missing?" I prompted.

"Flossie had a way with men. And it wasn't just her looks. She knew just how to wrap them around her finger. All sugar and spice if you know what I mean. Ernest, the under gardener, was crazy for her. Thought she was going to marry him. I tried to tell him not to take her too serious. That for all her flirty ways the girl had a head on her shoulders and wouldn't settle down until she was ready, not if she hadn't done so till now. But of course he didn't listen. Not to me, or to Mrs. Snow, saying that there was bigger fish in the sea and Flossie was a girl out for the main chance."

"Eaten up with spite, some people!" Mrs. Malloy with her saintly expression and hat on looked as though she should be seated in church.

"Course I really shouldn't be sitting here gossiping." Mrs. Hasty displayed less conviction than Mrs. Beetle had done, as she continued to stroke the cat.

"Don't think of it that way. In our business it helps to get a sense of the personalities that have left their imprint on a house." I spouted this hogwash while again listening for further movement out in the hall. This time I was sure I heard a tiptoed step. My hands clammily gripped the arms of my chair.

"It's got to be said that Sir Horace—Lady Krumley's late husband that is—had taken a fancy to Flossie. But that's not to say there was any funny business going on. And when she let on she was in the family way I never thought about anyone but Ernest being the father. And he wasn't slow at owning up to it."

"But Mrs. Snow . . . ?" I queried softly.

"Went around hinting at things and giving those sly looks of hers. Oh, I did feel sorry for Lady Krumley, because when someone plants the seed of suspicion, it's hard to get rid of it, isn't it?

So when she couldn't find that brooch, well, who could blame a wife—ladyship or not—from seizing the opportunity to get rid of a pretty young woman that she'd been made to believe was a threat to her marriage? Mrs. Snow told Lady Krumley she'd seen Flossie coming out of that room where she'd no business being, so it did look suspicious. And when she wouldn't explain what she was doing there," Mrs. Hasty looked momentarily doubtful, but concluded stoutly, "I expect her pride was up at the injustice of it all."

"Sad the way some people treat their household help." Mrs. M. cast a meaningful look my way. "Sent packing on the spot, was she?"

"Out the door in half an hour, she was." Mrs. Hasty sucked hard on another lemon drop.

"Did she and Ernest marry?" I could have done with a sweet myself.

"No, ducks. Maybe all the upset turned her a bit funny. She wouldn't have none of him. Fair broke him up, it did. He stayed on for several months . . . close on a year from what I remember, but his work suffered. Too much time spent down the pub, and in the end he was let go too. I've always hoped he got himself sorted out in time and met some other girl that was fond of him, for he weren't a bad-looking lad. Tallish, with the most wonderful head of auburn curls that's I've ever seen on a man. My husband was always a bit thin on top, bless him."

"Was he also employed at Moultty Towers?" I was genuinely interested.

"No, Mr. Hasty was the milkman. And although he made a good living he was agreeable to me continuing working, seeing we wasn't blessed with little ones. When Mrs. Snow finally retired I took over from her. Mr. Hasty's been gone ten years now, but her ladyship let me have this cottage, and I still manage to get out and about a bit. So all in all it's not been a bad life."

"What happened to poor little Flossie?" Mrs. Malloy displayed eagerness to get the conversation back where it belonged, and I couldn't blame her. We had been sitting with Mrs. Hasty for close on an hour, and Laureen was liable to stick her head in the door at any minute to be told by the elderly lady that we hadn't yet got round to talking about specific pieces of furniture.

"Flossie?" Mrs. Hasty was beginning to sound sleepy. "Went to live in a bed-sitter. In Mucklesby. Twenty-one Hathaway Road was the number."

"My, you've got a good memory." Mrs. Malloy inclined her hat in salute.

"I've a friend that still lives on that street. And every time I pass the house where Flossie was I get a tear in my eye. You see she had her baby there and died not long afterward. The little girl was given up for adoption. It was all so sad, and I often wonder if there was something I could have done to help. I did write—several letters—but Flossie never answered them. Perhaps she was too ill or didn't want any contact with anyone from Moultty Towers. I can't say as I blame her." Mrs. Hasty's head had begun to droop and after several moments said in a drowsy voice: "About this business of the furniture, what exactly are you looking for?"

"A rosewood secretary desk with brass ring handles that Lady Krumley believes used to be in one of the bedrooms, an oak library table with lion claw feet and a gentleman's wardrobe with marquetry panels," I told her.

"Don't remember any of them."

This was not surprising, since I had invented the lot on the spot.

"Then we'll just have to go and look in the attics." Mrs. Malloy got to her feet and signaled for me to follow suit. With a few murmured words of farewell to the now gently snoring Mrs. Hasty, we swiftly exited the sitting room and were about to walk out the front door when Laureen Phillips came down the stairs. She had probably been up and down several times, fetching and carrying as she tidied up. I told myself I was silly to have had that prickling feeling of unease that she or, even more unlikely, that someone else, had been eavesdropping on our conversation. She looked so sane and sensible in her severe gray blouse and cardigan. She couldn't possibly be involved in something as distasteful as murder. I was sure that Mrs. Malloy would concur that we would be wasting precious time by including this woman on a list of suspects in whatever nasty business was underway at Moultty Towers.

"I wonder if I might have a word with you both?" Laureen Phillips held open the door and followed us out into the garden. It was pleasantly said, with just the right touch of deference—something that had been missing upon our arrival at the cottage. Perhaps she wanted some advice for herself on the choice of lampshades or some tips on wallpapering. She might want to elaborate on her fondness for Mrs. Hasty or her concern for Lady Krumley's health. But I read Mrs. Malloy's glance as if she had spoken and agreed with her wholeheartedly—there'd be no standing chatting by the wishing well for either of us.

Fifteen

"I've been sitting upstairs in Mrs. Hasty's bedroom thinking about how to approach this," said Laureen Phillips, "and I've decided the only way is to say it straight out."

"Say what?" The wind tried to ram my voice back down my throat. And Mrs. Malloy, ignoring the fact that her hat was trying to turn itself inside out, kindly repeated the question.

"That I know you came here posing as interior decorators."

"What a bloody load of rubbish!" Mrs. Malloy added her own bluster to that going on all around us. "You need to sit your bottom down on a psychiatrist's couch, you do. It's a sickness going round being suspicious of people. Paranoia—that's the word for what you've got! For your information my partner and I have great big diplomas from R.A.D.A."

"That would be the Royal Academy of Dramatic Arts," Ms. Phillips pointed out.

"Same as for the decorative arts," Mrs. Malloy continued to hold her head high due to the fact that she was standing on tiptoe to retrieve the hat that had blown onto the lamppost outside the cottage. Her blonde coiffure had flattened to her head like a bathing cap, leaving her all painted eyebrows and purple lips. As for myself, I was sure I looked every bit as ruffled as I felt, which left only one of our trio with every hair in place and with a composure to match.

"It so happens that I trained at R.A.D.A.," Ms. Phillips informed us. "I was a stage actress for some years. One can be a good actress, working steadily without acquiring either fame or fortune. And one thing you do learn is how to recognize when someone is playing a role."

"As it happens, I am an interior designer," I said.

"But that's not what brings you and your colleague to Moultty Towers."

"So what does, Miss Clever Dick?" Mrs. Malloy had recaptured her hat and was punching it back into shape.

"Why don't I paint a scenario for you?" suggested Laureen. It being regrettably clear that we were in the process of becoming matey, it made sense to think of her on a first-name basis. "Lady Krumley drove off in her car a couple of days ago—something she hadn't done in years—which would suggest she wasn't keen on having anyone know where she was going. She became unusually flustered on her departure when her nephew Niles Edmonds, whom you have both met, said he felt an asthma attack coming on. He has them frequently, which leads one to wonder if her ladyship's agitation was due to a fear of being late for an appointment. Are you both with me so far?"

"One might also ponder," I deliberately matched her manner, "whether Mr. Edmonds had a suspicion as to the nature of that appointment and was eager to prevent her keeping it."

"What an interesting thought! Congratulations. You sound just like the detective in the last play I was in! Is it coincidence, or could Lady Krumley have left to meet with a private detective? Or, better yet, a pair of them."

"No wonder the poor old ducks don't go out often if it caused all this fuss." Mrs. Malloy had her hat back on and looked ready for the fray. But I had a strong suspicion that she and I were on the losing side of a game whose rules were yet to be made clear. All I could see to do for the moment was try to keep my eye on the ball.

"Getting back to Mr. Edmonds, why would he be worried if

what you suggest were correct?" I smiled to prevent my face from caving in under the buffeting the wind was giving it. Laureen continued to stand with her arms at her sides, seemingly impervious to the elements.

"He's the nervous sort. It's probably a result of having blown up his nursery and his parents along with it when he was a kiddy."

"Boys will be boys!" Mrs. Malloy replied loftily. "I almost married a mad scientist once." She forgot herself sufficiently to smile fondly. "Talk about chemistry! Could he ever make the sparks fly!"

"A sense of humor helps in any business, and I am sure you need one in yours." Laureen paused and, when neither Mrs. Malloy nor I replied, went on: "So far as I know, Mr. Edmonds is principally occupied with three things: his health, keeping out of his wife Cynthia's way and handling his aunt's business affairs."

"Fiddling the books, you mean?" Mrs. Malloy prided herself on being receptive to the helpful hint.

"I'm a maid, not a spy." Laureen gave a dismissive wave of the hand. "I don't poke and pry through private documents, or listen at keyholes—unless I feel a moral obligation to do so."

"As you did just now in the cottage?" I stared her straight in the eye.

"What do you mean? I never came downstairs until I heard you come out of the sitting room. But let's stop all the fancy footwork." Other than waving her hand that once, Laureen hadn't moved a muscle. "You two women know what was on Lady Krumley's mind that day, because it was you she went to see. We made the mistake of thinking the investigator was a man, but there was no doubt about what had put her ladyship in such emotional turmoil. It was that wretched brooch turning up."

"And you're the one what found it!" The words shot out of

Mrs. Malloy's mouth in the form of an accusation, but her sub-
sequent apologetic look was directed at me. "There! I've gone
and done it, Mrs. H.! Let on that Lady Krumley told us that!"

"So did Mrs. Hasty just now."

"I forgot and thought I'd blown our cover. Sorry. Too late,
now."

"There is something Lady Krumley wouldn't have told you."
Laureen glanced back toward the copse and for the first time
looked uneasy, although it was highly unlikely that anyone
lurking there could have picked up even a few isolated words of
what we were saying. We were standing close to the cottage, a
good hundred yards from the closest trees, meaning that even
without the wind we should have been safe from pricked ears.
And surely by standing out in the open we would appear less
likely to be discussing anything of a secret nature. Even so, I
was glad that when Laureen continued it was even more qui-
etly. "Lady Krumley wouldn't have told you because I didn't
tell her. . . ."

"What?" Mrs. M. and I whispered back.

"That the brooch wasn't there jammed in behind the skirting board on the day before it was found."

"Are you sure?" Again the words were barely mouthed in
unison.

"Absolutely. I had dropped a hairpin"—she touched a hand
to the heavy coil at the back of her head—"right in that same
spot, and I bent down and searched along the whole board. I
found the pin, but there wasn't any brooch. I'd have seen it. I
know I would, just as I did . . . after it had been put there for me
to find."

I retied my raincoat belt that had come undone and been
flapping about in the wind. "Why now? Why would someone
choose this moment to resurrect the past?"

"Why not any other time in the last forty years?" Mrs. Malloy clapped a hand on her hat as it tried to make another break for it. "What's different about now? That's what I'd bloody well like to know."

Laureen cast another glance back at the copse. "It could be that someone only recently got his or her hands on that brooch. What's needed is to find out who that someone is, so we can understand what's to be gained."

"By scaring Lady Krumley out of her wits." Mrs. Malloy's scowl did Milk Jugg proud.

"She didn't strike me as the type to be easily frightened." I was picturing that face with its black hooded eyes and beak of a nose. "What I saw was a woman consumed with remorse. If that is the object to play games with her conscience then it's working perfectly. She has set about doing what is required to locate Flossie's child. But why? What is so desperately important about Ernestine?"

"We can't stay talking here." Laureen looked at her wristwatch. "I need to go back in and get Mrs. Hasty something quick for lunch and then return to the house. But I could make an excuse—pretend I need to go into the village to buy something. It's not as though I've all that much to do with her ladyship in the hospital. I could meet you at the café to the right of the green. It's called The Copper Kettle; you can't miss it. Say in about an hour's time?" She acknowledged my nod and started to walk away, but Mrs. Malloy caught hold of her sleeve.

"Not so fast. I've been wanting to know who you was talking about when you said 'we'."

"When I said what?"

"Don't look daft, ducky." Mrs. M. stuck her nose in the air and should have thought herself lucky not to have it pecked off by the blackbird flitting past. "It was when you was talking about Lady Krumley going off in the car. You said 'we' made the mistake of thinking the investigator was a man. Now that would be you and who else?" She shot me a triumphant look at having beaten me to the post on that one.

"Be at the café and I'll tell you." Laureen disappeared into the cottage, and Mrs. Malloy and I headed back through a gathering mist to Moultty Towers to reenter the kitchen where we found Mrs. Beetle taking a rice pudding out of the oven. She nodded and smiled but did not attempt to engage us in conversation when we said were on our way up to talk to Mr. and Mrs. Edmonds about taking a look in the attics, something Mrs. Malloy and I had decided was a good idea in order to maintain our fast-fading aura of credibility. Besides, there was the question of the birds. We went out into the hall, but before either of us came within knocking distance of the drawing room door, Watkins came out of an apartment on the other side of the hall. In the glow from the vast overhead chandelier his white eyebrows appeared faintly orange and his bald head shone as if he took a professional pride in assiduously polishing it along with the silver. His stooped shoulders did not diminish his stately progress toward us.

"Ah, Mr. Hopkins!" Mrs. Malloy shot me another of her smug looks at having his name on the tip of her tongue.

"Watkins, madam. Hopkins was the name of the prior butler. A common mistake, one made by Mr. Vincent Krumley upon his arrival the other evening. Had I known that his visit was to be curtailed I would not have taken the liberty of correcting him. He was so delighted to see again, as he thought, someone from his past. A very great tragedy despite his advanced years." He cleared his throat. "Do you wish me to advise Mr. Edmonds that you need to speak with him? He is currently engaged in the drawing room with Sir Alfonse Krumley, who is just arrived from France to discuss the"—another gentle cough—"necessary arrangements for Mr. Vincent Krumley's funeral. Miss Daisy Meeks is with them."

"Then we won't disturb Mr. Edmonds." I did a good job of keeping the relief out of my voice.

"That might be as well, madam. Miss Meeks is an excitable lady under normal circumstances and she was displaying a great deal of agitation, when I went in a few moments ago with the tea tray, at the prospect of the inquest. It will make for something of an occasion in Biddlington-By-Water, and Miss Meeks was concerned that she did not have the right hat. She had hoped to find one in the attics. Something neither too plain or too fancy." His eyes went to Mrs. Malloy's headgear, but he did not ask where she'd had the good fortune to purchase it, perhaps because it was looking rather the worse for wear following its tussles with Mother Nature. Instead he apologized for allowing his tongue to run away with him, to which Mrs. Malloy responded kindly that it was entirely understandable in the circumstances.

"An inquest you say, and I suppose there had to be a postmortem? Horrible it must be for you to think that just the other night the poor old codger was cutting into his dinner and now . . . well, best not to go thinking about it, ducks. I suppose the police are sure it was an accident? They wouldn't go thinking that it was anything else, would they? I mean that he threw himself down that well on purpose, while the balance of his mind was disturbed over the disappearance of his little doggie?"

"Constable Thatcher was here a half hour ago. I met him outside the kitchen door and presumed to have a word with him. He made it clear that the inquest would be a formality. Mr. Krumley was over ninety and very tottery on his legs, all the more so at the time because he had indulged in a glass or two of brandy to calm himself down before he went looking for Pipsie. He had informed me upon his arrival that he had given up drinking and would not partake of wine at dinner, so perhaps he was more strongly affected than he would have been in the past." Watkins again cleared his throat, and I felt my heart sink. From the sound of things the police weren't going to be of any help. I pictured Mrs. Malloy and myself showing up at the police station and reeling off our tale off deathbed curses, missing brooches and Krumleys dropping of the family twig like windfall apples. The only thing that might make this Constable Thatcher sit up and listen was our encounter with Have Gun, but then the question would arise, why hadn't we reported on him sooner? My head started to spin. I hadn't eaten much breakfast, I'd had that terrifying experience with the birds, and it was more than time for lunch. Steaming away in the kitchen was Mrs. Beetle's steak and kidney pudding. My mouth watered. If Mrs. Malloy and I didn't hurry we would be late for our appointment with Laureen, where with luck we would again get to settle for baked beans on toast. I thought about giving the attics a pass, but we had to check for those birdcages. Mrs. Malloy had brought them up to Mr. Watkins and he was already requesting that we follow him up the staircase. Perhaps he regretted not having escorted us on our prior trip.

After toiling up several additional flights above the bedroom floor and in the process meeting the steely-eyed gaze of a series of family portraits, we reached a door crouched below a sloping ceiling, which Watkins opened with the aplomb of a museum curator. His hand found an inner light switch that murkily illuminated a labyrinth of caves with wooden rafters festooned with cobwebs, below which stood forlorn groups of furniture and trunks. I thought of Kathleen Ambleforth and how she would have had the removal vans loaded within five minutes of being told she could have this lot for her charities.

"I really must speak to the girls who come in to clean about keeping up with their dusting up here." Watkins shook his head and said that he hoped we would be successful in our endeavors. "No doubt it will do Lady Krumley a world of good upon her recovery to involve herself in redecorating the house. If you will forgive the presumption, the addition of a handsome library table and secretary desk should particularly lift her spirits. The library was, to my understanding, Sir Horace's favorite room, and Lady Krumley enjoys tending to her correspondence."

Mrs. Malloy and I thanked him, whereupon he retreated down the stairs, leaving us facing what now struck me as a hostile mob of wardrobes, armchairs and chests of drawers. We stood for a few minutes regretting the bag of lemon drops she had given to Mrs. Hasty, then discussed how desperately we both wanted a cup of tea and whether Laureen would already be waiting for us at The Copper Kettle. I climbed over a footstool in search of the birdcages, while Mrs. Malloy parked herself on a rush-seated chair. As might have been supposed I was the one who spotted them. There were two behind a brass bed piled end to end with boxes. They had been used and duly replaced. Methodical, I had to hand that to our murderer.

"Nice to be proved right." Mrs. M. was already heading out. "Where's your bag? You won't want to come back for it."

"I left it in the hall."

"And don't forget we promised to bring Mrs. Beetle an autographed copy of one of Mr. H.'s cookery books," she reminded me as we scurried down the first set of stairs. "Tina, she said her name was. I wonder what that's short for? Christina most likely, don't you suppose?"

"Probably."

We had descended to the bedroom floor with speed, but even with thoughts of lunch abounding my steps slowed. All this exercise might be good for me, but my legs were starting to complain. Pain, however, was not what brought me to a dead halt outside a door that was cracked open an inch.

"You could have signaled," Mrs. Malloy complained.

"Shush!" I backed up along the wall, drawing her alongside me.

"Don't you go shushing me! We're not back at Merlin's Court, you know!"

"Listen!" I whispered. "There's someone in there talking. . . . Something about the brooch."

"That's Cynthia Edmond's voice."

I nodded, pressing a finger to my lips as I strained to catch the words, spoken with a deliberation that intensified their venom. Mrs. Malloy was breathing heavily down my neck.

"I know you put it there." Cynthia gave a throaty laugh. "I came across it in your jacket pocket the previous day. I wouldn't put it past you to have suggested to gullible Aunt Maude that it would be a good idea to have that girl Laureen give the skirting board a good dusting, by way to making sure she learned the importance of being thorough. What a crafty thing you are, with your blank face and that voice that drives me up the wall. How we have all underestimated you. And how you are going to be made to pay, in substantial installments adding up to a great deal of money. Don't worry, you won't have to take it out of the piggy bank. It should be a simple matter of fiddling the books."

"I bet that's gone down like a plateful of fish and chips," Mrs. M. whispered in my ear.

"Quick!" I mouthed back at her. "They're walking about. They could be coming out!" I caught my breath. Something silky had brushed against my ankle. I looked down and a Maltese terrier looked up. First it gave a pitiful whine and then it nosed growling and yipping toward the door. This was all we needed! Yanking my fellow snoop's arm I tiptoed at a run toward the stairs and only ventured to look back when we were almost at the bottom. That door hadn't opened. And no one was in the hall where I grabbed up my bag. But my breathing didn't slow until Mrs. Malloy and I were in the car driving toward the gates.

"So that's what Cynthia Edmonds meant by that remark in the drawing room about a business venture bearing fruit,

Mrs. H. She was talking about blackmail. Who do you suppose was with her that she got the goods on?"

"Her husband springs first to mind. He's an accountant. He handles his aunt's financial affairs. Who better to fiddle the books?"

"Well," Mrs. Malloy said, applying fresh lipstick, "I could almost feel sorry for the man. As for that Cynthia she's playing a dangerous game. He may love her, but a man who'd kill his own parents won't likely let that stop him."

"We don't know that he did kill them. It probably was an accident. And it may not have been Niles in that bedroom with Cynthia. It may not even have been a man," I said as we parked outside The Copper Kettle, which as Laureen had promised was on the other side of the green from the Biddlington-By-Water police station."

"You've got a point." Mrs. M. sounded only vaguely interested.

"A pity that little dog can't talk. There was someone in that room that it didn't like."

"Mmm!"

"What have you got ticking away inside your head?" I asked sharply.

"Oh, nothing all that exciting." She returned the lipstick to her handbag and snapped the clasp. "I've just solved it, is all."

"But you can't have. We haven't found Ernestine yet."

"Oh, I don't mean the case." Mrs. Malloy swung her high heels onto the pavement. "It's even better than that. I know why Watkins's face seemed so familiar. He's the man I told you about, the one I talked to a few years back when I came to play bingo with the Biddlington-By-Water senior citizens."

Sixteen

Trust Mrs. Malloy to have added Watkins to the list of men included in what she was fond of referring to with capital letters as Her Past. I told her I was happy for her, that I vaguely remembered her mentioning some old geezer from that night at bingo. But I didn't recall her sounding all that smitten. Hadn't there been something about his feeling guilty about gambling because his wife didn't approve?

"No one's perfect, Mrs. H., and seen in daylight he's not a bad-looking chap."

"And handy around the house. That's not to be sneezed at."

We were entering the café, typical of its sort, with closely grouped tables between which a waitress with a fierce look of concentration on her face was squeezing her way. One turned head, one shift of a customer's foot, one poke of an elbow and there would go the loaded plates she was carrying. The wall, shelf-lined with copper kettles, provided another hazard, being at just the right height to ensure that anyone seated at a table beneath it would get a cracked head if failing to exercise extreme caution when getting up from a chair.

"It wasn't his wife." Mrs. Malloy narrowly missed being sideswiped by one of the plates. "It was his daughter or granddaughter or maybe a niece."

"Not a nephew?" I was sidling toward the only empty table.

"Oh ho, aren't we getting snippy, Mrs. H.?"

"I'm sorry," I said. "I'm hungry and worried that we're only going to make matters worse by sticking our noses in this business. It will probably take ages for us to be served. And it has begun to dawn on me that we have too many nephews cluttering up this case."

"Do we?" Mrs. Malloy looked genuinely nonplussed.

"Don't get me wrong," I said, moving the bottle of sauce as though it were a pawn on a chess board, "I'm not blaming you for insisting that there be a nasty nephew involved, but one per murder plot is usually considered adequate."

"That's all there is, Niles Edmonds."

"Wrong." I shifted the pepper pot. "I can count two more already. Mrs. Beetle mentioned the vicar had a nephew who was something of a disappointment because he'd gone on the stage. And Mrs. Hasty told us that Mrs. Snow, the horrible housekeeper, paid her nephew's boarding school fees."

"And I'll bet he's been made to pay through the nose ever since, the poor sod. He's probably at her beck and call this minute, trotting up and downstairs with cups of tea and extra pillows for her poor old back. And then there's someone like Milk"—she threw out a hand, knocking over the salt shaker that I had just set up in position—"off doing what real men do: getting mugged in alleyways and boozing it up in some back room. It just don't seem fair."

"You're right. It isn't the least bit fair to Lady Krumley that we're playacting at handling her case because we've no means of getting in touch with Mr. Jugg, who must surely have enough credibility with the police to get them to take a closer look at Vincent Krumley's death. He might also tell us how to set about finding Ernestine pronto." In my agitation I shot back in my chair and pilloried the waitress.

"You all right, ducks?" Mrs. Malloy asked her. "There's not

room to swing a cat round in here. Now, what was it we was saying, Mrs. H.?" She began unbuttoning her raincoat as the woman sucked in her stomach and sidestepped away.

"That you and I are caught up in something we're not equipped to handle."

"Rubbish! Faint hearts never won diddle, let alone the five thousand pound her ladyship has promised us. I'd say we've made a lot of headway in one morning, what with Laureen Phillips falling all over herself to spill the beans. And we'd do a lot better if you'd stop fixing on piddly stuff like who's got a nephew and who hasn't. Now, don't go telling me it's always them little details that helps solve the case in detective stories. I know that and I'm not saying they aren't important in real life, but the point is we need to keep our eyes on the big picture first and then see how and where the small things fit in to be important. If they do, which probably most of them don't, being mainly red herrings as they say. Ooh, and that does make me think . . ."

"What?" I leaned forward hoping to hear that she'd just had a brilliant revelation as to who was the most likely person behind all the peculiar goings-on at Moultty Towers.

"That I could kill for a couple of kippers with poached eggs on top."

"Is that all?"

"You rather I dropped dead of hunger before Laureen Phillips shows up?"

"If she ever does. Maybe she's had second thoughts." Not so, it would seem. I glimpsed a shadow, felt rather than heard someone approach our table, and a moment later Laureen Phillips, wearing a raincoat gapped open to reveal her gray blouse and cardigan, sat down.

"Sorry I'm late, ladies," she said. "I ran into Mrs. Thatcher outside the corner shop. She was going in to pick up a comic for her son who's home from school with an upset tummy."

"Thatcher." Mrs. Malloy sat looking wise beyond her years (which were always open to interpretation). "Now would she be the constable's wife?"

"That's right." Laureen broke off when the waitress hobbled our way and asked what we would have. Mrs. M. and I settled on sausage, baked beans and chips, that being all that was left on the menu, and a pot of tea to be shared with Laureen who said she didn't have time for anything else. "And anyway I had a slice of toast while getting Mrs. Hasty's lunch. She was in a chatty mood after her nap, and I didn't like to rush away after the shock she's taken. It's a wonder she isn't having nightmares along with Ronald."

"Ronald?" I wished I could look as intelligent as Mrs. Malloy, who now sat pouring our tea from an earthenware pot almost as big as the table.

"The Thatchers' boy. He's nine-years-old and has proved a bit of a handful, having been one of those change-of-life surprise packages and coming after three model brothers, all of them grown up now and living away from home. But if you ask me he's not a bad kid. He comes over to see Mrs. Hasty quite often. Well, mostly he comes to see the cat." Laureen smiled, and I decided that, unprofessional though it might be, I liked her, and surely a private detective had to sometimes rely on instinct. "Ronald's desperate for a cat or a dog, but his father says he can't have one until he demonstrates some responsibility and maturity. So I don't give much for his chances at the moment."

"Why's that?" I asked.

"And what does it have to do with the case?" Mrs. Malloy frowned so severely that the waitress inquired in a trembling voice if the meals she had set down looked all right. It took my raptures over the burnt sausages to get her to hobble away. And then my heart went with her, so that it took me a moment to refocus.

"I'm not sure." Laureen sat sipping her tea.

"You said that Ronald's been having nightmares," I said, "and now he's home from school with an upset tummy. I used to get them as a child when I was worried about something."

"The kid should be worried. He's in big trouble with his dad for throwing a flower pot at Lady Krumley's car the day before yesterday when she was driving past the green." Laureen looked toward the café window. "There was another boy, a classmate of Ronald's, who was in on it. They were on their school dinner hour, and Constable Thatcher saw what happened and chased them down."

"Her ladyship mentioned the incident." I laid down the knife and fork I had just picked up. "It made her late for her appointment. She had to stop at a garage to get her car window temporarily fixed."

"Mrs. Thatcher said that if her husband had realized Lady Krumley was driving the car he would have checked first to make sure that she was alright before leaving the scene. I imagine," Laureen shrugged, "that he was in such a temper that he wasn't thinking clearly."

"Your bringing this up explains something Mrs. Beetle, the cook, had to say when we was talking to her earlier." Mrs. Malloy had polished off her sausages and chips and most of her baked beans.

"That's right," I said, "she mentioned that Constable Thatcher hadn't been informed of Vincent Krumley's death when he showed up at Moultty Towers."

"On the night in question"—Mrs. Malloy reached out a fork to spear one of my sausages—"he got a phone call about it just after he arrived. So something else brought him to the house. Must have been to own up to his son's naughty behavior and find out how her ladyship was doing. Who'd be a parent? Quite makes up me mind for me, I'm not having no more kids."

Laureen smiled, but I didn't dare.

"Did the boy say why he and his friend threw those flower pots at the car?" I asked Laureen.

"No."

"And his father, a policeman, can't get it out of him?"

"That's what's got Mrs. Thatcher so worried. Usually Frank's only got to look at the boy to get at the truth. She thinks Ronald's frightened . . . badly frightened. She said it could be of the other boy. He's almost a year older and much bigger than Ronald, and Mrs. Thatcher—as most mothers would—thinks he's the ringleader. But she is also wondering if it has something to do with Vincent Krumley's death."

"Now, what makes her think that?" Mrs. M. poured more tea.

"It's not just the nightmares. Ronald's been talking in his sleep. Muttering stuff about the old man and the dog."

"What does his father say?" I asked.

"That he should be having nightmares after what he did."

"And the other boy isn't talking?"

"Not a word. His parents are saying it was all Ronald's fault, along with Frank's for being too strict." Laureen spooned sugar into her cup. "I'm afraid those two boys came over to see Mrs. Hasty and the cat, or to play in the copse, and saw something they are now afraid to talk about."

"Did you say that to Mrs. Thatcher?" I had finished as much as I could of my meal.

"No, she was already upset. And I could be wrong. Maybe the two incidents, Ronald's hooliganism and Mr. Krumley's death, which is of course the talk of the village, get mixed up in his head while he's sleeping. Perhaps he's heard it said that Vincent was a heavy drinker and not much good for anything, and he's scared in case it really is true that people who do bad things come to a bad end." Laureen pulled a wry face and said that if such were indeed the case she was in deep trouble.

"You've lost me, ducky." Mrs. Malloy eyed her sternly.

"Sorry. I'm bracing up to getting the topic back to the reason I asked you both to meet me here." The smile was still in place and included me. "I want to confess."

"Oh, you do, do you?" Mrs. Malloy opened her handbag with the exaggeratedly casual air of one about to whip out a gun. It was a little disappointing when she produced a tissue instead and dabbed her lips. "And would there be an accomplice involved in this confession? The same person you mentioned as having, along with yourself, made the mistake of thinking Lady Krumley had gone to see a man detective? The world's full of surprises, isn't it? But I don't suppose it'll catch you all that unawares when I tell you that me and Mrs. H. here have been in the business long enough to put two and two together. Oh, yes! Ever so good at our sums, we are. So instead of you confessing, why don't we tell you what we think?"

"Yes, why don't we?" I was all encouragement.

"It's about a man that showed up waving a gun shortly after Lady Krumley left our office."

"Do continue," said Laureen.

"Well, like you can imagine," Mrs. Malloy continued, preening in her most unbecoming way, "the two of us have been in that situation often enough to know when there's something that's not just right. And it seemed to us that on this particular occasion it was what we call a putup job, a sham . . ."

"A charade." I felt entitled to put in two words, particularly when I was the one who had originally suggested to Mrs. Malloy that there had been something stagey about Have Gun's appearance on the scene. I was silenced with a flick of the eyelashes.

"Playacting, that's what it seemed to us. And this morning you went and let slip that you'd been an actress."

"I thought I said it straight out." Laureen bit her lip.

"Very crafty. But I'll give you this, it wasn't you playing the gunman. If you was that good, you'd be world famous. In all likelihood it was some fellow actor, possibly a friend, that like you wanted to make sure her ladyship's talk about Flossie Jones and deathbed curses wouldn't be dismissed as so much nonsense from an old woman."

"Who do you think that friend would be?" Laureen sipped her tea.

Mrs. Malloy's look dared me to get in ahead of her. "The man that disappointed his dear old uncle by going on the stage. Mr. Featherstone the vicar's nephew, that's who!"

"His name is Tom Stillwaters."

"Runs deep, does he?"

"He's not much of an actor."

"But a nice man and you're fond of him." Mrs. Malloy wiped the smirk off her face. She was always susceptible to the whiff of romance, even when she was not the party involved.

"And he's devoted to Mr. Featherstone."

"Who in his turn," I said, "is devoted to Lady Krumley."

"He's in love with her, always has been. She must be the only one who doesn't seem to know. Never having been a beauty, or even verging on pretty, it probably wouldn't occur to her that any man could live out his life harboring a grand unrequited passion for her—certainly not a clergyman. They're not supposed to be that sort, are they?" Laureen pushed away her teacup. "And from the sound of it, Sir Horace never did much to boost her self-esteem as a woman. Tom overheard his uncle talking to Lady Krumley about her disappointment with a private detective. He was clearly afraid that she was working herself into such a state of agitation over her feelings of guilt toward Flossie that she would have another heart attack. One that might prove fatal. And when I told Mr. Featherstone what I knew about the brooch he became even more concerned. He agreed that someone seemed bent on malicious, wicked mischief. Tom and I knew we had to do something. And the scheme popped into our heads."

"It was foolish and dangerous." Mrs. Malloy peeked into her

compact mirror and adjusted her hat. "It could have been me and Mrs. H. here that got the heart attacks, if we wasn't the professionals we are. But seeing as how you've tried to be helpful, we'll say all's forgiven and go on from here. If that waitress ever shows up with the bill, that is."

Taking the hint I reached into my bag for my purse while Mrs. Malloy assured Laureen that there was no need for her to contribute toward the pot of tea, because the meal would go on the expense account. This sounded all well and good until I reminded myself that we wouldn't receive a penny from Lady Krumley until we found Ernestine. Would locating her lead us any closer to the shadowy figure who was responsible for putting her ladyship in a hospital bed?

This topic was the focus of conversation between Mrs. Malloy and me as we drove out of Biddlington-By-Water and took the road to Mucklesby, which was the shortest way back to Chitterton Fells. It was now 2:30 in the afternoon, and I was eager to be home with Ben and the children. I wasn't used to being gone for most of the day. But when I came to Hathaway Road, a street lined with late Victorian houses about a mile from Jugg's Detective Agency, I slowed the car and turned the corner.

"Remember," I said, "this is where Mrs. Hasty said Flossie had her bed-sitter."

"Of course I do." Mrs. M. had her nose pressed to the car window. "Look, there it is. That's the house, number twenty-one. Stop! There's a woman coming out the door."

"And what's she going to be able to tell us?"

"Probably not much. But it don't hurt to ask, does it?" She was using her wheedling tone, which always reduced me to meekness. But whether or not I was destined for regret on this occasion remained to be seen.

Seventeen

"Can I help you?" The woman walked toward us as we stood hovering by her front gate like a pair of diffident souls expecting to be told by St. Peter that they had come to the wrong place and if we didn't buzz off he would have to summon the man in charge.

"This is a long shot," I said, smiling into the pleasant friendly face, "but we were wondering if you might happen to know who owned this property forty years ago. You see we're trying to trace someone who lived here back then. I'm not explaining very well. It was only for a short time—a matter of months while she was a baby. Her mother was a young single girl, who died."

"When the house was broken up into bed-sitters?"

"That's right." Mrs. Malloy rested her handbag atop the gate.

"And the mother's name?"

"Flossie Jones." I felt a little bubble of excitement rise in my throat.

"Well, Florence really," said Mrs. Malloy. "The way we understand it she came here before she had the baby. But of course it's a long time ago and as my colleague here was saying it's a bit much to hope you can help us."

"How are the two of you involved?"

"We're private detectives. Look, hold on a tick, I'll show you me card." Mrs. Malloy rummaged inside her handbag. "We'd be standing here all day if we waited for Mrs. H. to find hers. That's teamwork for you. I keep us organized, and she does most of the legwork. Me knees isn't what they once was, you'll be sorry to hear. But I just couldn't abide to sit put at the office for this case, not when we've gone and promised a very ill old lady that we'll find Flossie Jones's daughter for her. You see there's an inheritance involved. And our client won't die easy until everything's settled." While rattling away Mrs. Malloy had flashed the card, which I knew from its pale lavender color to be her membership card for the Chitterton Fells Charwomen's Association. Fortunately our new acquaintance failed to peruse the fine print. Looking duly impressed she opened the garden gate and beckoned us to come inside.

"A inheritance you say, for that little baby!"

"If we can locate her." I felt the excitement bubble grow bigger. This woman had information. It might not be much, but anything was better than nothing. Maybe it would turn out that we hadn't done Lady Krumley a major disservice by taking on the case. Maybe in finding Ernestine we could prevent another murder. I reminded myself that we still had a long way to go, but it was difficult not to do a jig on the path.

"We are talking about a great deal of money." Mrs. Malloy compressed her lips as if the mentioning of it were somehow irreverent.

"How lovely! And won't my parents be delighted!" The woman beamed over her shoulder as she led us to the house with its stained glass panels on either side of the front door and lace curtains at the windows.

"Your parents?" I was saying as we entered the hall dominated by a rather dark staircase with massive newel posts.

"They've lived here most of their married life—fifty-five years next month. My husband and I moved in with them when our kids were grown, and my Mum and Dad needed some extra help."

"Could we speak with your parents?"

"Well, Mum's not home at the moment, but perhaps you can come back again. And in a minute I'll ask Dad to come in. I'd do it now, but he's out in the garden practicing his golf putting. A very keen golfer is Dad. He should have gone professional; people are always telling him that. But when he left school he had his widowed mother to support so he went into selling insurance, which is always a bit up and down. When he and Mum had a family—me and two brothers—they needed a bit extra, so they turned the upstairs and even the attic into bed-sitters, dad doing most of the construction work himself. "

"Well, fancy that!" Mrs. Malloy looked up the staircase in awe. "What, including the plumbing and electrical? Marvelous! I don't suppose your Mum has ever thought of passing him along to some other deserving woman?"

"Never in a million years," the woman spoke with a laugh. "They got married when they were both nineteen and are still like a pair of lovebirds even in their seventies. By the way, my name's Janet Joritz, but everyone calls me Jan. Come on into the front room, why don't you? We can have a sit down, while you ask me what you need to know."

"Do you remember the young woman and baby?" I asked as Mrs. Malloy and I followed her into a pleasantly cluttered room in the Victorian style, but with a large modern sofa and matching easy chairs arranged around a sensibly large coffee table. On this were scattered magazines and books and a piece of pale blue knitting that looked as though it had just been set down.

She urged us to be seated, and asked if we would like a cup of tea. When we declined, explaining that we had just had lunch, she took her own seat.

"You were asking if I remember them? The young woman and the baby?"

"And do you?" I asked. Unfortunately I had made the mistake of sitting next to Mrs. Malloy on the sofa. She accompanied a derisive chortle by an elbow in my side.

"What a question! Why, it's obvious from looking at her that Jan here couldn't have been more than a toddler herself at the time."

"Why that is kind of you to say," came the smiling response. "But I'd have been twelve or thirteen. Yes, that would be right." Mrs. Joritz was counting off on her fingers. "I'm fifty-two now. . . ."

"Who would have thought it! Why you don't look a day older than Mrs. H. here, and she claims to be in her early thirties." Mrs. Malloy was really overdoing things. It took all my restraint as a grown-up and a phony private detective not to poke her with my elbow. Mrs. Joritz might be rather too trusting, but I sensed she was no fool. Had she not been caught up in the excitement of our visit, she would surely have found Mrs. Malloy's flattery highly suspicious.

I breathed easier when she picked up her knitting and began clicking away, and immediately I sensed something else: Mrs. Joritz didn't want to rush things. Here was an event to be savored and later dwelt upon and talked about at length. She wouldn't enlarge upon the part she had played. She didn't strike me as a self-centered woman; it would be more like rewatching a favorite television program. It wouldn't be the beginning or ending that mattered half so much as the middle.

"I don't think much about how I look. It's never been all that important to me. It's how you feel on the inside that counts, or so I tell myself, and having my granchildren helps keep me feeling young these days. This little cardigan I'm knitting is for my eldest granddaughter, Julie. She's seven and does she ever think she's grown up! Her mother, my daughter Susan, let her get her ears pierced. My husband didn't think it was right, but I told him no one thinks twice about it these days, anymore than they do when someone has a baby without being married. It's all different. And just as well if you ask me, when you think back to what girls like the one that died upstairs went through, cast off by their families and left to fend all on their own when the bloke that got them in trouble washed his hands of his responsibilities."

"Sometimes these situations can be complicated." I was thinking about Ernest who had wanted to marry Flossie and then remembered Sir Horace who couldn't or wouldn't accept responsibility for the child.

"Such a pretty girl, she was too. It was still there even when she took ill." Mrs. Joritz laid down her knitting. "I suppose thinking back that's what made me realize looks aren't every-thing. That poor lass should have had the world at her feet."

Mrs. M. had reached out her hand to some grapes in a bowl before realizing they weren't real. "But a nice decorative touch," she proffered kindly, "cheerful but classy you might say, which gets me to wondering if that would describe Flossie Jones?"

"I didn't get to know her well enough to say. I just passed her coming in and out the door, that sort of thing. She wasn't un-friendly, but you couldn't expect her to go out of her way for a twelve-year-old girl. And it was clear she was hard up. She'd be weeks late with the rent; my parents were always a pair of soft-ies when it came to putting anyone out. I remember when the baby was born the doctor coming in the middle of the night. That made for a lot of excitement. And then of course Mum and Dad talked about her being ill. That part happened very quick, the way it does with pneumonia. It was the same doctor that came then. A Doctor Green, he was, and it was him that arranged things for the adoption."

"He did?" Mrs. Malloy and I bolted forward on the sofa in unison.

"There was this couple, patients of his, that couldn't have children; it's often the case, isn't it? Those that want them can't have them and those that don't find themselves in a pickle." A sharp crack, as if from a ball hitting a window, cut Mrs. Joritz short and caused Mrs. Malloy's hat to slide from her head to mine. I had a suspicion that it did nothing for me, but before I could request an opinion Mrs. Joritz began chatting away in a nervous voice about how she had enjoyed her daughters' growing-up years. Some five minutes later the door opened and an athletically built, dapper gentleman entered the room, nonchalantly swinging a golf club.

"Oh, Dad! You didn't!" Mrs. Joritz addressed him in a softly rebuking voice.

"That's your father, sweetheart! Another hole in one!"

"Through next door's dining room window?"

"The exact same spot as last time."

Mrs. Joritz pressed her hands to her cheeks. "Tell me you didn't smash any more of Mr. Warren's Royal Doulton character mugs? You know that man lives and breathes for his collection. He's finally got all of Henry VIII's six wives."

"And a few moments ago one of them's had her head chopped off for the second time. Now don't go upsetting yourself." Her father grinned. It was a very attractive boyish grin and knowing Mrs. Malloy's tendency to become distracted under certain conditions, I replaced her hat, pulling the brim down over her eyes. "It's alright, Jan. Mrs. Warren wasn't the least put out. She not only downright refused to let me pay for the window, she invited me to start practicing on her lawn, which does have the advantage of that little pond and the children's sandbox to make me feel more like I'm playing at the club. The woman hates those mugs. She says they're always leering at her. And she has nightmares about being up on the mantelpiece with them. But what will these two ladies be thinking of me, chewing on about my game." He propped his club against a table and extended his hand, first to me then to Mrs. Malloy. "We haven't met previously, have we?"

"No, but isn't it nice that there's a first time for everything?" It was clear to me from Mrs. Malloy's limpid gaze that the image of Watkins, the butler, had been wiped from the horizon of her memory. She introduced herself with the bashfulness of a schoolgirl while making adjustments to the hat. Knowing she was desperate to get at her lipstick, I shifted her handbag out of reach.

"I'm Bob Songer." He sat down, hitched up his crisply ironed trouser legs to display an inch of robin's egg blue sock and leaned toward us, eyes twinkling. "You must be new friends of Jan's, or we'd have met before. She's always been great about including her Mum and me when she has people in, never making us old folk feel underfoot, the way you hear of some people doing to their parents."

"Dad"—Mrs. Joritz returned his twinkle—"you're forgetting it's your house."

"That wouldn't stop some." Mr. Songer's grin faded. "Mrs. Warren was telling me this morning how she'd read in the local paper about some ninety-year-old man that died from falling down a well."

"Well, I never!" Mrs. M. avoided my eye.

"A nasty accident from the way it was written, but as Mrs. Warren pointed out, accidents can be made to happen. 'Mark my words,' she said, 'that old codger was in the way, getting on someone's nerves, always harping on about the old days. Probably couldn't remember if he'd had breakfast, but could describe down to the last button on his overall what the grocer's delivery boy looked like." Mr. Songer's grin had a rueful curve to it this time. "There is no denying the tendency to live in the past as we age."

"But not you, Mr. Songer!" Mrs. Malloy dipped her eyelashes.

"That's where having Jan and her husband here is such a blessing." His face glowed. "There's always something going on with their family. She'll have told you about her daughters and how well they've done for themselves? Both of them with university degrees and married to successful and very nice men. Susan's husband is a barrister, and they have seven-year-old Julie who, though I suppose I shouldn't say it, is as bright as a penny. She's in a class with children two years older than her, and has no trouble keeping up. None at all. In fact she came top last term, isn't that right Jan?"

"Oh, Dad!" Mrs. Joritz blushed. "You really shouldn't boast. I'm sure to other people our Julie's just a nice ordinary little girl."

"Not too many children can speak Spanish."

"Dad she can count to ten; that doesn't make her fluent." Mrs. Joritz picked up her knitting. "Of course she can do it backward as well as forward. And her teacher did say her accent is exceptional."

"She also dances like a little fairy." Mr. Songer's wide boyish smile displayed an excellent set of teeth for a man of any age. But Mrs. Malloy no longer eyed him with quite so much enthusiasm. Indeed, when he continued to tout little Julie's accomplishments I got the impression she was wondering what she had seen in him at the beginning of their now ten-minute-old relationship.

"Did Jan mention that the child is musical?"

"Not that I remember." Mrs. Malloy's eyes were beginning to glaze.

"She plays the triangle."

"How splendid," I responded with genuine feeling. Hadn't I been overwhelmed with pride when Tam blew what sounded like two or three notes of "Ba Ba Black Sheep" on a comb wrapped in toilet paper?

"The only child to perform solo in the school concert."

"Fancy!" Mrs. Malloy glanced around as if hoping to spy a well that she could tip him into.

"Gifted, I heard someone say."

"Dad, that was her father." Mrs. Joritz smiled fondly at him over her knitting.

"There's nothing like listening to stories about other people's kiddies." Mrs. Malloy rallied to add, "Bless their little hearts. But me and Mrs. H. here don't want to go taking up your whole afternoon."

"The boot's on the other foot!" Our hostess dropped the knitting and now looked acutely embarrassed. "Dad, I should have explained at once! These ladies are private detectives. They're wanting to locate Flossie Jones's baby. The one that was born here and given up for adoption all those years ago. I was just telling them, before you came in, about Dr. Green's involvement."

"A good man," replied Mr. Songer. "He told me he urged the young mother when she was dying to let him get in touch with the baby's father. He felt the man was entitled to be made aware of the situation—to take the child and raise it if that was his wish—but she refused to name him. And so the doctor talked to this couple who had been hoping to adopt for some time."

"Do you know if Dr. Green is still alive?" My heart was thumping hard.

"I wouldn't think it likely. He was close to sixty at that time."

"Never mind." I tried not to sound as disappointed as I felt. "That would have been too easy, wouldn't it?"

"So it would." Mrs. Malloy got to her feet. "But fortunately my partner and I have the experience to turn a dead end into," she valiantly lifted her chin, "into a shortcut." As this made no sense I began voicing my thanks to Mrs. Joritz and Mr. Songer for the information they had given us, only to be interrupted by that nice woman.

"But we haven't told you the name of the couple who adopted the baby. It was Merryweather. They managed to track our family down through a blanket I'd knitted for the baby that went with her when she was taken from here. I'd done several of the same pattern for the church bazaar."

"Jan was a whiz with her knitting even at twelve years old," enthused her father.

"Well, it's not to be expected you've kept in touch with the Merryweathers all these years," said Mrs. Malloy somewhat ungratefully.

"Isn't it?" Mr. Songer's boyish grin was back in place as he turned to his daughter. "Jan, where does your mother keep the address book?"

Eighteen

Mrs. Malloy was in a major snit when I dropped her off at her house in Herring Street. She thought me derelict in my professional duties in refusing to go rushing off to the address we had been given. Time, she reminded me sententiously, was of the essence, a point on which I agreed with her. At close on 4:00 in the afternoon it was time for me to get home to my family. Tomorrow would be soon enough to attempt making contact with Ernestine's adoptive parents, to which statement she responded darkly that she hoped I wouldn't live to regret them words.

It was already dusk when I parked the car in the stables and entered the house by the garden door, feeling foolishly like a child who had stayed playing outside beyond the time I had been allowed. Freddy was alone in the kitchen. And I have to say I was shocked. Usually in such a situation I would find him lolling back in a chair with his feet up on the table and a bulging sandwich in each hand. Not the case this time. He was standing with his back to me chopping onions. It has never pierced my soul to see a man slaving away in a kitchen, especially when it is my kitchen. But there was something about my cousin's lackluster ponytail and the dejected sway of his skull-and-crossbones earring that temporarily wiped all thoughts of Ernestine and the motley goings-on at Moultty Towers out of my head.

"You're worried about your Mum, aren't you?" I said as I hung my raincoat on one of the pegs in the alcove. "Any word?"

"Not a peep."

"Oh, Freddy! I am sorry."

"It's been seven days now, and Dad's contemplating having her declared legally dead."

"That's Uncle Maurice. Always the stiff upper lip." I stowed my handbag on the Welsh dresser and went and placed a hand on his shoulder. "But surely there's no reason to think something terrible has happened to her. Hasn't she done this sort of thing before? Gone off on one of her shopping expeditions and . . ." My voice petered out.

"Lost track of time?" Freddy laid down the knife and turned to face me.

"Or met someone—an old friend from boarding school— and gone to stay with them for a few days, quite forgetting in the excitement of getting caught up on all the gossip to phone home. Let's face it, she can be a little feckless, in the sweetest possible way of course."

"Yes." Freddy lounged over to a chair and sat head bent, hands lolling to the floor, "Mum has done a bunk before, usually when Dad's been narking on at her to cut down on her shoplifting, if she's going to come home with the same hat three days running."

"While's he's needing a new cardigan." I put the kettle on and reached into the cupboard for cups and saucers. "I suppose some people would say he had a point."

"In certain ways, Ellie, theirs is one of those old school marriages, with Dad laying down the law and Mum every so often deciding she's had enough."

"There you are then." I handed him a cup of tea and a biscuit. "This is just another of those times. She's setting out to teach him a lesson and when she thinks he's had time to get the idea she'll come home."

"That's what I've been trying to tell myself, coz." Freddy sipped at his tea but set the biscuit down on the table—not a good sign, given his usual willingness to eat anything that didn't run for cover before he got within a yard of it. "But I've got a bad feeling this time. I suppose it's Dad telling me about her being down at that pub, The Wayfarers, or whatever it was called. Mum just isn't a pubby sort of person. She thinks they're places for amateurs, getting their start by pocketing those cardboard coasters. The Red Lion and such just aren't her scene."

"What aren't you telling me?" I sat down across from him and stirred sugar into my tea. "You were worried this morning, but not to the point where you are now."

"This is going to sound stupid." He brushed a strand of hair out of his eyes.

"Tell me."

"Okay, it's like this: Mum has always sent me a card on the anniversary of the date when I cut my first tooth."

"I think that's dear."

"Don't go all sloppy on me, Ellie. She doesn't remember my birthday, but this is different. She never missed until this time."

"When should you have received the card?"

"The day before yesterday. But you know how the post can be. Sometimes you get a letter before it's been sent and other times you'd think someone was hanging on to it hoping the value of the stamp would go up."

"So why panic?"

Freddy got up and strolled back to his onions. "Mum always sent the card off early to be on the safe side. And when it didn't show up today," he resumed chopping, "I've got to tell you, Ellie, my blood ran cold."

"Have you talked to your father?"

"I got him on the phone just before you came in. He had nothing to report, other than he was having to make do with poached eggs on toast for the third night in a row. And that there was nothing but tinned peaches for afters. What really got him splattering was that they were an off brand. And his blaming that on Mum just didn't wash. She never thinks price when she goes to the supermarket. She always takes the very best. Says it's more economical in the long run."

"Less seasoning to add," I concurred. "Freddy, what are you doing with those onions? And where"—I hadn't wanted to bring the subject up before—"where are Ben and the children?"

"He took them out somewhere about half an hour ago. To the library I think. And since I'd invited myself to dinner I thought I'd get a meal started. I'm making spaghetti bolonaise."

"That's really thoughtful." I was now standing refilling my teacup. "But you know Ben always has containers of pasta sauce in the freezer. Why not just relax?"

"Thanks, but I need something to do."

"Then would you help me lay the table? Or, better yet, fix a salad?"

"All right." Freddy set down the knife before wandering over to the fridge and returning with a head of lettuce in one hand and a couple of tomatoes in the other. "What do you think, coz, about my calling in a private detective to help find Mum? What about that bloke Mrs. Malloy works for?"

"He's still on holiday and impossible to reach. Remember? I told you that Mrs. Malloy and I have been filling in for him on that case. We had quite a chat about it this morning."

"Missing my mother does not mean I'm losing my mind. Or maybe it does." He tossed aside the knife and leaned morosely against the sink. "Most sons would have disinherited her, shown her the door, told her to get lost years ago, done all the things that outraged parents do when their offspring don't turn out well. It's no joke, although I know I make it sound like one, having a mother who'd rob the Pope of his little skullcap while asking for a papal blessing. But I can't send her back and ask for a new Mum, can I?" Freddy stood with his eyes closed plucking at his scroungy beard. "I've looked and I can't find the box she came in."

"I wish there was something I could do to help."

"You wouldn't be willing to talk to Mrs. Malloy about taking on a missing person case? It would be right up the same alley as the one you're working on now. My cousin opened his eyes and gave me a threadbare smile. "By the way, how's that going?"

"We made some progress today. In fact I think we may be close to finding Ernestine. We have the name and address of the people who adopted her."

"Great!"

"It was mostly luck. Several things fell into place. Freddy"— I was struggling into an apron, getting my head stuck in one of the armholes in the process—"about your mother: I don't feel equipped. You need someone who really knows what they're doing. Not someone who's playing detective." I felt sick when I heard what I was saying. It was just fine to practice on strangers, was it? But not when it came to my own family. Any exhilaration I had felt on leaving the house on Hathaway Road was wiped away. It didn't help to tell myself that, given Milk Jugg's absence, Lady Krumley could have been stuck in her hospital bed with no one believing a word of her fantastical tale. I was staring glumly back at Freddy when the garden door opened and my three children came bouncing into the kitchen, followed by Ben with his hands full of white cardboard boxes and several books under one arm.

"Fe fi fo fum! I smell Chinese food." I felt a smile slide over

my face as little Rose wrapped her arms around my legs and
Tam and Abbey raced to pick up Tobias, whose furry face had
appeared out of nowhere.

"I needed to go to the library, and the children wanted to
come along." Ben was unloading onto the table. "So we decided to make a treat of it and get a takeaway."

"That's wonderful. Freddy can stop slaving away chopping
onions."

"Sorry, I thought I told him . . ."

"He's a bit preoccupied at the moment about Aunt Lulu."

"Still no word?" Ben straightened up and began unbuttoning his coat. I could see the concern in his face as he looked at
Freddy. And I had one of those moments when my love for him
welled up inside me. I felt comforted and sheltered without his
eyes shifting my way, or his hand reaching for mine. It had
nothing to do with his dark good looks or his way of giving el-
egance to an elderly sweater and even older pair of trousers. It
had to do with the knowledge that he would always be there to
rescue me in times of trouble. And, possibly even more important, he would be equally willing to let me rescue him.

I bustled the children out of their coats as Ben stood talking
to Freddy. And after that the three of us got down plates, set
out the cutlery and opened the cartons, while the kettle boiled
for a fresh pot of tea.

"This is a feast." I removed the apron while surveying it.

"I was in the mood for chicken fried rice," announced Tam,
climbing on to his chair.

"And I wanted shrimp slug bug." Abbey pranced over to
give me a kiss before taking her place.

"That's sub gum," corrected her brother.

"Is it?" Abbey appealed to me.

"Darling, it's delicious. That's all that matters." I was getting
Rose into her booster chair, while Ben poured the tea and
Freddy produced beakers of milk for the children. He was still

looking strained, but he made an effort to appear his usual self when asking Ben what books he had got at the library.

"Ones on computers."

"Oh, dear, so you're still having trouble?" I was thinking that I must get back in touch with Kathleen Ambleforth to find out what luck she was having in tracking down the typewriter and other items from the study. It didn't matter that Ben was no longer upset with me. I still had to put things right. Before he could answer Tam started to talk about his library book.

"It's about a little train that gets lost. And the people inside get very cross because they wanted to go to London. But they don't. The train takes them to the seaside. Then they look out the windows and see the sand and the children with buckets and spades and . . ."

"My book's about a bunny rabbit. It's sad because it can't find its Mummy." Abbey looked at my cousin with her bright blue eyes. "Is that why you're sad, Freddy? Do you want your Mummy?"

"Do you, Freddy?" Tam was shaking soy sauce onto his plate of fried rice, which he had shifted away from Rose after she reached out to take a handful. Being the typical two-year-old she always preferred one of her siblings' plates to her own.

"They must have heard me on the phone talking to Dad." Freddy was pushing his sub gum around with his fork and completely ignoring his mandarin beef. "Don't worry kids." He forced a grin. "I'm fine. After dinner you can read me those books of yours, while your parents have fun by themselves doing the washing up."

"Sounds like a plan." Ben spooned out the remains of the cartons.

And so the evening went. Eight o'clock rolled around, and it was time for the children to get ready for bed. I insisted on doing the honors. I sensed that Ben was eager to get into the study and crack open those computer tomes. He had asked me how my day had gone. Not wanting anything to break the lovely harmony of the moment I had said it had been fine and I'd tell him about it later. I thought about what I would say while giving the children their baths, tucking them into bed and singing "Jesus Tender Shepherd Hear Me" in my untuneful voice before turning on their night lights and giving them each a final goodnight kiss.

I was halfway down the stairs when the phone rang. I picked it up to hear Kathleen Ambleforth's voice on the other end.

"Ellie, cousin Alice has come through."

"Splendid!" It took me a moment to realize whom she was talking about.

"Remember, she made out the lists of where the donations were sent?"

"Yes." If Aunt Lulu hadn't been missing and people getting killed at Moultty Towers I would have erupted into a song and dance number.

"Do you have a piece of paper handy?"

"And a pen." I picked it up.

"Then here's the name of the organization and the telephone number. Are you writing it down? Am I going too fast?"

"I've got it." To reassure her I repeated the information back. It was all just letters and numbers to me. My mind was in a whirl. But I did remember to thank Kathleen profusely before putting down the phone and slipping the piece of paper into my skirt pocket. I would telephone first thing in the morning. Ben came out of the study as I crossed the hall. I was so tempted to tell him, but then I risked disappointing him if something went wrong. Better to wait and surprise him.

"What are you thinking about?" He drew me into his arms and kissed me in full view of the twin suits of armor. It was a wonderful kiss, both tender and passionate, and when I opened my eyes and looked into his I saw the promise of even better things to come. It was going to be one of those times for my sea

The Importance of Being Ernestine   183

green nightgown with its lovely foaming of lace, and that bottle of wickedly expensive perfume that was hidden away in the box where I kept the first letter he had ever written me, the first rose, the first wrapper from the first bar of chocolate . . .

"I'm thinking about what you're thinking about." I rested my cheek against his neck. "But Freddy's here."

"He went back to the cottage."

"Was he still feeling down?"

"He didn't look very chipper."

I sighed. "Poor, dear Freddy. But this does give me a chance to talk to you about what Mrs. Malloy and I have been up to." I drew him into the drawing room, switched on the lights and settled beside him on one of the matching ivory brocade sofas.

"You sound as though you don't expect me to approve." He cupped my face in his hands and kissed me, gently this time.

"That's because I don't fully approve myself, but somehow we got caught up in it." I could hear myself stammering. "It began the night of our quarrel, and I couldn't seem to find my way to talk to you about it." I floundered on, aware that it all sounded highly colored and more than a little preposterous. He stopped me now and then to ask a question, but his black eyebrows did not descend over his nose as they were wont to do when he was outraged. Neither did he blanch nor catch me in a vicelike hold, saying he would never let me out of his sight again for fear that the dark forces of evil that had descended upon Moultty Towers would claim me for their next victim. Indeed, I thought there were a few times when he was stoically restraining a laugh.

"So what do you think?" I asked at last.

"That it sounds as though you and Mrs. Malloy are having the time of your lives."

"There's no need to pat my head like I'm a child of six." I inched away from him and sat hugging a cushion.

"I'm not doing anything of the sort." A mendacious state-

ment if ever there was one. "Why shouldn't you enjoy yourselves? You're attempting to provide ease of mind to a troubled
old woman and from the sound of it you'll probably succeed.
You'll tell her how to get in touch with Ernestine and leave it
up to the two of them to sort out their past history."

"But what about the murder?"

"What murder?"

"Ben, haven't you been listening? Vincent Krumley. Remember him?"

"Sweetheart." His lips were twitching. "You said yourself
that the man was ninety-years-old. I don't expect to be too
steady on my feet at that age. You don't believe those other relatives of Lady What's-Her-Name were all deliberately done
away with, do you?"

"No, but they may have put ideas into someone's head."

"And you don't believe in deathbed curses?"

"Possibly not. But what about all those other things I told
you about?"

"Such as?"

"Why did Constable Thatcher's son Ronald throw those
flower pots at Lady Krumley's car? And why is he now having
nightmares that seem connected with Vincent Krumley's
death? I get the feeling that could provide a vital piece of the
puzzle. And at the back of everything—first and last—there's
the emerald brooch."

"You're taking a lot of what that woman, the lady's maid
Laureen, had to say for granted."

"Why would she lie?"

"To cause trouble. To make herself feel important. All sorts
of reasons. Or she could merely have been mistaken about
when the brooch was there and when it wasn't. Ellie," he removed the cushion from my clutches and tossed it onto a chair,
"do your good deed. Find Ernestine. Hope that Lady Krumley
wills her an enormous fortune, so she never has to work an-

other day in her life. And then leave the inhabitants of Moultty Towers to fend for themselves."

"So you're not the least bit worried that I'm walking into danger?" I sounded like Abbey at her poutiest.

"You are at this moment in very great danger"—Ben lowered his face to mine, his blue green eyes taking on unfathomable depths as he drew me close—"of being kissed back to your senses."

"Then you don't think it bothersome that Mrs. Malloy and I overheard Cynthia Edmonds demanding blackmail money from someone?"

"You could have misheard. The door was closed. Or such may be her usual method of getting extra cash out of her husband, threatening to tell Auntie that he hasn't been a good boy." Ben sat back with pained resignation. "Possibly this time he had done something really naughty, like buying himself a new train set."

"We can't assume it was Niles Edmonds in there with her. When Mrs. Malloy and I went up to the attics he was in the drawing room with the newly arrived Sir Alfonse Krumley. It could have been anyone in that bedroom with Cynthia. Including," I grabbed another cushion, "Daisy Meeks?"

"Who's she?"

"The woman who came into the room after the bird incident. Some sort of cousin."

"You think she was checking to see how badly you had been scared?"

"She seemed a dim bulb, but that could be an act."

"Shall we make her the prime suspect?"

I caught Ben's laughing gaze and tossed the cushion at him. Why couldn't he take me seriously? Wasn't it clear that Vincent Krumley had been murdered because he somehow posed a danger to the plot afoot, just as Cynthia Edmonds knew something best kept under wraps . . . unless she had taken precautions to protect herself? But what was at the back of it all? Revenge? Hate? Love? Greed? All classic motives and surely—I sat up straighter on the sofa—all applicable in this case. Revenge and hatred born of the injustices done to Flossie Jones. . . . A mother's love denied, and greed for what might be deemed one's rightful inheritance as the unacknowledged daughter of Sir Horace Krumley? Who else but Ernestine herself? Not some shadowy figure, but a woman who had made herself a diabolical presence in the ancestral home. Someone I had already met . . . talked with . . . thought not only harmless but also rather nice?

The doorbell interrupted my racing thoughts. By the time I had pried myself off the sofa, Ben had gone to answer it. I heard the murmur of a woman's voice. Mrs. Malloy, I wondered, come post haste with some vital piece of new information? Wrong. It was Freddy's mother, Aunt Lulu, who proceeded Ben into the room. My enormous relief at seeing her was mitigated by her woebegone face and unsteady gait, the more pitiful because she usually resembled a grown-up Shirley Temple, all dimples and curls.

"Hello, Ellie," she mustered the weakest of smiles, as I settled her into the nearest chair. "I've run away from that awful place."

"What place, Aunt Lulu?" I asked, as Ben pressed a glass of brandy into her trembling hand.

"One of those rehabilitation ones. I went in voluntarily. I thought it might make for a bit of a change." She sipped her brandy. "You often meet such interesting people at these places. But the most depressingly dedicated woman ran this one like a reform school. And every single person there wanted to be helped. Well, of course so did I, but not all at once or quite so thoroughly. I tried to escape from my third floor window. There was the nicest oak tree right outside, but some horrible do-gooder dragged me back in. After that I was watched all the time. It wasn't until this morning that I was able to get away after managing to sound the fire alarm. That created just enough chaos to give me a headstart down the drive to the road, where I hitchhiked a lift to the closest town from a passing lorry driver. And I've been thumbing my way here ever since."

"What's the name of this place?" Ben asked.

"The Waysiders. It's not a religious based setup, but I suppose it comes from the Bible, rescuing those that fall by the wayside."

"Freddy thought it was a pub," I said.

Aunt Lulu was beginning to revive, and the dimples appeared in her cheeks when she smiled. "My son's not just a pretty face. He must have been thinking of 'Tales from a Wayside Inn'."

"Yes, now I think about it he did say something about Longfellow the other day." My voice was drowned out by Freddy's eruption into the room from the hall. While he and his mother were falling into each other's arms Ben was filling another brandy glass. I reached into my skirt pocket to pull out the piece of paper on which I had written the address and phone number of the charitable organization where Kathleen Ambleforth's cousin Alice had dispatched the items from Ben's study.

It was as I thought. They had gone to The Waysiders, 109 Bottlecreek Road, Battersea. Looking at Aunt Lulu's now beaming face as Freddy set her back on her feet after a prolonged hug, I decided it might be best not to mention my connection to her when I telephoned to plead my case.

Nineteen

"I do wish you'd make up your ruddy mind." Mrs. Malloy had replenished her handbag with another bag of lemon drops and was sucking fiercely away as we drove through a green light that shone palely through the mist. "This morning it's Ernestine that's the villain of the piece. And that's after you saying the other day Lady Krumley could be telling fibs about her reasons for wanting to find the poor unsuspecting woman—to say she's sorry and wants to leave her gobs of money in her will. When," she continued, cheek bulging, "what she was really after was to get Ernestine out of the picture for good and all, for reasons that aren't nearly so nice."

"For all we know that may still be the case," I replied soothingly. "I merely suggested we look at the situation from the opposing angle. We've taken her ladyship's word that she, not Sir Horace, was the one who brought the money into the marriage. But what if she's lying about that? Or she signed her fortune over to him at some point in their marriage?"

"So that she gets to live on the income but hasn't a dickie bird to say about who gets what when she kicks the bucket." Mrs. Malloy shook her head at the vagaries of life.

"Meaning," I replied, turning on the car lights as the mist briefly thickened to fog, "Sir Horace could have left a will making Ernestine the major beneficiary, under certain circumstances, such as if other family members had died off first."

"He could even have put her ahead of some on the list. Daddies can be quite soppy about their little girls." Mrs. Malloy rustled into the bag for another lemon drop. "Me own father couldn't bear to deny me nothing. Called me his Little Twinkle Toes, he did. Course Mum had to go and say that was because he couldn't never remember me name. And, to be fair, he was like Sir Horace, not rushing to accept his responsibilities at the beginning. Then again, knowing Mum, he couldn't be blamed for not being quite sure, not until anyone with eyes in their head could see I was his spitting image. Ooh, but he was a handsome man, me Dad!"

I waited until the count of ten to make sure she was finished before picking up the threads of how Sir Horace might have left things in his will. "Supposing Niles Edmonds, of whom Lady Krumley appears to be fond, would only come into a fortune if Ernestine predeceased him? That would provide her ladyship with an incentive for finding her husband's love child and making sure she comes to grief."

"Well, there you are, then Mrs. H." Mrs. Malloy shook her fist out the window at a cyclist who was weaving along side of us. "You've gone and talked yourself right round. And a good thing too, because I don't think it right trying to make poor little Ernestine into a murderess after all she's been through. Besides, I've quite set me heart on it being that Cynthia—a right nasty piece if ever there was one, ranting on about the hairdresser messing up her new do, and not a word about how nice I looked in my hat. I'd feel quite sorry for her husband if he wasn't such a weasel. Last night I got to thinking, as I laid in bed drinking me gin and tonic, that it was most likely him we heard her talking to in the bedroom. But not being one to think meself the big know-it-all, I'm quite prepared to try and see things your way."

"About what?"

"Lady Krumley playing us for fools." Mrs. M. shook her

head. Today she was wearing a cherry red hat and her fake leopard coat. "It could've been her Cynthia was talking to on the telephone, letting her know what she'd seen."

"Her ladyship dropping Vincent down the well before setting off in the car for Mucklesby?" I slowed for a stop sign.

"It would explain the flower pots, wouldn't it?" Mrs. Malloy sucked on another lemon drop. "Those two boys—Ronald Thatcher and his little mate—saw what happened and being frightened, ran off, is my guess, but when the car drove past them they went into a rage."

"Surely if they'd witnessed the murder they would have run and reported it to Ronald's father or the first person they saw. There might even have been a chance of getting to Vincent Krumley while he was still alive."

"They're kiddies. They panicked, wasn't thinking straight. And now Ronald's having them nightmares thinking about what he should have done. But afraid to speak out for fear of being blamed."

"Isn't it more likely that they saw something that upset them, without their realizing its full significance until later, when word spread about the purported accident?" I drove cautiously past a car that was crawling along in the mist.

"Have to nitpick don't you?" Mrs. M. folded her gloved hands over her handbag. "What we needs to do is talk to them two boys. As quick as possible too. Because the way things stand, I wouldn't place any bets on Cynthia keeping her next appointment for a wash and set. Now you could say, Mrs. H., as that would be doing the chap that fixes her hair a favor, but we can't go getting too softhearted. We've just got to swallow our feelings and do our professional best to keep the woman from getting herself murdered."

"Maybe we should have gone to Moultty Towers before coming here." We had now entered Chandlers Point, a market town situated midway between Chitterton Fells and Muck-

lesby. This was where Ernestine's adoptive parents lived.
Mrs. Malloy had informed me on entering the car that she had
telephoned them the previous evening. "Mr. Merryweather
sounded surprised to learn I was a private detective wishing to
talk to him and his wife about their daughter, and he kindly
gave me directions to their house." She proceeded to reel off to
the accompaniment of much hand waving.

"Keep going down the High Street, Mrs. H., till you pass
Woolworth's on the right . . . or would it be the left? Never
mind, it has to be one or the other, don't it? And then you'll
see a florist. You just went by it. No, don't back up! Keep going
another hundred yards and turn left onto Seashell Crescent
and the house is . . . right there. Not the one with the green
front door, the one next to it: number seventeen with the curtains like bunched up petticoats at the windows and all them
gnomes in the garden. Now I do hope you won't go in there
looking like you can't stop thinking about that film *The Bad
Seed*."

"You have my word," I promised meekly while turning off
the ignition.

"As I said, I'd rather it wasn't Ernestine herself up to tricks."
Mrs. Malloy came around the car to join me on the pavement.
"I suppose it comes from picturing her as that poor little baby,
but that's not to say me hard-nosed objectivity has gone out
the window." She eyed me severely from under neon-coated
lids. "I've been Milk Jugg's right hand long enough to know,
you can't overlook a single possibility. Everyone's a suspect.
Course, I can't help thinking that could be because the job
pays more that way, if you bill by the number, I mean. So, even
if it is strictly for business reasons, we got to include Laureen
Phillips and Mrs. Beetle."

We were at the front door, and I had just rung the bell. Before she could say more we were being ushered into a fun fair
hall of mirrors. The number of fractured images flashing at us

from all sides was disorientating. Adding to the kaleidoscope effect was the Hawaiian shirt worn by Mr. Merryweather. It was an intense blue, patterned with teacup-sized flowers and birds of paradise. He was short and stout with tufts of wiry gray hair surrounding a bald pate. His complexion was brick colored and he was beaming at Mrs. Malloy and me as though we were a pair of long-lost relatives.

"What a pleasure! The wife has been on pins and needles. Was up at 6:00 this morning getting ready for you. Just a few scones and a loaf of plum bread. She loves to cook, always has done, as you can see from looking at me!" He patted his protruding tum. "Do let me take you into the sitting room. She'll be fussing with the cushions. You know what women are like. Well, of course you do!" His chesty chuckle carried with it a whiff of cigar smoke heavily scented with what the Reverend Ambleforth would refer to, in his most dubious voice, as "strong spirits." I could not fail to notice Mrs. Malloy's suddenly hopeful expression, given that it was reflected from all angles in the assembly line of mirrors. And, if anything, she looked even more optimistic when Mrs. Merryweather came toddling toward us, with hands outstretched and a smile as broad as the River Thames. This roly-poly woman, sporting the oversized cherry-framed glasses and a shift that screamed Hawaii even louder than her husband's shirt, exuded a hospitality that would extend beyond a cup of tea to accompany the scones and plum bread. Indeed a glass-fronted liquor cabinet, displaying an impressive array of bottles and glasses, was prominently positioned in the room.

"It's very good of you to see us." I included husband and wife in my smile, which was somewhat constrained by the anguish of having my fingers squeezed in a vicelike grip that didn't quite go with Mrs. Merryweather's baby pink lipstick and lavender hair. Then again, she had a marvelous golden tan, meaning she might be seriously outdoorsy, setting up her tanning bed on the lawn at every available opportunity. One just never knew about people. She might even be a keen rider like Cynthia Edmonds, a thought that brought with it a prickle of unease, along with a desire to speed up this meeting with the Merryweathers and immediately report our findings to . . . whom? Lady Krumley? I wasn't sure. If only, I thought, while my eyes traveled around the lime green walls to light on a painting of a fleshy nude woman with a ribald smirk who might not be, but probably was, Mrs. Merryweather, someone would kick in the door, and that someone would turn out to be Milk Jugg, intent on taking over the case on his terms with no further interference from a rank pair of amateurs. It was a lovely thought.

"Fancy you two ladies being private detectives." Mr. Merryweather had wheeled a tea trolley alongside the sofa and was handing us little plates and paper serviettes. "Never a dull moment, cracking cases the police aren't up to, bringing families back together." He sighed inexplicably. "Now what will it be, scones or plum bread?"

"Would you listen to Frank!" His wife flapped her pudgy little paws at him while winking at Mrs. Malloy and me. "Have both and come back for more. And be sure and pile on the butter. We don't do margarine in this house, not any more that is." Her expression faltered as she caught her husband's eye. "There's jam if you'd like it in the dish and," she added, toddling toward the liquor cabinet, "how about we go wild and have a glass of something?"

"Just to celebrate." Mr. Merryweather was now winking at her, rather frantically it seemed to me. Either that, or he had something in his eye. "Unless you two ladies have views, that is, about the consumption of alcoholic beverages. We've nothing against people that disapprove. Some of our best friends don't drink. We're not narrow-minded in that way, me and Ethel. Are we, love?"

"Never! Each to his own is what we say." Mrs. Merryweather stood with her back squarely toward the liquor cabinet. "But perhaps you ladies would rather have tea. It will be just as quick to brew up a pot. Or then there's coffee. How about coffee? Unless you only drink the decaffeinated sort. We pitched it the minute the sell-by date came up."

Husband and wife now wore matching sheens of perspiration on their faces, which, coupled with the similarity of their Hawaiian outfits, made them look remarkably alike, as is said to happen to couples over a period of years. My gaze was drawn back to the nude portrait. A discreet draping of shadow might have ruined the integrity of the piece, but I wouldn't be sitting with the uncomfortable feeling that I ought to avert my eyes while handing it a dressing gown, along with an apology for entering the room without knocking. My taste runs to landscapes and the sort of family photos you can send out on Christmas cards. It suddenly struck me that the only photos in view were of Mr. and Mrs. Merryweather. Had Ernestine grown up camera shy? While I allowed my mind to wander Mrs. Malloy got down to business.

"Oh, don't go fussing with pots of tea or cups of coffee. Me and Mrs. H. here wouldn't think of putting you to all that trouble." Treading down on my foot with a spiked heel.

"Absolutely not," I spluttered through a mouthful of scone.

"What else is on offer?" Mrs. Malloy gave the liquor cabinet her undivided attention.

"Pretty much anything you'd like."

"You name it, we've likely got it."

The Merryweathers spoke as one, simultaneously mopping their brows and in their beaming smiles displaying that their faith in humanity was restored.

"Then I'll take a gin," Mrs. Malloy proffered graciously. "With just the teensiest splash of tonic, if you'll be so kind.

Mustn't," she said, eyeing me smugly, "spoil the integrity of the drink."

Just great! I fulminated. Had she forgotten that she didn't need to sound like a decorator, except when visiting Moultty Towers? And where were her priorities? Our objective was to find out how or where we could find Ernestine, not to booze it up. I ignored the fact that I was on my second piece of plum bread and kept giving the scones encouraging smiles, hoping one of them would get up the nerve to leap onto my plate. It was hardly wrong to desperately long for an invigorating cup of tea. But a small sherry it would have to be.

"That we don't have." Mr. Merryweather straightened up after poking around among the bottles. "Very nice sherry, but not much bang for your buck." He wheezed out another chuckle. "How about a nice spearmint cordial? Ethel and I first had it in Florida."

"Las Vegas, Frank. Remember that night in the casino?" His spouse reached out to tickle his arm. "Then later in the hotel? Me in my pink nightie out on the balcony and you in that nice new pajama top? And that couple in the next room phoning down to the desk. No fun in some people. No spirit of adventure." Her plump face seemed to collapse in on itself. "It breaks your heart, but there it is. How about a glass of wine?"

I was afraid to refuse in case she broke down and wept. What was going on here? My mental image of Ernestine was adjusting rapidly from a forty-year-old woman with a sweet baby face to a brassy blonde dancing on tabletops in some seedy joint, where the booze never stopped flowing and susceptible, unprepossessing men could be made to think they were sexy and talked out of—or even married for . . . their money. But what if, I turned the thought this way and that in my mind, it should turn out after the knot was tied that the man was financially dependent on an elderly aunt, and would remain so until the wife took matters into her own hands? Hadn't her ladyship, my heart beat faster, said something about Vincent Krumley accusing Cynthia Edmonds—in what she took to be a befuddled way—of being a go-go dancer? But if it were Cynthia who killed him, then why would she be blackmailing anyone? Unless, she had persuaded Niles to do the dirty work for her and could produce evidence to nail him.

"Don't sit there in a trance," Mrs. Malloy muttered in my ear. "We're not getting paid by the hour. Do you want a glass of wine, or don't you?"

"That would be lovely." I scrounged up a smile for the Merryweathers.

"Anything in particular?" Ethel beamed back at me. "We've all flavors and colors."

"We're into our own wine making," explained Mr. Merryweather. "Took it up last year after Ethel sprained her back at a senior limbo festival in Hawaii," he said, patting his shirt front. "It was her chiropractor that suggested we take this up. Very good for the lower back stomping on the grapes or the gooseberries, or whatever else comes to hand. Or I should say"—he planted a loud kiss on his wife—"to foot?"

"Makes for a very nice bouquet, I'm sure." Mrs. Malloy sipped her gin with ladylike precision.

"Have our own label, Chateau Frankethel. Clever, don't you think?"

"It'll keep me up half the night chuckling," said Mrs. Malloy.

"Here," he filled a glass with a murky liquid and handed it to me, "see how you like our April vintage."

"Thank you." I took a pretend sip. "And now if we may, my partner and I would like to get round to discussing . . ."

"Oh, yes, please do tell us what you have discovered about our darling girl." Mrs. Merryweather leaned against her husband's shoulder to be lovingly supported by him to a chaise lounge, where they sat clinging to each other's hands as if aboard a raft that was doomed to sink at any moment.

"Well, it's wonderful news like I said on the phone." Mrs. Malloy elbowed me back against the cushions. "Mr. Songer and his daughter Mrs. Joritz was very nice about helping us get in touch with you. Took quite a bit of legwork to get to that point, but me and Mrs. H. here are used to that in our line of work. They told us how you tracked them down, something about a baby blanket that Ernestine came with when you adopted her."

"Yes," Mrs. Merryweather said, dabbing at her eyes with a crumpled serviette, "the prettiest shade of pink and beautifully knitted. One morning I was going down the High Street with Ernestine in her pram and I just happened to stop alongside a woman pushing her baby, and would you believe she had the exact same blanket? It was an unusual pattern with a very fancy fringe, so I asked her where she'd got it. Didn't I Frank? You remember me telling you?"

"So you did, love." Mr. Merryweather squeezed her hand and blinked back his own tears. "She told you she'd bought it at a church bazaar in Mucklesby. And I said that seeing that our little girl came from that area there likely was a connection. So we checked around and found out the blanket from the bazaar had been knitted by this young girl, Janet Songer. We got the address and went round to see her parents. What a day that was! Mrs. Songer and her husband filled us in on Ernestine's first months of life in that bed-sitter.

"Enough to break the hardest heart it was . . . thanks, Ethel love, . . ." he said as Ethel handed him a serviette to blow his nose, "that poor young girl dying like that, all alone in the world, and the father never showing his face around the place."

"And her being sacked for stealing, without any proof from the way I understand it. Why didn't she sell that brooch if she had it? That's the question I'd have liked to ask those high-

and-mighty Krumleys." Mrs. Merryweather withdrew her hand from her husband's to pound a fist on her knee. "They should be downright ashamed of themselves."

"Lady Krumley wishes to make amends." I slid my untouched glass of wine onto a side table.

"She's a bit late." Mr. Merryweather tucked the serviette into the pocket of his Hawaiian shirt. "When I think of the shadow cast over Ernestine's life and the effect it's had on her, I could howl like a baby."

"You told her what you knew?" I was aghast.

"We didn't want to." Mrs. Merryweather sounded defensive. "But right from an early age Ernestine asked a lot of questions. And it didn't seem right to lie to her. This is a small place and stories leak out, people gossip. We didn't want her accusing us later of telling her a bunch of fairy stories."

Having Rose, I could understand the difficulties. Ben and I were both concerned about how best to handle the situation when the time came to explain that she had been born to my cousin Vanessa and came to us when she was three months old. Mrs. Malloy, perhaps in an attempt to shift the conversation back to calmer waters, asked the husband and wife if they had thought about changing Ernestine's name.

"We considered it." Mr. Merryweather pecked his wife on the cheek. "We'd have liked her to be Gloria or possibly Darlene. Something with a bit of sparkle."

"Ernestine," his wife explained, spreading her hands in a hopeless gesture, "well, it's . . . so very earnest, isn't it? And she was such a sweet baby. We doted on her from day one."

"Isn't that lovely!" Mrs. Malloy looked misty eyed herself.

"We always hoped . . . we tried so hard to be the right kind of parents, but it just wasn't to be. And it's no good asking the question where did we go wrong? Sometimes nothing you do is enough. They turn out the way they want to turn out, and you just have to keep on loving them the way they are." Mrs. Merryweather's voice cracked. "You focus on the small comforting things like the fact that Ernestine always enjoyed cooking. She got that from me. It's a bond. I tell myelf that when I wake up in the middle of the night. And maybe she'll be different now that she wants to come home. We have to hope so, don't we, Frank?" She sagged against his shoulder.

"Come home?" Mrs. Malloy produced a notebook and pencil from her handbag with a flourish. "Where is she living now?"

Both husband and wife looked completely blank, but it was Mrs. Merryweather who spoke: "But that's what you and this other lady," he said, waving at me, "have come to tell us, isn't it?

"No." Now Mrs. Malloy and I were wearing the blank expressions.

"You mean . . . but we thought . . ." Mr. Merryweather spluttered to a halt and had to cough himself back to coherence. "We somehow got the idea that Ernestine had decided to get back in touch after having washed her hands of us twenty some years ago, never so much as letting us have her address. And because we've moved several times since then, sometimes out of the area and back, it would make sense for her to use a detective service. We thought, Ethel and I, that you were sounding us out to find out if we were willing to see her. To be honest we've had mixed feelings. We love her, always will, but we're not sure we can go back to those days of having to hide the butter for fear of being lectured for hours about our cholesterol levels. Or of trying to keep the peace by drinking nothing stronger than decaffeinated coffee. And being reviled—that's not too strong a word—for listening to rock 'n' roll music."

"The day she packed her bags and walked out the door we shed a lot of tears." Mrs. Merryweather blinked hard.

"But then you know what we did?" Her husband grabbed her in a bear hug. "This little woman and I got back into life. She got her portrait painted. We went on our first cruise. And you know what helped most? Talking to other parents who'd learned to live with being a bitter disappointment to their children. So," he paused, "what do you have to tell us about Ernestine?"

"That Lady Krumley wishes to make amends by leaving her a sizeable inheritance." I said.

"Well, isn't that nice." Mrs. Merryweather dabbed at her eyes. "That calls for a drink. How about a nice clove cordial?"

Twenty

U pon our departure from number seventeen Seashell Crescent, Mrs. Malloy and I drove to the Cottage Hospital where Lady Krumley was a patient. We now prowled its corridors, hoping to find a lift before our food supply—the bag of lemon drops and the half bar of chocolate in my handbag—ran out.

"Next time perhaps you'll think to bring a map." Mrs. Malloy teetered around to look back the way we had come. "I'm beginning to understand how Moses managed to spend forty years getting lost and relost in the desert. But I'm not blaming you, Mrs. H. I'm worn out after a morning spent talking to those Merryweathers. Them and their limbo dancing! It makes me wonder what it was like for Ernestine being their kiddie. Probably worn out by the time she was four and ready for the rocking chair at age twelve. But then again some little tinkers would have thrived on it and gone hot air ballooning out their bedroom window every chance they got. Or maybe it was like they said, that they didn't discover their wild side till after she was gone. What did you think of that rude picture of Mrs. Merryweather?"

"Very realistic."

"You can say that again, Mrs. H.! I've heard of them paintings where the eyes follow you all around the room, but this was worse. It wasn't the eyes, it was the other—boobs and bobs—that kept staring at me, even when I squeezed me eyes shut. You can tell me it would be spoiling the integrity of the piece, but if that thing was to be hung in my front room I'd have to paint on a pair of knickers and a twenty-four-hour support bra. But we've got to be fair. Mr. Merryweather said it wasn't done till Ernestine was out of the house. Rebelling against authority is what it's called."

"Whose authority in this case?"

"Ernestine's. From the sound of it she was rather a strict child—on at them every minute about one thing or another. That sort of thing can wear you down in a hurry. My George tried it with me a few times, saying I should dress more me age and cut back on bingo and me occasional gin and tonics. Well, as you can imagine, Mrs. H., I soon told him what he could do with his advice. And it wasn't to stuff it up his jumper. But likely the Merryweathers don't have my backbone."

"It's very sad to think of parents not having any contact with a daughter in twenty years." I kept on walking and Mrs. Malloy came teetering alongside me. Her sideways glance at my face was shrewd.

"You can stop that this minute Mrs. H.!"

"What?"

"Fretting about little Rose. What went on between Ernestine and her Mum and Dad had nothing to do with her being adopted. Children is children however they get here."

"We can't assume that Ernestine wasn't affected. And you know how it is," I said, quickening my pace, "whenever there are problems with an adopted child. People tend to throw up their hands and say what can you expect!"

"What people? Probably the ones who'd like to come up with an excuse for why their own kids is all messed up."

"Possibly." After the damp chill of the outdoors the hospital hallways felt unbearably stuffy. A few moments later I decided Mrs. Malloy had reached the point of hallucinating. Flinging out an arm she queried in a faltering voice, "Is that a wheel-chair I see before me, the handles toward my hand?"

"Not that I can see. But if you want to get in I'll push you."

She heaved an irritated sigh. "I was just trying to lighten things up, taking the mickey out of Shakespeare. Didn't take me for the highbrow sort, did you, Mrs. H.? Always a big mistake that is, making assumptions." Her voice mellowed. "It's why we're both feeling so low at this minute. We showed up at the Merryweathers's door thinking they'd tell us what Ernestine is up to these days and how to get in touch with her. Never a thought that we'd come up short."

"We should have been more realistic." We came to a water-cooler, but I decided it had to be a mirage. "If it were that easy everyone would be private detectives, which wouldn't be good for the likes of Milk Jugg."

"We wouldn't want that." Mrs. Malloy didn't sound as sure as I would have expected. "But I've got to thinking as how there's something to be said for being new at this work. Not going by the book like Milk would do."

"How does our muddling along from one moment to the next work in our favor?"

"Muddling isn't the word I'd choose. I'd call it taking a fresh approach." Mrs. M. flung a vexed look my way. "If Milk was on the job, talking to the Merryweathers and such—like we've gone and done—I can't see him stuffing his face with scones while they rambled on about this, that and the other, or sitting watching that Mrs. Joritz knitting. Being a busy man with other cases on the books he'd have had to speed things up, take control of the interview. It's the way he'll have been taught. But you and me, we haven't been to private detective school. So, for the most part, we've just let people chat. And maybe that'll end up being more help than them just answering questions."

"Because it's the little things—the seemingly unimportant

snippets—that help build up the picture, or suddenly turn it around. Yes, I know exactly what you mean, Mrs. Malloy. It happened to me this morning. Only it wasn't the Merryweathers; it was something you said." I broke off because we found ourselves standing in front of a lift. Its doors opened. People—mostly hospital staff—got out. We stepped into the empty space, and I pressed the button to Lady Krumley's floor.

"So what does that make me? The dim-witted sidekick that can't figure out how he's helped, while the detective just stands there combing his moustache and looking clever?" Mrs. Malloy stuck her nose up so high it almost knocked off her hat.

"Of course not, but this isn't the best time to get into it. Anyway, it's only a thought to be picked over when we're not in the middle of something else, such as deciding what we are going to say to her ladyship."

"I thought we'd been over that." Mrs. Malloy sounded only slightly mollified. "We'll keep it simple. Tell her we've located Ernestine's adoptive parents and that we believe Vincent Krumley was murdered."

"And not by some phantom figure. I'm still not sure what's best to be done about Cynthia Edmonds. What are the odds of her owning up to the blackmail if Lady Krumley were to warn her to be careful, or she'll end up the next victim?"

"Slim to none, I'd say."

"We have to persuade the police to cooperate."

"No harm in being optimistic, Mrs. H.!"

The lift doors opened, and we emerged within a few yards of the nurses' station. It was presently a hive of activity. Personnel came and went, some holding clipboards, some scribbling down notes and the majority with stethoscopes dangling around their necks. It was a couple of minutes before Mrs. Malloy and I were able to get the attention of a nurse. She was a motherly-looking woman and managed to seem as though she welcomed another interruption. But when we asked to see

Lady Krumley, her expression altered dramatically. We were about to be given some very bad news.

"I'm sorry, she's gone."

"You mean she's been discharged?" I croaked.

"I'm afraid not."

"Was it very sudden like?" Mrs. Malloy grabbed hold of my arm, which no doubt gave her some support but forced me almost to my knees.

"Very. A nurse was in the room when Lady Krumley received a phone call. So she left. And when she went back in just five minutes later, her ladyship had done a bunk."

"Well, I don't think that's a very nice way of putting it," said Mrs. Malloy. "Couldn't you say had been called above?"

"I suppose I could, if she'd died." The nurse's face now expressed bewilderment. "But that's not what we're talking about here. Oh, I'm sorry." Light belatedly dawned. "Lady Krumley didn't take an unexpected turn for the worse. The doctors were very pleased. The tests showed she hadn't suffered a heart attack. They believe the problem—her fainting or passing out in the car the other night—was stress-induced. She was to be released tomorrow. So why she'd just walk out of here like that is a complete puzzle, unless it could have had something to do with that phone call."

"That must have been it." I was speaking more to Mrs. Malloy.

"I shouldn't have discussed this with you." The nurse's kindly face turned anxious. "You haven't told me what your relationship is to Lady Krumley, and we're only allowed to discuss a patient with close family members."

"That's us," Mrs. M. assured her.

"Oh, what a relief!" The woman was more than ready to accept this as fact. "We try not to let our emotions get in the way of our work. But I've got an elderly grandmother myself, and I'd be worried sick if she pulled a stunt like this. Her ladyship's nephew who lives with her was contacted as soon as we realized she was gone. He promised to get in touch the minute she showed up. Which of course she's bound to do."

"We'll go to Moultty Towers at once," I said and joined Mrs. Malloy in thanking her and promising not to breathe a word to anyone about having been told what had happened. We eased away, got into the lift that luckily was waiting and, on stepping out onto the ground floor where we had spent so much time getting lost, found ourselves facing the exit door. The car wasn't hiding in the parking lot. We walked straight to it and were speedily upon our way heading out of Mucklesby in the direction of Biddlington-By-Water.

"I'll bet you my share of the five thousand pounds her ladyship promised us, Lady Krumley got bad news about Cynthia Edmonds." Mrs. Malloy opened the bag of lemon drops and for once offered me one. "She'll have met with a fatal accident or been fed bad mushrooms. And we could say it serves her right, but that wouldn't be Christian and is probably against the ethics of our profession."

"You admitted just a short while ago that we're amateurs."

"The word never crossed me lips. I said we was just starting out, and wasn't yet bogged down by a lot of rules and regulations." Mrs. Malloy closed her mouth on another lemon drop, and we drove in silence until reaching the outskirts of Biddlington-By-Water. "I've been thinking," she informed me as we approached the village.

"Yes?"

"You're not the only one that can do it. Or keep their little inspirations to themselves till they're ready to talk about them. What I want you to do, Mrs. H., is stop the car. Outside the café where we met Laureen Phillips will do nicely. We're coming up to it now."

"What's this about?" I asked upon dutifully parking.

"We can't let things drag on any longer. Not with the bodies beginning to pile up. It's clear to me that our best hope of cracking this case is to talk to Constable Thatcher's son, young Ronald. I'm not saying you haven't been thinking along them lines too," she said and poked her head sideways to peer in the rearview mirror, "but the question has been how to go about it."

"And what have you come up with?"

"I'm going to be the truant officer."

"But you don't know he's ever been improperly absent from school."

"Well, I don't think it likely he got back on time from his dinner hour after throwing them flower pots at Lady Krumley's car and all the rest of what went on. I'll find out where he lives and march over to his house and insist on talking to him. He was off school yesterday and with luck he'll have stayed home another day. And I'll want to know why, won't I? If not I'll have to slide one by the headmaster or whoever I talk to and have Ronald pulled out of class."

"But he won't even talk to his parents."

"That's different. I'll be official. But I won't be his constable Dad, or his Mum, who sounds the soft sort, going out to buy him them comics after him being so naughty, on the face of it that is. I'll make it clear to young Ronald that he can't have anyone better on his side than yours truly, so long as he don't keep me twiddling me thumbs while he tries to feed me some cock-and-bull story. My George knew how far he could play me; I'm sure it'll be just the same with Ronald. And it will end up with him sitting on me knees feeling a whole lot better for getting things off his little chest."

Her confidence boosted my spirits. Having arranged that she would walk over to Moultty Towers when she was done, I waved and after seeing Mrs. Malloy disappear into the café to ask directions to the Thatcher's house, drove the short distance through gathering gloom. It made the day seem closer to evening than early afternoon and gave the house a grimmer aspect than on yesterday's visit as I proceeded up the drive. Upon ringing the doorbell, my feelings of trepidation returned full force. Cynthia Edmonds might not have been a nice person, but I shrank from hearing that something awful had happened to her.

I hadn't completely gathered myself together when I was ushered into the house, not by Watkins the butler, but by Mr. Featherstone the vicar. He recalled in the kindest of voices having met me at the hospital and simplified the situation by saying that he was aware, from having talked with Laureen Phillips, that I had been hired by Lady Krumley as a private detective, not as an interior designer, and he had told her ladyship a short time ago while driving her home from the hospital that he was privy to the secret."

"Your partner is not with you this afternoon?"

"She'll be here shortly. But tell me about her ladyship?"

"I think under different circumstances she would have enjoyed making her escape." His distinguished face creased into a smile. "Maude has always been a woman of remarkable spirit. She telephoned me from a kiosk near the hospital, and asked me to come and fetch her. It was unfortunate that when Niles rang her, he made Cynthia's condition seem worse than it was, an understandable reaction on the part of a husband. But I do feel he leans too heavily at the best of times upon his aunt for emotional support. However well she has come through this episode, she has had a couple of heart attacks."

"I've been fearing the worst," I said. "That Cynthia was dead."

"Neither has she suffered any severe injury. You had anticipated she would be the next victim?" There was no one visible in the hall or on the stairs, but Mr. Featherstone beckoned me into a small room fitted out like a parlour. "This is better. It wouldn't do to risk being overheard." He looked and sounded profoundly concerned. "For quite a time now, I have felt something in this house—the presence of a disturbed personality. Call it evil if you will. This could come from my subconscience, triggered by some half-formed recognition. I've tried to puzzle it out, with no success, Mrs. Haskell. Do I have your name correctly?"

"Yes, Mr. Featherstone. Please tell me what happened to Cynthia Edmonds."

"She was out riding several miles from here at around noon, when her horse bolted onto a main road—something it has never previously done. Cynthia is an excellent rider of many years' experience, but even that might not have saved her. It is a heavily trafficked road, but God was with her. One could call it a miracle. It happened when there wasn't a vehicle in sight."

"Does she routinely ride in that area, at the same time of day?"

"I believe so. Maude describes Cynthia as a creature of habit. She keeps a detailed calendar and rarely varies from it. An exacting woman in many respects. I say this," Mr. Featherstone met my eyes squarely, "because for you to accomplish what you have come here to do, it is imperative that you have an insight into the personalities of all those involved."

"Yes," I said. Exacting was very likely an excellent description of Cynthia Edmonds. It meshed with the fuss about her hairdresser making her the wrong shade of blonde. And when taken further it could provide the sort of ruthlessness necessary for blackmail. "How badly was she hurt?"

"A few bruises and a scraped elbow. The worst injury appears to have been to her pride in falling off her horse."

"You don't think she will take it out on the animal?"

"No." Mr. Featherstone smiled. It was a gentle and serene smile. "Cynthia loves that horse. It brings out what is best in her. We all have something that does that for us. A redeeming force. And sometimes in the end it is enough to turn back the darkness."

I was tempted to say it was a pity Cynthia ever had to get off the horse. Instead I asked if I was right in assuming that Mr. Featherstone didn't believe her to be the source of what was going on at Moultty Towers. He replied that he did not, and then brought up the subject of Laureen Phillips and his nephew.

"Laureen told me she had confessed to you and your partner about the stunt they hatched up between them. I very much regret and disapprove of Tom scaring you by showing up with that gun."

"We should have realized it wasn't real."

"That doesn't lessen the seriousness of his shocking behavior."

"There was no harm done, in fact quite the reverse. It convinced Mrs. Malloy and me that there might be something in Lady Krumley's story that needed investigating."

"You're very kind, and there is another bright side." Mr. Featherstone's eyes twinkled. "His performance convinced my nephew that acting wasn't the career for him, and he has decided to go into the church. Laureen also seems to have discovered her true calling. She has found so much pleasure spending time with Mrs. Hasty and other elderly people in the village that she has decided to make working with them her chosen path."

"That's wonderful!" I really meant it and could not resist asking: "Any hope of wedding bells?"

"An engagement is imminent."

What a special man he was, so freely rejoicing in the romantic happiness of others when his own hopes for a life with Lady Krumley had not been realized. But surely it wasn't too late even at this stage in their lives. Maybe, once she was able to put all this business of Flossie Jones and Ernestine behind her, she'd come to the realization that the years she had left could be filled with renewed happiness. I thought of my grandmother who had recently and blissfully married the love of her life and I made a wish for Lady Krumley and Mr. Featherstone. I completely forgot that I'd harbored suspicions of her motives for searching out Ernestine, and they didn't reoccur when I asked Mr. Featherstone if it was possible for me to see her ladyship.

"Or is she in bed?"

"She wouldn't hear of it and threatened another health episode if anyone brought pressure to bear. You'll find her in the drawing room with Sir Alfonse. Niles and Cynthia are upstairs in their rooms, but I believe Daisy Meeks is with them. No one in the family had met her prior to a few years ago, when she came on a visit to Moultty Towers and shortly afterward bought a house in the village." Mr. Featherstone then led me across the hall and walked with me into the drawing room. As on the previous day my appalled gaze fixed on the array of game heads on the walls. All those furry faces with their antlers and reproachful glass eyes! They reduced everything else—including the people in the room—to a backdrop for a powerfully visual appeal for animal rights. I jumped when a voice spoke from a chair near the fireplace.

"Admiring the family portraits?" A man got to his feet. He was of a portly build and of medium height with a head of glossy black curls and a luxuriant moustache. His accent was faintly continental and his attire—a beige linen suit and a yellow and navy blue bow tie—also suggested that he wasn't English or liked to project the image of a widely traveled man of the world. So this was Sir Alfonse Krumley, inheritor of the title, but not the heir to Moultty Towers.

With his emergence the rest of the room sprang to life. My eyes went to Lady Krumley who beckoned me forward with an imperative hand. Seated beside her on the sofa was Daisy Meeks. Her badly permed hair gave her every right to complain to her hairdresser, but her frumpish frock suggested she had little interest in her appearance. I stood in a whirl of introductions made by her ladyship in a voice charged with vigor and found myself seated in the chair vacated by Sir Alfonse, who remained standing. Mr. Featherstone left us, saying he needed to return to the vicarage and when the door closed behind him the room sank into a silence that had a muffled sort of quality to it. A small fire burned in the very large grate and it wasn't until a log broke apart with a sharp crack that animation returned with Lady Krumley addressing me in her deep voice, while her black eyes snapped glances at Sir Alfonse and Daisy Meeks.

"So, Mrs. Haskell, how are you proceeding with the plans for the decorating?"

"We've come up with some ideas, but this may not be the best time to talk about it with you so upset about your relative's death." Would this clue her in that I would return at a more convenient time?

"Alas, poor Vincent! He came to Moultty Towers to meet his fate." Her ladyship now looked at Sir Alfonse, who was to be congratulated on looking suavely anguished.

"I was fond of the old roue." The foreign accent deepened, the moustache quivered and the rather protuberant dark eyes moistened to a shining gloss. "Many's the night we sat in a Parisian nightclub, discoursing on the most eclectic of subjects—Russian art, the advent of Esperanto, the proper making of porridge. A man of many parts was Vincent. Do we remember him as a drunkard, a gambler or do we recall only what was in him sublime? His devotion to that little dog?"

As if summoned to contribute to this eulogy, Pipsie, if I remembered the name rightly, appeared out of nowhere to leap at a linen trouser leg and begin devouring what I guessed, from the forthcoming reaction, to be a cherished cuff. Far from smiling fondly down at Vincent Krumley's dog, Sir Alfonse attempted to shake it off with a vengeance, and I thought I caught words, "revolting animal." Meanwhile Daisy Meeks had entered the conversation in a small flat voice that strained the ears of her listeners.

"What's comforting is that we were all together when Vincent passed away."

"We weren't all with him," Lady Krumley contradicted. "And he didn't pass away. He went down a well."

"What I meant to say," Daisy continued, shuffling her feet away from Pipsie who was trying to burrow under the sofa, "is we were all with him the night before he left this earth."

"He hasn't left it." Lady Krumley was growing more provoked, which explained perhaps why she hadn't thought to ask me to return at a more convenient time or suggested that the other two leave us to talk. "He's still on a slab in the morgue. That's what we've been sitting here talking about: how to get him buried."

"Before he get's too well settled in and refuses to move." This quip from Sir Alfonse was in line with his initial remark to me about the family portraits. Clearly the man prized his sense of humor as much as his trousers. I was sure that there were women somewhere who would appreciate his well-practiced charm.

"We must decide on the hymns for the funeral," barked Lady Krumley.

"It's some consolation to remember how much he enjoyed the stew Mrs. Beetle made for dinner that night." Daisy turned to me. "Do you make stew?"

"Yes."

"The coffin must be selected," her ladyship addressed Sir Alfonse.

"May I lift that burden from you, Aunt Maude? I believe I know just what Vincent would like."

"That's all very well but I don't think we can put him in a brandy cask." Lady Krumley's hooded eyelids were beginning to droop.

"I always put turnips in my stew."

"If you would also be so good, Alfonse, as to arrange for the flowers."

"And a couple of bay leaves."

"The service is set for noon, followed by internment in the family plot." Her ladyship's voice had grown gravelly with fatigue.

"We must make it an occasion. It's what Vincent would have wanted." Sir Alfonse turned away to hide his emotion.

"And a little garlic powder."

Not having known Vincent Krumley I didn't have a clue what he would have wanted for his funeral, but I was beginning to wonder if he really had been the doddering old duffer her ladyship had described to Mrs. Malloy and me at the hospital. She had talked about his being muddled in his perceptions. But had he been wrong about Cynthia having been a go-go dancer? And had he said Daisy Meeks had a twin as reported by her ladyship, or that he hoped she didn't have a twin? Words get altered in the recounting. Or elaborated upon.

At the moment when I realized Lady Krumley was soundly asleep Watkins entered the room to inform me that Mrs. Malloy was waiting for me in the hall. After making my farewells to Sir Alfonse and Daisy Meeks, I joined her and made all speed out to the car.

"Well," I asked as we drove off down the drive, "did you talk to Ronald Thatcher?"

"Didn't I say I would?" She was looking unbearably smug.

"And?"

"And what?"

"Were you able to get anything useful out of him?"

"Enough to make we wonder if we haven't found our murderer. But I wouldn't want to start discussing it today, Mrs. H., if you're not in the mood." She proceeded to make a production out of going into her bag and taking out a lemon drop. Of course I was consumed with curiosity, but when she added insult to injury I responded in my own mean-spirited way.

"I don't suppose Ronald gave you Ernestine's address?" I deserved to be punished for that, but God is remarkably forgiving. When I got home Ben came out of the study to provide me with a vital piece of information that he'd found on the internet while playing, as he cheerfully told me, on his wonderful new computer.

"That's nice, dear." I did my wifely best to sound excited.

"I looked to see if the Waysiders had a Web page or whatever it's called, Ellie. And low and behold I came upon the name Ernestine Merryweather. She runs the place. She's the woman who may have frightened Aunt Lulu into going straight rather than be returned to reform school. Of course," he put his arm around me, "She may not be your Ernestine."

"She'd jolly well better be," I said, "or I'll set Pipsie the Maltese terrier on her. That little dog is itching to make someone pay for Vincent Krumley's death. And I would just as soon it wasn't me or Mrs. Malloy."

Twenty-one

I t was the following evening and Mrs. Malloy and I were having a last cup of tea before what we hoped would be the final scene in the melodrama being enacted at Moultty Towers. We were in her tiny kitchen, with its bead curtain screening the washing machine from view. The dangling fringe on the tablecloth and the red shaded lamp always reminded me of a fortuneteller's parlor. Usually I didn't mind the absence of a crystal ball, but at this moment it would have been helpful. We had spent the day getting everything set up and had been fortunate in the cooperation we had received from those we had assigned as stage managers. Mrs. Malloy and I had divided up the workload and were fairly well satisfied that we had everything covered. All-important had been Lady Krumley's eventual willingness to accept our hypothesis, for that's all it was up to this point. The information given to Mrs. Malloy by young Ronald Thatcher had convinced us as to the who, and last night had been spent putting together all those bits and pieces that seemed to provide us with the why. This was still a far cry from hard evidence, leaving us dependent on squeezing out a confession. That's where the difficulty had been with her ladyship. It had been necessary to convince her that the dark forces she had talked about so often were clothed in human flesh. Not being confident that Mrs. Malloy or I would be able to bring her over to this way of thinking, I had telephoned Mr.

Featherstone and enlisted his help. He promised, with his old world courtesy, to do his best. Within two hours he rang back to say that Lady Krumley had responded to the effect that there was no point in hiring a pair of private detectives and barking oneself. He wasn't certain that she had given up on Flossie's deathbed curse, but we had her agreement to stage our scene in the drawing room at Moultty Towers at 8:00 that evening.

"Very kind of the reverend to pitch in." Mrs. Malloy stirred her tea. She looked very much the fortuneteller in her black taffeta dress with the jet beading. The silk turban perched on her blonde curls heightened the impression. "But then he, being a man in love, was ready and eager to help. It was different with Constable Thatcher. I had to exercise all the force of me personality to bring him into line. But after I mentioned what a shame it would be if Lady Krumley pressed charges against his Ronald and the other boy for throwing them flower pots, he came round very nicely. Course, Mrs. H., I'm not saying I had him a hundred percent convinced his son had spotted a murderer laying the groundwork, so to speak. But my guess is there's now this question mark in his mind. Would be nice if it'd light up and flash and go Bing! Bing! every so often, but medical science hasn't progressed that far. They're too busy cloning sheep and other such silliness."

"You gave Constable Thatcher his instructions?"

"Told him and then wrote them down, so's there'll be no mistakes. He's to position himself outside the drawing room after everyone troops in. And right before we gets started the vicar will sidle over to the door and open it a crack, like to see if there's anyone outside, and then not close it properly, so Constable Thatcher can hear what's going on and write things down in his little book if he fancies. Men!" She smiled indulgently. "They do like to make themselves feel important. Well, if it keeps them happy, why not? There was you all stirred up thinking Mr. H. would leave you after your redecorating and updating. Now he's like a kiddie with a new toy. Can't tear himself away from his computer now."

I was rubbing at a drop of tea that had landed on my sage green sweater. "I know, we were completely at cross purposes. I thought he was still angry with me for getting rid of his old typewriter. Instead he was feeling guilty about having made such a fuss because within minutes of turning on the computer he was hooked and feeling even guiltier about all the time he was spending on it. He told me he loves the study the way it's redecorated; it gives him more room, and more storage. It's as though he finally has his very own space instead of being shut up in the cupboard under the stairs."

"Surprises me you didn't give his head the back side of a frying pan." Mrs. Malloy eyed the cookoo clock that wasn't known of its truthfulness. She must have decided it was fast this time rather than slow, because she not only settled back into her chair but also poured herself another cup of tea.

"Who could have guessed that my shipping those items off to Kathleen Ambleforth's charity drive would have this much impact?" I had succeeded in making the tea spot worse. "But for my row with Ben I wouldn't have turned out that night to meet you at Jugg's."

"Thanks ever so!"

"I wouldn't have been so depressed that I smoked and got sick drinking that whisky, which was why I got talked into working with you on this case. And if I hadn't been so desperate to get the items back I wouldn't have pestered Kathleen for the name of the organization where they had been sent. She wouldn't have finally told me it was The Waysiders, right before Aunt Lulu showed up with her horror stories about her stay there, making for such a coincidence that my harping on about it got the name stuck in Ben's head. So that's when he was next at the computer . . ."

"And don't let's forget me finding that address card in Vincent Krumley's wallet that lets us know he was also familiar with The Waysiders." Mrs. Malloy yawned behind a heavily ringed hand. "So don't go letting Mr. H. get too chuffed, or he'll be expecting a cut of that five thousand pounds. And you know what that'll mean. He'll be buying himself a laptop, so he can take it to bed with him and there goes your marriage. I tell you what," Mrs. Malloy said, adding a drop more tea to my cup, "I'll send Mr. H. a nice thank you card, and you can do likewise for the Reverend Featherstone who's been more than good handling things with Lady Krumley and Ernestine too. A busy day for a man of his age having to go here, there and the other. If her ladyship don't appreciate him after this she never will. And either you can get a divorce and marry him or I'll do it. Come to think of it that might be a little more special than a card." Mrs. Malloy made a production of getting to her feet and again looking at the clock. "You did say you talked to Laureen?"

"Yes, just as we discussed."

"Never a dull moment in this business." Her face sobered. "It'll be a bit of a letdown when it's over."

"Let's hope we're around to enjoy it."

"What's that supposed to mean?"

"We can't be absolutely sure that things won't get out of hand. Constable Thatcher could doze off clutching the doorknob. And our murderer may not take kindly to be brought out into the open. Naturally I didn't plant that little seed in Ben's mind. I assured him that you and I were safe as houses."

"How many policemen did you tell him there was going to be on hand?"

"A few."

Mrs. M. was flapping powder onto her nose with a large puff. "I'm shocked, that's what I am! Telling lies to your very own husband."

"Only a white . . . well, maybe a gray one. For all I know Constable Thatcher could be a very large man, the size of at least three regular-sized ones."

"He's nothing of the sort, he's built just nice. Quite a pleasant jolly sort of chap for all we've heard of him being so strict with young Ronald. He asked me if I'd ever thought of going into the police force. There was quite a meaningful look in his eyes when he said it."

"He wasn't suggesting that with you being such a whiz at solving murders you should be well up the chain of command by now?" Mrs. Malloy did not dignify this with a response. I followed her into the hall where we got into our coats, picked up our handbags and went out the door into the mildest evening we'd had in weeks.

The drive to Biddlington-By-Water seemed shorter because it was now so familiar. We didn't talk for several miles or rather I should say neither of us said a word out loud. I was reciting my lines for the upcoming production inside my head. And Mrs. Malloy, from the way she was moving her lips and her frequent frowns, appeared to be doing the same thing. But after a while I reverted to thinking about the problems ahead. It was all very well for Mrs. Malloy and me to be conducting dress rehearsals whenever we could spare time during the day. It was hardly surprising that each of the players did and said exactly as wished when we were playing all the parts. The reality was unlikely to go as smoothly. And in the end would it all be for naught? Mrs. Malloy's thoughts were flowing right along with mine.

"Here's me fretting that it won't be a legal confession, no matter how many people hear the bugger say it. Not with all this silly business of the courts insisting that criminals be read their rights first or it all goes out the ruddy window. But what if we don't get nowhere at all? What if there's no voice piping in with, 'It was me! I know it's not right to go around scaring old ladies out of their wits and murdering people, but a little dickie bird told me to do it'?"

"We'll still have accomplished something, Mrs. Malloy. The scheme will have been exposed. That should put a damper on things and provide the Krumley family with some security. An admittance would be nice because then we'd know with certainty that we were right and so would the others. But we're just going to have to take what we can get."

"I suppose you're right."

"We're together in this." I turned and smiled at her, and she snuffled into a hanky.

"I guess I've just got a touch of stage fright. Me knees is knocking. It was the same way when I was in that play at the church hall."

"On that occasion you made the mistake of trying to bolster up your courage with a stiff bottle of gin. This time you stuck to tea."

We had now reached Biddlington-By-Water, which looked charmingly Dickensian in the glow of its streetlights and utterly incapable of harboring a jaywalker let alone a murderer in its midst. But soon Moultty Towers, looming before us and in the dark stillness of an almost moonless night, gave off the aura of a place where one might likely spot a discreetly placed sign indicating that "Doctor Crippen Slept Here." After parking under a skeletal tree, I gripped Mrs. Malloy's arm, half hoping in cowardly fashion that one of us would slip, spraining an ankle that would demand immediate medical attention. But there was to be no escaping the business at hand.

We were admitted to the house by Watkins, who removed our coats before leading us in his stately way into the drawing room, where we found Lady Krumley enthroned on a high-backed chair in the midst of her family members. The mantelpiece clock gave eight tinkling chimes as Sir Ambrose Krumley and Niles Edmonds rose to acknowledge our entry. There was some murmuring and an inclining of heads, but it was rather like birds fluttering and twittering overhead, something that required a minimal input and response. Cynthia sat, looking glamorous, ill-tempered and with no visible signs of her riding accident, several chairs away from her husband who appeared transfixed. His spectacles somehow seemed more real than the rest of him. Sir Alfonse wore a pale blue suit this evening and a pink and lavender bow tie. They dramatized the appeal—if one were inclined to be enamored to that type of man, which he clearly was—of his portly figure, glossy black curls and swirling moustache. Daisy Meeks, dumpy and dowdy, was the only one whose voice carried above the rest.

"The egg custard we had for a sweet was very tasty. Mrs. Beetle called it a crème caramel. I always put a little lemon rind in mine." No one paid her any attention, perhaps because at that moment Mr. Featherstone walked into the room.

"Are we finally all here?" Cynthia Edmonds stirred irritably in her chair. "This whole business strikes me as a joke. First these two women," she said and jabbed a manicured finger in Mrs. Malloy's and my direction, "are interior designers and now we're told they're private detectives, and we're expected to listen in raptures to them telling us that someone in this room is a murderer."

"Not necessarily!" I said. "The gathering is not yet complete."

"Some people don't care for egg custard," said Daisy Meeks more for her own edification than anyone else's.

"Where's the little dog?" demanded her ladyship. "Animals are very sensitive to the dark forces." My heart sank. It would seem Mr. Featherstone had not been successful in bringing her round to the concept of a living-breathing villain. But I felt better when her hooded eyes searched out Mrs. Malloy's face and mine. "I'm talking about the evil that inhabits the hearts and minds of those blighted souls who will do whatever they must to achieve their own ends."

I thought Mrs. Malloy was about to clap, but she restrained herself. The door had again opened and this time it was Laureen Phillips, followed by Mrs. Beetle and Watkins who carried a silver tray loaded with glasses. The gathering was indeed now complete. Far from looking relieved, Cynthia Edmonds glowered in disgust.

"Why are the servants to be present?"

"Mrs. Malloy and Mrs. Haskell made the request and I approved it," Lady Krumley addressed the room at large. "Once Watkins has provided everyone, including himself and the two other members of the staff, a glass of wine, I would appreciate having the proceedings begin. Damn!" Her voice had deepened into a growl. "What I wouldn't give for a cigarette even if it killed me."

Twenty-two

S omewhere beyond the drawing room a floorboard creaked. Here was a moment ripe with disaster should anyone other than Mr. Featherstone open the door to find Constable Thatcher with his ear to the keyhole.

"This is highly nervewracking," Lady Krumley said. "Has to be for all of you. But as I'm at the center of this sorry state of affairs, you'll have to allow me to feel the need for a courage booster. Laureen," she said to her maid, "fetch me one of those nerve pills the doctor sent home with me. The bottle is on the table behind you, or did I put it on the bookcase?"

All was well for the moment. Mr. Featherstone opened the door and peered out into the hall and, as arranged, left it an inch or two ajar when returning to stand by Lady Krumley's chair. Laureen located the pills on the secretary desk and handed one to her ladyship along with a glass of water.

"Well, isn't that nice," Mrs. Malloy said, edging in front of me. "Seems like everyone's finished fussing around and we can get down to business. Me and Mrs. H. here are private detectives sent to investigate the recent carryings on in this house undercover of being interior decorators." A defensive muttering from Mrs. Beetle the cook interrupted her. "Don't get your knickers in a twist, ducks," Mrs. Malloy smiled kindly upon her. "No one's accusing you of pinching the teaspoons or using margarine instead of butter in the cakes."

"Then why am I here? That's what I'd like to know. I didn't understand it when Watkins talked to me this afternoon."

"You're not being picked upon, Tina. He's here and so am I," Laureen pointed out, only to be ignored by Mrs. Beetle.

"All he'd say was something had cropped up and I was wanted to stay over past my usual time."

"Those were her ladyship's instructions, and it was not my place to embellish." Watkins admonished her.

"My husband's not going to be pleased. He's a man that likes dinner at 6:00 on the dot, and it was to be his favorite tonight. A beef ragout. Just like the one that I served the night Mr. Vincent Krumley arrived. From the cookery book," she said, sending a fuming glance my way, "that one said her husband wrote."

"Can't solve a murder without telling a few lies here and there, Tina," murmured Laureen consolingly.

Mrs. Beetle's red face, having ballooned with annoyance, slowly deflated. "Oh, is that what this is about? Something to do with the way Mr. Vincent Krumley died?"

"You've hit the nail on the head, Mrs. Beetle," I said.

"He was murdered out there in the garden, while I was bustling about with the pots and pans?" She groped her way over to a chair and sank into it without so much as a glance at Lady Krumley. "And you want to find out who knows what? Well, I'm sorry, but you're barking up an empty tree in my case. There's nothing I can say that could be the least bit helpful."

"You mustn't think that." Mrs. Malloy reached out a hand to pat her shoulder. "You've already helped enormously."

"When? How?"

"We'll get to that soon," I told her.

"Charmingly, I'm sure!" bespoke Sir Alfonse.

"I'm sure we all hope this doesn't go on much longer." Cynthia Edmonds tapped away a yawn with an elegantly manicured hand. "Or am I the only one being bored out of my mind."

"My dear," her husband said, withdrawing deeper into his chair, "Aunt Maude is understandably upset and if having these two women make their presentation helps ease her mind we must endeavor to be supportive."

A small spiteful laugh. "Really Niles, you can occasionally be quite amusing. You make it sound as if they are here selling Tupperware."

"Are they?" Daisy Meeks clasped her hands together, and her dull drown gaze brightened. "I've lost the lid to my salad bowl."

"All hearts are breaking." Sir Alfonse stood twirling his wineglass.

"Or maybe it's called a lettuce shaker? Anyway, is it possible for me to get a replacement?"

"I wouldn't know," Mrs. Malloy replied stonily.

"Proceed." Lady Krumley waved a hand in our direction.

"Oh, but surely Aunt Maude," Cynthia Edmonds said, now looking quite vicious, "we should ask the vicar to say grace . . . or something of the sort first."

"I have already prayed to our God of truth, justice and mercy." Mr. Featherstone inclined his silvery head obscuring his expression, but I could read his annoyance in the stiffness of his posture. He wanted this to be over for her ladyship's sake, and I sensed, for the guilty person in our midst. The vicar was not a man who would gain any satisfaction from twanging away at anyone's nerves. I didn't like it either. But I hadn't stemmed the series of interruptions, my hope being that a rising panic on a certain person's part would make a blurted out confession more likely. Mrs. Malloy and I had discussed our strategy beforehand, but there came the point where we had to get down to business.

"Lady Krumley met with me and my partner here on the day Mr. Vincent Krumley kicked the bucket." Mrs. Malloy stood tapping her fingers on a folded arm. "She wanted to hire us to find Ernestine, as Flossie Jones's baby was called before it was given up for adoption. What had brought her to this decision was all the deaths there had recently been in the family. They was all elderly, but it's got to be said some of them did pop off in odd sort of ways—getting mauled by kangaroos, dying in bungee jumping accidents and the like. Not the sorts of ways you'd expect from folk tottering around on sticks and putting their dentures in to soak at night. That's what got her ladyship to thinking about how Flossie Jones had put a deathbed curse on the family."

"And you are so stupid as to believe in such things?" Cynthia Edmonds uncoiled like a snake in her chair.

"What we believed," I said before Mrs. Malloy could open her mouth, "was that someone had taken pains to frighten her ladyship into suspending disbelief by making sure that the brooch that Flossie had been accused of stealing would be found after nearly forty years. Lady Krumley assumed, as was intended, that it had been there all the time behind the skirting board in her bedroom. Her reaction could not have been better. She was consumed with remorse, convinced that she had leaped at the opportunity to believe Flossie guilty because of her relationship with Sir Horace, a relationship that her ladyship sorrowfully accepted had resulted in the birth of Ernestine, a child soon bereft of a mother and denied the financial and emotional support of its father."

"It is true." Lady Krumley sipped at her glass of water as though it was poisoned. "I forbade my husband to see Flossie or the child, threatening to divorce him and take my money with me if there was any contact, leaving him without the means to keep Moultty Towers going."

Her Ladyship bleakly surveyed the assembled group. Sir Alfonse continued to exude his man-of-the-world appeal. Niles Edmonds fidgeted in his chair. His wife, Cynthia, leaned back against the spreading waves of her blonde hair. Mr. Featherstone appeared deep in thought. The staff—Watkins, Laureen and Mrs. Beetle—shifted into a cluster. The animal heads on the wall monitored every stir of motion. And Daisy Meeks observed that it was a green Tupperware bowl, but she believed the missing lid had been clear.

"A nasty business for all concerned"—I prevented Mrs. M. from again edging in front of me—"one made all the worse by the venomous housekeeper Mrs. Snow. Before she got her tongue lashed around the situation it was thought Ernest the under gardener was the one that got Flossie pregnant. And we do have to ask ourselves why she named the little girl for him?"

"To tick off Horace for not coming through for her." Cynthia shot me a look that let me know just how dim a bulb she thought me. "It's what I would have done."

"I'm sure you would, ducky," said Mrs. Malloy in quite a nice voice. "But there could be another explanation, couldn't there now? Like this Ernest really being the Dad, and Flossie wanting to let him know it after her play for Sir Horace and a life on easy street didn't pan out. A tricky piece that girl, if you asks me. To my way of thinking she'll have had her reasons, none of them good, for trying to patch things up with Ernest." Mrs. Malloy now swiveled on her high heels toward Mr. Featherstone. "Spit it out, ducks!"

"What?"

"Got something on your mind, haven't you vicar?"

"I do indeed." He clasped his hands and flexed his shoulders as if seeking to ease a burden. "One dislikes to betray a confidence, especially one made by a now-deceased man to his cleric, but I believe I must under the circumstances speak out, as I urged Horace to do on the advent of his marriage to you, my dear Maude." His voice betrayed his consternation as he looked down at her ladyship.

"What is it?" She sat ramrod straight as she returned his gaze.

"Horace told me he was unable to father children, the cause being a severe case of the mumps when he was a boy. I believed I had persuaded him of his obligation to tell you so before the wedding, but it appears he did not do so."

"Never a word." Lady Krumley's eyes shone blacker and glassier than those stuck in the furry faces on the wall. "I imagine he was afraid I would decide against marrying him, and there would go my fortune. I always thought our failure to have children was due to my age being against me. We talked about it, and he allowed me to think . . . and not even to relieve my suspicions regarding little Ernestine was he prepared to tell me truth. One must assume he knew me well enough to believe that whilst I might forgive his infidelity I would never be able to get past such a monumental deceit."

A hush fell heavily upon the room. We might have been participating in two minutes of silence in response to some national tragedy. Mr. Featherstone looked distraught, Cynthia bored, Sir Alfonse suavely pained and the rest, especially the staff with Watkins at the forefront, intensely uncomfortable.

"I'm very fond of that Tupperware bowl." Daisy Meeks's flat voice brought the room back to life. "I've used it for making salad for sixteen years."

"A family heirloom, I'm sure." Mrs. Malloy essayed deep sentimentality. "You'll likely want to leave it to someone near and dear, even though the lid's missing. Wills are highly interesting in our line of work, isn't that so, Mrs. H.?" She responded to my nod with a bright magenta smile. "So it got our attention in a big way when her ladyship here told us as how she wanted to leave the bulk of her fortune to Ernestine. That being the case it wouldn't have been surprising if some interested party had sought Ernestine out for the purpose of making sure she was put out of the picture. But that didn't explain Mr. Vincent Krumley, did it now? So me and Mrs. H. looked at things from the other way round."

"Meaning?" Niles croaked out the question.

"That a certain person," I responded, "was determined to make sure that no one, including Mr. Krumley, would put a spanner in the works of Ernestine receiving what was due her, in the light of past wrongs."

"Such as?" Cynthia elevated a perfectly arched eyebrow. "Considering she wasn't Sir Horace's child."

"If I may be pardoned for speaking out." Watkins cleared his throat in a deferential manner. "There is still the matter of the brooch, isn't there?"

"And a terrible thing that was." Mrs. Beetle had clearly decided there was no point in her continuing to just stand there like a lamp. "I don't know that I'd ever get over it if I was falsely accused of stealing from my employers. The very idea of me working for such people," she said, fixing a stare at Lady Krumley, "would send my husband up the wall. "

Laureen remained silent, every glossy chestnut hair in place.

"Let's assume Flossie wasn't falsely accused," I said. "That she did steal the brooch, but didn't take it with her when she was ordered off the premises, had no chance to retrieve it from where she had hidden it and knew that both her person and her possessions would be searched. Then comes the question, who would she ask to bring it to her?" I took my time looking from one face to the next. "Not Sir Horace. And not her friend Mrs. Hasty, who seems a decent and honest woman."

"No one's saying otherwise," said Mrs. Beetle, "but what I'd like to know is why she hasn't been dragged in here along with the rest of us."

"She's old as well as being the one to suffer the shock of finding Mr. Vincent Krumley's body," retorted Laureen. "What you didn't give Mrs. Haskell time to explain is why it's clear Mrs.

Hasty didn't help Flossie out by getting the brooch to her. Had she done so the girl wouldn't have been living in a bed-sitter without a bean to her name. She would have sold the brooch and been living off the proceeds."

"That may be." Mrs. Beetle's face was again ballooning up. "And it's true she's not staff anymore, but she lives on the grounds and was around when all this stuff was going on, which is more than you can say of me and Watkins, or yourself for that matter."

"Now, I've got to say," Mrs. Malloy flashed one of her infuriating smirks, "you do seem to be taking a bit too much for granted, Mrs. Beetle. It's true enough that you and Laureen wouldn't have been here, unless it was as toddlers, but the same can't be said for Watkins, now can it?"

The butler looked severely puzzled. "Did her ladyship not advise you that I have only been in her employ for the past five years?"

"Most certainly I did." Lady Krumley was sipping her glass of water.

"As Watkins, yes," I said, "but as Ernest . . . that would be an entirely different matter."

"Look, it's like this." Mrs. M. took the bit between her teeth. "I got the feeling I'd seen you somewhere before when you let us into the house that first morning. It took a while coming back to me, but then I realized I'd talked to you at bingo one night a few years back in Biddlington-By-Water, and you told me you had a daughter that wouldn't approve if she knew you was gambling. That's the effect I have on men," she said, fluttering her eyelashes, "always tell me more than they mean to, poor saps."

"A daughter?" Niles poked his head out from his chair. "You mean Ernestine?"

"Well, it did seem to fit when me and Mrs. H. here talked to the couple that adopted her. Grew up in to a bit of a prude, she did, a backlash against what she'd heard about her mother perhaps. But who's to know really?"

"I do not have a daughter." Watkins retained his calm.

"Only when you slip up and mention her to a stranger," Mrs. Malloy chortled. "And you don't have much hair left, do you? Came in handy when you decided to return to Moultty Towers and didn't want to be recognized. Mrs. Hasty said Ernest had a lovely head of auburn hair—'his most striking feature' I think was the way she put it. Funny, the little things that can give you away. You was standing under a light in the hall when Mrs. H. noticed you'd got an orange tinge to your eyebrows. Made her wonder if you'd once been a redhead. And then when you was taking us upstairs to the attics you mentioned a couple of items—a library table and a secretary desk—as we might find up there."

"And why was that relevant, madam?"

"Because when we was sitting with Mrs. Hasty in her cottage we made out we was looking for just them pieces. Perhaps to be overheard by whoever was creeping about outside the sitting room. It could've been Laureen who was there helping the old lady by straightening up and fixing a meal, but then again it could just as easy have been you, Mr. Watkins."

"I don't think it's Christian picking on him like this." Mrs. Beetle's face grew fierce. "Why, even if he is this Ernest chap, why would he murder a doddering old man like Mr. Vincent Krumley?"

"Your turn." Mrs. M. nudged with her elbow.

"Because Vincent recognized him as Ernest."

"The only one to do so after all this time!" Cynthia sneered.

"They may have met more recently." I was not prepared to elaborate at this point. "And it seems to Mrs. Malloy and myself that it was Mr. Watkins," I added, eyeing his impassive face, "who led Lady Krumley to believe that Vincent was no longer in full possession of his faculties by asserting that he had mistaken him for Hopkins the former butler. The names are not that dissimilar, making this plausible to anyone who had witnessessed or overheard the exchange between the two men upon Vincent Krumley's arrival. But the more my partner and I assessed Vincent's other apparently foolish comments, the stronger became our suspicion that despite a lifetime of heavy drinking and his advanced age he remained surprisingly . . . dangerously sharp."

"Perhaps I should purchase a new bowl rather than try and replace the lid," Daisy Meeks mused, while continuing to sit like a bundle of old clothes.

"Oh, for God's sake, keep quiet!" Cynthia rounded on her. Her apparent boredom was replaced by a jerkiness that could be explained as her nerves spinning out of control. Did she sense what was coming next?

"A pity you didn't have the sense to keep quiet about what you knew," Mrs. Malloy said smugly. "Blackmail's a risky business, as you must have realized when you was thrown from your horse. Of course you'll know better than Mrs. H or me what was done to cause it to rear or whatever it did—some sudden scary noise perhaps, or a dart shot into its poor rump? And all because you wanted to get your greedy hands on some quick cash."

"Niles!" Cynthia now directed her rage at her husband. "Are you going to just sit there and let this ignoramus insult me?"

"I don't know." He trembled from head to foot. "What do you think, Aunt Maude?"

"That I hope you are in no way involved in your wife's doings. It is one thing to have a nephew who may have blown up his parents on purpose—these past few days have perhaps made me cynical—but blackmail is quite another matter. Vulgar is the word that springs to mind. And now let us continue to hear what my private detectives have to say." Upon her ladyship pointing her formidable nose our way, Mrs. Malloy gave me the elbow and said it was my turn to hold forth, possibly indicating she had forgotten what she had been going to say next or that she wished to be at the ready should Watkins make a bolt for the door. Up to this point he had admirably retained his impeccable calm.

"Our first suspicion, Mr. Edmonds, was that you were the object of your wife's blackmail. After all you do manage Lady Krumley's finances. However, when we began to zero in on Watkins we recalled being told—by Mrs. Beetle I think it was—that he did her ladyship's banking along with other errands on a regular basis. Who would question him if he were to sign Mr. Edmonds's name to an extra check, or a number of checks for that matter supposedly for household expenses? Which money he would then turn over to Mrs. Edmonds. And how likely was it that Mr. Edmonds, a man possibly far more interested in his train sets than business, would think twice about the additional withdrawals?"

"If I may be forgiven for intruding myself into the conversation." Watkins might have been announcing that dinner was served. "What do you believe to be the subject of Mrs. Edmonds's attempt to blackmail me?"

"There again we can thank Mrs. Beetle for the answer." I nodded at the bewildered-looking woman. "During our talk in the kitchen the other day, she mentioned that the door to the cellar was kept locked, only to be opened by the key in your jacket pocket, Mr. Watkins. But we saw you hang your usual jacket on a peg, where anyone needing that key could help themselves to it, when you changed into one for cleaning the silver. Mrs. Beetle also told us that in addition to the wine stored in the cellar there was also a supply of apples. And," I continued, glancing at a still highly resentful-looking Cynthia, "that Mrs. Edmonds was in the daily habit of taking apples to her horse, which would on occasion have presented a problem when you were not available to unlock the cellar door for her, Mr. Watkins."

"Indeed so, madam, and what I presume you to be suggesting is that on one recent day Mrs. Edmonds went into my pocket for the key."

"And found the brooch that was soon to turn up behind the skirting board in her ladyship's room."

"Is that what happened, Cynthia?" Niles was nibbling on his nails.

"Why should I deny it?"

"You let dear Aunt Maude believe it had appeared out of thin air as a result of Flossie Jones's deathbed curse?"

"Can I help it if she's a gullible old fool?"

"I say, enough of that!" Sir Alfonse protested.

"Mrs. H. here doesn't think there was any deathbed curse." Mrs. Malloy could not contain her bitterness. "She goes for the idea it was just another of Mr. Watkins's stories, put around way back when he was working here as Ernest, for the purpose of getting even with the Krumley family. All mixed up in your feelings you was," she continued, returning the butler's steady gaze without a twitch of an eyelash. "Leastways that's how Mrs. H. and I sees it. Angry with Sir Horace for having a fling with Flossie, and bitter against her because she'd convinced you the baby wasn't yours. It wasn't till years later, after wasting your life on drink—not that I've got anything against the occasional gin and tonic—that you realized you'd been hoodwinked. That was when you came face to face with Ernestine. It was the same as with me own father—something I mentioned and Mrs. H. picked up on. He didn't believe I was his daughter until he saw with his own eyes that I was the spitting image of him. When that happened to you Mr. Watkins you was driven to coming up with your plan."

"Which was?"

"To take the post advertised for a butler at Moultty Towers

and search for the brooch Flossie had told you she'd hidden in the grounds, is my guess. Maybe you've been looking for it for most of the last five years. Could be she'd hidden it near a tree that's been chopped down, and you couldn't pinpoint the place. Or maybe you felt you had to wait for the moment as would give you the best hope of success. Wouldn't do to bungle things at this stage of the game would it? Lucky you when all them relatives began dropping off the family twig, putting Lady Krumley in just the right frame of mind to think Flossie had finally got round to dishing up the curse. You were very clever in some ways, Mr. Watkins. Those birds were a nice creepy touch. But you made your mistakes, such as not cleaning the brooch properly after digging it up. Perhaps your eyesight's not all that good. We thought you hadn't polished that candle stick, remember, but it must have looked all right to you."

The moment had come for me to play my ace. "Now then, Mrs. Malloy," I chided, "it isn't fair to lay all the blame at Mr. Watkins's door. He might never have embarked on this wicked scheme if not egged on by Ernestine. The naughty girl was not averse to getting her paws on the Krumley fortune the moment her ladyship could be stowed underground, having conveniently succumbed to another heart attack resulting from recent stress."

"Now you sound truly mad!" Watkins's imperturbability had finally slipped.

"And I suppose you'll claim I am lying if I say that Ernestine is here." I took my time looking from one face to another. "Right now, in this very room."

"I would . . . yes, I would and all you wretched women!" His careful diction was gone, replaced by that of a man who had been brought up rough and had never pictured himself swanking around the insides of a house the likes of Moultty Towers.

"Let's consider Mrs. Beetle as Ernestine," I said.

"What me?" Her voice came out in a squeak, far too small

for her size of face. "There's things that fit." Mrs. Malloy was plainly beginning to enjoy herself. "Like you speaking so sympathetic like about Mr. Vincent Krumley's dog, calling it a poor little orphan, which is what someone that had been orphaned herself might well say. And then there was you giving Mrs. H. and me to understand as how you are deeply religious—Roman Catholic I think you said. Now the Merryweathers that adopted Ernestine didn't say nothing about her being partial to any particular faith, but they did let us know she saw sin everywhere she looked, which isn't to say that's not a stage young people go through and you'll have come out of it if you did join up with your father. . . ."

"Watkins is not my father!" Mrs. Beetle gave a bounce that shook the room.

"Well, you don't look much like him, I'll give you that," Mrs. Malloy conceded, albeit begrudgingly. "And one thing I'll say for Roman Catholics is that they do like their bingo, so I can't see why—if you really are one that is—you'd object to your old Dad enjoying an evening of it now and then. Besides, as I can see Mrs. H. is itching to say, there's someone else here as is another likely candidate for being Ernestine, and that is . . ." She took her sweet time before pointing her finger toward Daisy Meeks.

"What? Did I say something?" That lady blinked as if coming out of a trance filled to the brim with Tupperware. "Why is everyone looking at me?"

"We're wondering about your life before you suddenly showed up at Moultty Towers claiming to be a long-lost relative and then bought a house in the village," I said. "It's not always easy to tell a woman's age these days, when one can be confused by makeup, or the lack of it, into adding or subtracting ten or even more years."

"I'm fifty."

"So am I on a bad day," Mrs. Malloy shot back at her. "The

rest of the time it's twenty-nine. And maybe for you it's forty, like if you was Ernestine."

"I'm not following?"

"Or you don't want us to think you are, ducks. Playing like you're muddleheaded so that people lose patience and ignore you, while all the time you're thinking deep inscrutable"—Mrs. M. brought out the word with a flourish—"thoughts."

"I am?" Daisy Meeks looked vaguely pleased.

"Stop it! Put an end to this cat-and-mouse game, Father!" This exclamation came from Laureen as she flung herself toward Watkins. They know from this," she said, wildly tugging at her auburn hair until it tumbled out of its carefully arranged coil to cascade over her shoulders, "that I'm your daughter."

"No." Watkins was losing it fast. He backed away from her as if persued by the devil. "You're not my Ernestine."

"What are you afraid of?" Her voice spiraled into rage. "That I'll reject you as my mother did? Well, let me tell you I've done more than that. I've helped these women—these two private detectives—because someone had to be made to pay for my life as the child of those appalling Merryweathers. And you made it so easy for me to settle on you."

"Liar. You're nothing to me! My Ernestine is sweet and gentle!" Watkins had collided with Mr. Featherstone who clamped hold of his arms from behind. Lady Krumley sat as if turned to stone, while the rest of the group was reduced to a blurred photograph.

"I led these dear women step by step to Constable Thatcher's boy, Ronald." Laureen waved a hand at Mrs. Malloy and me and continued remorselessly. "In picking up bits and pieces from Mrs. Hasty I knew he had seen something that had aroused his suspicions about Vincent Krumley's death. And when this one," she said, poking at Mrs. Malloy's shoulder, "got him to open up, he told her he had seen you dragging Pipsie into the shrubbery and beating on it when it yelped. Ronald is very fond of animals. He's been begging his parents for a dog of his own, and he was charging to the rescue when he and his friend both pitched into a ditch. By the time they managed to scramble out you were nowhere to be seen, Father, and neither was Pipsie. They thought you had killed him, instead of locking him inside the cottage, so that when you offered to help Vincent look for him in the grounds he would start barking and you would follow the sound and suggest looking down the well. That's why Ronald and the other boy threw those flower pots at your car." Laureen whirled around to throw herself at Lady Krumley's feet and clutch at the skirt of her black dress. "They thought Watkins—Father—would be driving. He was the one who most often did so. They never meant to hurt you. And neither did I. Yes, I knew what he was up to, and I played along, giving him enough rope to hang himself. Let him play his little tricks with the brooch! And then I'd expose him. I never thought of murder."

"Oh, come off it!" Cynthia was back in form. "You were in it up to your neck, hoping to get your hands on a fortune."

"It does look that way." Niles appeared to be reviving now that the focus had shifted. "What do you think Aunt Maude?"

"My dear, how are you holding up under this emotional strain?" Mr. Featherstone spoke with deep feeling. But Lady Krumley's response was cut off by Watkins releasing a roar that knocked a couple of moose heads sideways. Staggering out of the vicar's clutches he swung around to pummel his fists in the air.

"You," he said, glaring at Laureen's kneeling back, "you're not worthy to speak my Ernestine's name let alone pretend to be her. She's a good woman. None of her mother's ways about her. It broke my heart the moment I first laid eyes on her after she'd been kept from me all those long years. I made up my mind I'd make it up to her. And it was like a sign when I saw in the paper a few months later that there was a job going here. It didn't bother me none when I had trouble finding the brooch. I knew inside here," Watkins thumped his chest, "that I'd find it when the time was right. And so I did. But I never told my Ernestine nothing. Not even that I was her father. To her I'm still just another of the men who've found their way to the organization she set up to help people with problems. It's called The Waysiders. I went there when I realized I needed help with my drinking, and it's there I met Vincent Krumley. He didn't remember me from the days when I was gardener here, but I had to go and tell him, didn't I, before I got sober enough to think straight." He was now clawing at his bald head. "In all this time I've been back at Moultty Towers the old geezer never once showed his face, until that other night when I made up my mind I'd be damned before I let him ruin things for me."

The drawing room door swung inward and a man in police uniform stood in the opening. This had to be Ronald's father, Constable Thatcher. Beside him was a woman in her late thirties to early forties—quite a pretty woman, despite a severe hairstyle and nunlike attire. It seemed to me that there was an aura about her, but that might have been because the atmosphere was so highly charged with emotion.

"Father," she said in a softly compelling voice, "it has all been explained to me, and I have come to help you." She held out her arms, and Watkins stumbled into them, sobbing like a brokenhearted child. As she stroked his bowed head she looked over her shoulder as if drawn by a magnet to meet Alfonse's bemused gaze across the crowded room. I'd heard of such things happening . . . and didn't get the chance to glory in witnessing it because Laureen had risen slowly to her feet. For a moment I mistook the look on her face for exhaustion from playing the role Mrs. Malloy and I had assigned to her.

Then when I saw her lift Lady Krumley's hand my heart sank. That nerve pill she had taken, what had it been really? And why, oh why hadn't Mrs. Malloy and I suspected that Watkins had chosen this moment to commit the murder he had been working toward all these years?

Twenty-three

"What completed Watkins's disintegration," I explained to Freddy the following morning while I did the breakfast washing up and he watched, "was when the little dog Pipsie burst into the room like the angel of vengeance and made snarling leaps at his ankles, the throat being for a dog of his size the equivalent of a mountain peak."

"So the police got their confession?"

"Signed, sealed and official."

"Well done, coz!" Freddy ambled over to plant a congratulatory kiss on my cheek and help himself to a remaining rasher of bacon in the frying pan. "Any thoughts of you and Mrs. Malloy staying in the detective business?"

"Oh, I don't know." I rinsed off another plate. "Milk Jugg will return to reclaim his office and her heart into the bargain. So who knows how much I will see of her. Besides it's harrowing work. You can't imagine what I felt like when I thought Lady Krumley had so speedily joined Victor in the hereafter. I blamed myself for not thinking that Watkins might have tampered with those pills."

"But he hadn't."

"Luckily not. The prescription was for a very strong tranquilizer. Just one was enough to put her way under. I wasn't alone in thinking she was dead. It took about five minutes to convince Laureen she wasn't to blame for having put on such a powerful performance she had killed Lady Krumley in the process."

"She sounds quite a woman. I hope the vicar's nephew appreciates her."

"So do I and that neither of them will regret giving up acting. She's certainly very good, but then Watkins was no mean performer. In fact he was so perfect in his butler's role that it got me to wondering if he was real. Or if he was copying someone he had seen on TV or on the stage."

"I wonder why Flossie named the baby for him."

"Remorse over having deceived him? Or her way of twisting the knife, letting him know that he'd lost out by not bringing her the brooch. What surprised me was that Ernestine didn't appear to me to bear any strong resemblance to Ernest. Perhaps what he really recognized in her was a likeness to Flossie, but that being unacceptible he decided otherwise. He wanted her to be his daughter, that much is certain."

"And such proved the case." Freddy ambled over to the refrigerator and poured himself a glass of orange juice from the carton.

"It would seem so from what Mr. Featherstone had to say about Sir Horace's condition."

"You think the vicar may have said that to give Lady Krumley ease of mind."

"No, he's not a man to lie, whatever the motivation." I leaned against the sink while drying my hands on a tea towel. "But we've all heard of men fathering children after being told it would be impossible. I'm sure Ernestine could find out, have some tests done, if she was so inclined. Just to be sure. But somehow I don't think she will. In all these years she's never made a push to find her father, or so she told Mr. Featherstone. And it wouldn't have been hard given all the facts at her disposal, just as it wasn't difficult for Watkins to substantiate that the Ernestine he had met at The Waysiders was Flossie's baby.

A word here and a word there! And look what quick results Mrs. Malloy and I got."

"You sound a bit glum, coz." Freddy poured more juice.

"Well, it would have been nice to talk things over with her this morning. But there was no answer when I phoned. Not any of the six times. And to make matters worse Ben decided right after breakfast to give me a break by taking the children to school before driving over to Moultty Towers to surprise Mrs. Beetle with a visit from the author along with a signed copy of his latest book. It was awfully good of him, of course, but here I am with nothing to do except . . ."

"Say 'Here's looking at you Freddy'?"

"I'll drink to that!" I said, reaching for what was left of his orange juice. But before I had taken more than a couple of swallows the garden door banged open and Mrs. Malloy marched into the kitchen to pound her bag, the one she used to carry her cleaning supplies, down on the table. Freddy and I exchanged meaningful glances but did not risk speaking while she peeled off her gloves a slow, methodical finger at a time, before unbuttoning her fake leopard coat.

"So this is what I'm reduced to." She tossed her hat onto a growing pile on the table. "Returning to work for you Mrs. H. and being subjected to the leers of that upended floor mop you call your cousin."

"I stand entranced by your blonde hair." Freddy circled her on tiptoe, his hands clasped to his chest.

"Well take one last look, sonny boy, because I'm about to dye it back to black. Me days as an aspiring Girl Friday is over."

"Did you say perspiring?"

"None of your cheek, or I'll give you a thick ear." Mrs. M. glowered at my incorrigible relative. "I'm in the mood to give anyone hell as comes within a mile of me. And that's the softer side speaking."

"You've spoken to Mr. Jugg on the phone, and he's not

pleased we took over the Krumley case?" I eased her down onto a chair and told Freddy to get the kettle going for tea, a task he set about meekly while his ears flapped a mile a minute.

"He's back. Walked into the office while I was tending to his bloody plants."

"The plastic ones?"

"They take just as much care as the real ones. You still have to talk to them if you want them to grow."

"Of course." I produced a cup and saucer.

"You're right about him not being grateful for all our efforts to bring peace and harmony back to Moultty Towers. Worked himself into a real state, he did, saying his Auntie would never forgive him for not handling the case himself. A man of his age having an Auntie. It put me right off it did. Me ardor cooled faster than that kettle's doing now Mr. Freddy's gone and took it off the cooker."

"I won't be able to hear you if it starts to whistle."

"That's the idea," Mrs. Malloy informed him with her nose in the air. "You're all the same, you men. Sweetness and light while it suits you and then . . ."

"It's off home to Mother." Freddy finished for her and a moment later he had pranced out the garden door without a backward glance.

"What's up with him?" Mrs. M. bestirred herself to a mild curiosity.

"Just what he said. He's gone home to his mother. You reminded him he'd left her down at the cottage where she could be having a relapse at this minute and if he doesn't gallop down the lawn she'll have emptied at least three rooms waiting for the vans to pull up outside. But back to Mr. Jugg. He's turned out to be another nasty nephew, has he?"

"And not just the ordinary sort. He's got the worst kind of aunt."

"What kind is that?"

"The Mrs. Snow kind."

"As in the snake-in-the-grass housekeeper Mrs. Snow?"

"The very same. It was her that advised Lady Krumley to go to him with her problem. Only now you and me are the ones with the problem Mrs. H. because he says he wouldn't dream of taking a fee from his aunt's former employer, not five pounds let alone five thousand. And he'll sue us for horrible damages if we go over his head. Well, let me tell you, I let him have it. I told him it wasn't the sort of case he'd have been any good at, seeing as it was one where the butler done it and nothing at all to do with the mean streets. Not that I'm now beginning to think he's ever been down one. Oh, was I ever taken in. But never again. I'm back here where I belong with Mrs. H. ruling the roost at Merlin's Court."

"That's just the way I like it," I told her.

"And I wouldn't be surprised if Ernestine's life has turned up trumps. I was talking to the Merryweathers on the phone before Milk, such a stupid name, walked into the office. And it seems they had a telephone call from her bright and early this morning. Quite over the moon about it, they were."

"Isn't that nice."

"Could be they didn't have it quite right, but they said Ernestine was leaving for France as soon as she knows what's going to happen with her father. It seems Sir Alfonse knows of some sort of mission he thinks he can interest her in. Another way of inviting her to look at his etchings if you asks me. And it was clear the Merryweathers are thinking along them same lines and are hoping like mad she'll turn over a new leaf and renounce all her good ways. I wonder if Lady Krumley will still leave her that money like she talked about?"

"I hope so. But I don't suppose it matters. She and Sir Alfonse did seem instantly besotted. Perhaps they'll bring French cuisine back to The Waysiders. That might make it more appealing to Aunt Lulu if she could be persuaded to go for another stay. She's a woman who will put up with a great deal for escargot."

Mrs. Malloy had gone to stare out the window while waiting for the kettle to boil. "Was you joking Mrs. H.?" she asked without turning around.

"About what?"

"Them vans you was saying Freddy's mother would have sent for?"

"Of course. Why do you ask?"

"Because there's a whacking great van pulling up the drive?"

"Oh, no!" I sighed in anguish. "It'll be the stuff from Ben's study being returned from The Waysiders. I made the mistake of bringing up the subject with Ernestine just before you and I left Moultty Towers, and she must have got right onto it. Quick! We've got to get out there." I propelled Mrs. Malloy toward the door. "They've started to unload."

We were standing on the path when I heard the front door open and Ben's voice calling to me from the hall. "Look," I told Mrs. Malloy, "I'll double your wages, I'll even take on another detective case if you twist my arm, but get out to those men. See there are two of them, big burly types with fire in their eyes and their very own teeth from what I can see from here. Say anything, do anything to get them to load that stuff back into the van. If Ben should get a glimpse of what he loved and lost, even the computer may not be enough to hold him."

"You're asking me to sacrifice meself." Mrs. M. was smiling as if her life was once more filled with promise.

"That's right. And take all the time you like. Remember if you come inside I'll make you scrub floors until your back breaks." I kissed her cheek and raced back into the house to close the kitchen door behind me as I went into the hall.

"Hello, Ben darling," I said as I went into his arms. "Did Mrs. Beetle like the book?"

"She was thrilled speechless."

"And that makes you deserving of a reward," I whispered against his lips.

"More new furniture?"

"Something better. Mrs. Malloy frightened me last night. She said you might become so keen on computers that you'd decide to buy another one to take to bed with you, and I'm going to show you why you don't need to do that."

"But isn't she here? I thought I heard you talking to her when I came in?" If he hadn't smiled at me in just that way while raising an enchantingly quizzical eyebrow I might have found the strength to tell him the truth. After all, hadn't I vowed never to be anything less than up front and straightforward with him ever again? But on the other hand, why should Ernestine be the only woman in the world to be blown away by a look . . . a glance from the right man?

"What? Mrs. Malloy here . . . in the house?" I took his hand and led him toward the stairs. "Trust me, darling, that woman has better fish to fry on a lovely day like this."

"It's cold and getting ready to rain."

"I know." I turned back into his arms for a delicious moment before sprinting ahead of him three steps at a time. "What's my prize if I race you under the covers?"

"I'll let you play with my computer."

"Perfect," I said. What more could any wife ask of life? Except hope that other women everywhere were just as happy.